T

By

David Johnson

Copyright © 2018 David Johnson

All rights reserved

ISBN-10:1986107124
ISBN-13: 978-198107129

Dedication

I dedicate *The Last Patient* to social workers, counselors, law enforcement officers, schoolteachers, and all those who have made the effort to help people who have found themselves in situations they did not know how to get out of or who made a bad choice that led to worse circumstances.

To make a difference in the life of one person—that is why you do what you do. It is not a calling for the fainthearted, and there are days you ask yourself if you can keep going. But the world needs you now more than ever. Don't give up. Don't ever give up.

>Truly I tell you, whatever you did for
>the least of these brothers and sisters
>of mine, you did for me.
>
>—Jesus Christ

Chapter One

MAGGIE—PRESENT DAY

With one hand on the steering wheel and the other on the bottle of vodka between her thighs, Maggie Stinson lets her foot off the gas pedal and glances at her hand-scrawled directions on the legal pad lying on the car seat beside her. This is the last thing she wants to be doing during her final days before retiring. She was hoping that the hospice agency she works for would let her just skate along by staying in her office and doing simple paperwork and tidying up a chart or two. However, as with most things in Maggie's life, things haven't turned out the way she hoped.

Yesterday, the administrator, Sheila, a woman half Maggie's age with a bubbly personality that grates on Maggie and whose life seems to be ruled by her ever-present cell phone, stopped by her office. "Hi, Maggie," she said cheerily. "Are you excited about retiring?"

Maggie started to tell her that she hadn't been excited by anything in a long time but instead decided to make the extra effort and be pleasant. "Retirement is what everyone is looking forward to, isn't it? Is there something I can do for you?"

Sheila's face took on a serious expression. "There's someone I'd like you to go see. It's a new patient that we've got, and he's . . ." She paused, seeming to try to find the right words. "He's complicated."

The word and the tone it was delivered with caused Maggie's rounded shoulders to slump even more. Even though she knew it was just another sign that she was burned out from being a social worker, she still said what she was thinking. "I'm tired of complicated. Complicated is all I've ever known." Sheila gave what Maggie was certain was a forced smile. *Quit trying to be so nice to everybody. Just tell me to get my butt out there and do my job.*

When Sheila responded, she sounded like she was talking to a five-year-old who didn't want to go to school. "But you're perfect for this situation. You always know just what to say and how to handle these kinds of people. I would send Jasmine, but she's only been working with us for a month, and I'm afraid she'd get a little freaked out by what she would face."

Maggie had to agree with Sheila's conclusion. Jasmine had recently graduated from college with her degree in social work and had the necessary knowledge, but having grown up in a life of privilege, she had no idea how to relate to and deal with the poor, which described the majority of the agency's patients. Maggie sighed and picked up a pen. "What's the patient's name, and where does he live?"

"His name is Israel McKenzie." Sheila cleared her throat and looked away as she added, "But he prefers to be called the Gravedigger."

Now, as Maggie looks through her windshield and squints against the bright summer sun, she mutters aloud, "Lord, he's out here in the middle of nowhere." She takes another swallow of vodka. *At least being out of the office and in the field like this makes it a lot easier to satisfy my thirst.* That's what she's begun calling it, rather than the distasteful-sounding "satisfy my craving."

Suddenly she slams on her brakes. To her right she sees a gravel lane disappearing into a thick grove of cedar trees. *This must be it.*

Pulling onto the lane, she eases into the dark shadows and drives past a three-gabled frame house that is gray with age; almost all the windows are broken out, the front door hangs by one hinge, and there are several holes in the wood-shingled roof.

A little bit farther, a small cemetery appears on her right. She stops and counts fifteen headstones, some of which look quite ancient. Anchoring the corner of the cemetery is a gigantic cedar tree—lightning has knocked the top off it, and she guesses it is easily over a hundred years old.

After traveling about a hundred more yards, she spies her destination—an old single-wide house trailer. The yard, if that's what you would call it, is populated by bald tires, two rusted-out cars, a pickup truck sitting on three wheels with a jack propped underneath the right front corner where the missing wheel is supposed to be, and two porcelain toilets sitting side by side. At one end of the trailer, looking completely out of place, sits a late-model Honda Accord.

As Maggie rolls to a stop, the front door of the trailer opens, and a woman dressed in bright green scrubs and carrying a clipboard steps out and walks toward the Honda. It's not until she takes off her surgical mask that she glances up and sees Maggie. There is a scornful look of disgust on her face that even her heavy makeup cannot hide.

Ah, Nurse Jones, Maggie thinks to herself. *What list of complaints will you toss at me today?* She'd just as soon not have to deal with the agency's number-one whiner and complainer. In describing her to another coworker, Maggie had said, "She's one of those people who has enjoyed being miserable her whole life."

Before getting out of her car, Maggie slips the vodka under her seat, then takes a look at herself in the rearview mirror. She wipes mustard off the corner of her mouth, left there from the McDonald's cheeseburger she ate on the way, and touches the area above her upper lip. *I've got to make an appointment to get my mustache waxed.*

After straightening the mirror and touching it three times with her right index finger, she grabs her clipboard and exits the car. Engaging with the nurse and attempting to look interested in what she has to say is the last thing Maggie wants to do, so she simply nods and says, "Hey, Delores," and heads toward the front door of the trailer. But Delores blocks her path.

"The way some people live ought to be against the law. Have you been in there yet?" Delores points at the trailer.

"Nope."

"Well, good luck is all I can say. I've been in some nasty homes in my time of working for home health and hospice agencies, but this place here is easily the worst. He just needs to go ahead and die; then somebody needs to set the whole place on fire."

Maggie stares at her with an expressionless face, hoping she'll get in her car and be on her way so that Maggie can get on with her own business of making a visit.

However, Delores has never been known as one who gets nonverbal messages—or verbal ones, for that matter. "You know what he calls himself? The Gravedigger. Who in the world wants to be called that?"

Maggie has heard enough and walks around Delores, who pitches one more disparaging comment toward her. "He's pathetic and isn't interested in getting any better. You know he refused chemo and radiation both. I don't know what you can do for him."

Maggie bristles at the insinuation that she has nothing to offer someone. She whirls around, unfortunately a bit too fast, and nearly loses her balance. It takes a second for everything to stop spinning. Then in an icy tone she says, "He asked to see a social worker. Perhaps he wanted to talk to someone who might show some empathy for him rather than having someone who wants him to hurry up and die so that they can burn down his home."

This finally shuts Delores up, and Maggie climbs the prefabricated fiberglass set of steps and knocks on the front door three times. Shifting her clipboard full of forms to her other hand, she rubs her arthritic knee.

When no one comes to the door, she opens it a bit and says, "Israel McKenzie? May I come in?"

"There's no Israel McKenzie here," a reedy voice from somewhere back in the trailer replies. "But if you're looking for the Gravedigger, come on in."

She tries to open the door wide enough for her to get her five-foot-four-inch, 190-pound frame through, but something behind the door prevents her. She peers into the unlit interior but can't make anything out. Leaning her shoulder against the door, she shoves a little harder, and whatever is behind the door gives just enough for her to squeeze inside.

She stands still for a moment, breathing through her mouth and not her nose. As a supervisor told her years ago, "It's the smells that'll get to you in this job much more than the sights will."

As her eyes begin adjusting to the dim light, tall stacks of magazines, books, and newspapers appear, some of them six feet high. At first it appears they are lined up like silent sentinels along a narrow pathway through what must have originally been designed as the living room of the trailer, but soon she sees that these are just the outer wall of a castle made up of the reading material. The room is jam-packed, wall to wall. *Looks like we've got ourselves a hoarder.*

With her hips brushing against the stacks on both sides, she moves carefully through the narrow aisle. "Israel?" she calls out.

"Back here," he answers, "but don't call me that. I'm the Gravedigger."

As she passes through a doorway and down a hallway, the piers of books give way to piles of white plastic garbage bags stacked two to three feet high. The squeaking sounds of foraging mice emanate from both sides of her. A thin ray of sunshine that has snuck past a pulled window shade spotlights a trio of cockroaches crawling down the walls.

"Don't touch nothing, and don't move a thing," Israel's voice rings out.

Maggie passes by a bathroom with a skylight in the ceiling. Pausing to look in, she sees a hole in the floor where a toilet used to sit and a bathtub completely filled with unopened bars of bath soap. There's movement in the black hole where the toilet used to sit, and Maggie freezes as a snake slowly begins to emerge. Quick as a wink, she grabs one of the bars of soap and throws it, striking the snake in the head and knocking it back into the hole.

"I heard that!" Israel yells. "What are you doing? You better leave my stuff alone!"

Maggie puts her hand on her chest and waits for her heart to slow, then says to herself, as she has often done during her career, *I've had to deal with worse than this.*

Looking down the hallway toward what has to be the bedroom, she steels herself for what she might find. As she is about to pass through the doorway, the Gravedigger issues a challenge. "Who are you, and what are you doing here?"

With a sharp and trained eye, Maggie quickly scans both the room and the patient. Scores of Pyrex dishes of various shapes and sizes are nestled against the walls of the room. Beside the bed is a table, the top of which is covered by several pill bottles and a shadeless lamp whose bare bulb is the only light she has seen burning in the trailer. In the corner of the room, an oscillating fan attempts to stir the hot, stifling air.

Israel is quite thin, as she expected he would be. His white hair looks as if he has stuck his finger in an electrical outlet. It's hard to tell if his receding chin makes his front teeth look pronounced or vice versa. At some point in his life, his nose was badly broken; it now follows a crooked path from between his eyes to its rather bulbous tip. An old scar runs vertically from his hairline to his left eyebrow. His skin tone is the yellowish-olive color she has seen many times in people with liver cancer. "My name is Margaret Stinson, but most folks call me Maggie. I'm a social worker with Tennessee Hospice." She offers to shake his hand.

He withdraws his thin arm from under the sheet that is pulled to his neck and sticks his bony hand in hers. "I'm the Gravedigger, and I want you to make sure that nurse that just left here don't ever come back."

Although she's not surprised to hear this, Maggie still asks, "Why is that?"

"She must have been weaned on green persimmons. I never met someone with such a sour disposition. I know she doesn't have to like me, but at least she can talk civil to me. I'm fifty-five years old, and I'm dying, you know. Dr. Wilson said it won't be long now, said I might could live longer if I did radiation and chemo, but I told him I was tired of living." Suddenly he breaks into singing, "'I'm tired of living and I ain't scared of dying, so Ol' Man River, he just keeps rollin' along.' You like how I changed those lyrics? I'm not scared of dying because there's lots of things worse than dying. You know that, don't you?"

Like turning off a spigot, Israel's flow of words stops as abruptly as it started.

Maggie says, "I'm glad to meet you, Israel."

"How can you say you're glad to meet me when you don't even know me? And don't call me Israel. Call me Gravedigger. You may have heard things about me, but that doesn't mean you know me. It just means you've been listening to gossip and wagging tongues. Once you get to know me, you might not like me. Will you tell me that if it happens, or will you keep up your fake smile and niceness?"

If you think you're going to bait me into an argument, you're wrong. Smiling, she says, "I don't have to like someone to be nice to them."

He blinks at her for a few seconds. Then his eyes narrow. "So you're just one of them hypocrites that pretends to be nice." He looks up toward the ceiling. "You hear that, Lord? She's one of them."

Unfazed but curious, Maggie says, "I guess that would depend on your definition of a hypocrite. I think a hypocrite is someone who pretends to be someone they are not. That's not me. If I'm nice to someone, it's because I choose to be, and the same is true if I'm not nice to someone." She pauses before saying, "Do you mind if I ask you a question?"

"Is this where you ask me my birth date, where I was born, how many schools I went to, and do I have any mommy and daddy issues?"

"I will, if that's what you want to talk about, but that's not what I was going to ask."

"Ask me whatever you want. That's up to you."

She gazes steadily at him. "Are you a hypocrite?"

"What gives you the right to ask me that?"

"Not a thing. It's just that we were talking about whether or not I was a hypocrite, and I was curious if you were one. I mean, if you are, it would make it a lot easier if I knew that up front." She lets a smile play at the corners of her mouth and sees that Israel notices.

His teeth become impossibly more pronounced as he grins. "I like you. I think we're going to get along just fine. I bet you're a straight shooter."

"I do believe in being honest with people. Don't you?"

"You're good at this. Been doing it a long time?"

"Long enough." *Probably too long.* "I'm getting ready to retire. I think you will most likely be my last patient."

Sitting still for a couple of moments as she lets him study her, she feels sweat trickling down between her breasts.

What I'd like to do is stand in front of that fan and lift my shirt.

"You going to retire before I die?" he asks.

She smiles. "It depends on how long you take."

This produces a laugh from Israel, which turns into a rattling cough that he almost strangles on.

Maggie quickly pulls some tissues out of a box beside him and holds them to his mouth. "Spit it out."

He raises his head and expels a wad of tar-colored mucus into the tissues.

Looking around, Maggie spots a small trash can lined with a Walmart shopping bag and drops the soiled tissue into it. Reaching into her purse, she takes out some hand sanitizer and squirts a nickel-size dollop into her palm. "So why are you called the Gravedigger?"

"Is that the most interesting question you can come up with? The answer to that is too obvious: because I dig graves, or I used to. I've dug graves for people I knew and people I'd never heard of, famous people and not famous ones, rich and poor, old and young. One thing I learned is that death is no respecter of persons. The grim reaper don't care about but one thing"—he raises his arm and makes a long swoop through the air—"taking his sickle and cutting you off from the land of the living. Some people die when they're too young; others die because their body is wore out. And some are dead because they deserved to die."

His last phrase carries an ominous tone that sends an unexpected chill up Maggie's back.

Chapter Two

ISRAEL—SEVEN YEARS OLD

Startled awake by the clanging of the iron triangle that hung in the hallway of the Little Boys' Dormitory, as it was called by everyone who lived at the orphans' home, Israel jumped out of bed with the other seven boys with whom he shared a room and began getting dressed.

In a voice that sounded as if it was being ripped from the throat rather than flowing naturally, the dorm mother, Miss Agnes, called out, "You boys better hurry up and get over to the mess hall and eat your breakfast, or you'll go hungry this day. I can promise you that!"

When Israel had been promoted from the nursery to this dorm at the age of four, he thought this to be an idle threat by Miss Agnes but quickly learned full well that she meant it.

Sunny Hill Orphans' Home was all Israel had ever known, having been dropped off there when he was an infant, or so he had been told. He never gave any thought to any other kind of life until he went to school and his teacher asked the students to draw a picture of their families. He sat looking at his blank paper, trying to decide what to draw. When he drew a picture of himself and all the boys in his dorm, with a stern-looking Miss Agnes in the foreground, complete with her ever-present bun sitting on the top of her head, his teacher whispered in his ear, "You can draw a make-believe family if you want to."

Because he thought it would please her, he obliged and drew the obligatory mother and father, with a house in the background, surrounded by a picket fence. But when he turned it in, he was told it still wasn't right.

"Where are you?" his teacher asked. "You're supposed to be in the picture, too."

Back at his desk, he'd drawn himself inside the house, looking out the window at his imaginary parents.

Now, the hallway of the dormitory began filling with sleepy-eyed boys as the four bedrooms emptied themselves of their nighttime guests. They lined up single file under the watchful eye of Miss Agnes, who said, "Keep in line, and no running," and followed her out the door.

In the mess hall, all two hundred of the residents who had gathered from the other dormitories stood behind their chairs except Anthony—the boy who had arrived at the orphanage the day before. He sat down in the chair beside Israel and began spooning hot oatmeal into his mouth.

Israel kicked Anthony's chair to get his attention. Out of the corner of his mouth, he whispered, "Get up, quick!"

Anthony gave him a questioning look, then looked around at everyone standing behind their chairs. He was about to stand up when Israel saw Miss Agnes bearing down on Anthony with a heavy wooden spoon in her hand. Just as she swung at the boy, Israel moved between them, keeping his back toward her and taking the blow of the spoon on the back of his head. He bit his tongue to keep from crying out in pain.

"Israel McKenzie!" Miss Agnes shrieked.

She swung for him again, but he was too quick for her. Grabbing a biscuit off the table, he sprinted toward the door. As he burst through it, he heard her yell, "You'll eventually have to come back, and when you do—"

He was out of earshot and couldn't hear her last words, but he was pretty sure what they were.

Making a turn toward the direction of the woodshop, he slowed his pace while eating his biscuit. Inside the shop, he was greeted by the familiar smell of resin from pine, hickory, and oak lumber and the high-pitched whine of wood being cut by the table saw as Darnell Williams, who had the bluest eyes he'd ever seen, pushed a board with his large hands slowly past the spinning blade. Israel waited until the saw had been turned off before he approached Darnell, just like Darnell had taught him to.

As the saw motor whirred to a stop, Darnell straightened himself and turned around. There was a look of surprise on his face. "Good morning, Israel," he said with a smile. "You're out here awfully early in the morning. Trouble?" He sat down and propped one of his feet on the chair, causing his pant leg to rise far enough to expose his wooden leg.

The first time Israel had seen the leg, he couldn't quit staring at it, but now he hardly noticed. "Maybe a little trouble," he said.

"Then that means a whole lot of trouble later today. Headmaster Tilley may get involved. You can't keep getting in trouble, Israel, or they're liable to send you somewhere else. I know you're a good boy, but you got to do a better job of following the rules."

"But Miss Agnes was about to wallop the new kid with her wood spoon. I felt sorry for him because he didn't know any better."

Darnell lit a cigarette and took a long draw from it. "Miss Agnes, she can sure get riled up about the least little thing." Looking at Israel, he added, "But now here's the thing: she's in charge. You have to do what she says. Rules are rules. You hear me? What does the Bible say?"

Israel parroted the answer he knew Darnell was looking for: "Children, obey your parents."

"That's right."

"But she's not my parent. I don't have any parents."

"When you live here, we're all your parents. We're just doing the best job we know how in raising you kids. Maybe some does it better than others, but at least we're here for you."

Israel nodded. "Yes, sir." Of all the people he knew, Darnell was the one he least wanted to disappoint. The way he asked for Israel's help and showed him how to do things, while most of the other boys had to work on the farm that produced food for the orphanage, made him feel special, even though it caused problems with some of the other boys, who felt like he was being treated as privileged. *I don't care what they think.*

"That's a good boy. Now, are you ready to help me sand the table we've been working on?"

Israel smiled. "Yes, sir!"

The rest of that day, he managed to make it through lunch and suppertime without ever seeing Miss Agnes, but as he headed to his dorm as the sun was setting, his legs grew heavy with dread. He had felt the sting of her belt before and tried to think of ways he might avoid it this time. But coming up with an excuse he hadn't tried before was impossible.

Grabbing one of the two towels that were allotted to him each month, he walked to the giant bathroom all the boys in the dorm shared. One side of the porcelain-lined room had a row of ten toilets, and on the other side, sixteen showerheads adorned the wall.

Standing under the shower with his face soaped up, he heard a boy beside him say, "She wants to see you, Israel."

Quickly rinsing his face, he looked at the boy. "What kind of mood is she in?"

"What kind of mood is she always in? You better hurry up."

Israel's stomach wrenched, and his hands trembled as he dried himself off.

Stepping out of the bathroom and looking down the hall toward her room, he thought of the train tunnel that he and some of the other boys would sneak down to, to watch trains pass through. This time, though, he felt like he was standing in the middle of the track with no means of escape.

He knocked lightly on her door in hopes she wouldn't hear him. That way he could go back to his room armed with the excuse, "But I knocked on your door."

But fate was not on his side tonight, as he heard her voice on the other side of the door. "Is that you, Israel?"

"Yes, ma'am."

"Come in and close the door."

With every muscle tense, he walked stiffly into the room that served as her living room. He was immediately confused as he was greeted by an overpowering sweet smell that reminded him of flowers and bath soap, but there was no sign of Miss Agnes.

She called from her bedroom in a tone that was unfamiliar to him, "Come in here, Israel."

To cross that threshold that all the boys had been told was forbidden made him feel like he was going to step into hell's lake of fire he had heard about on Sundays. In a small voice, he asked, "Are you sure you want me in there, Miss Agnes?"

"Yes, yes, Israel, it's okay if I ask you to. Come on in now. I need your help."

Taking tiny steps, he inched along until he was standing in the doorway and could see inside. The aroma that greeted him at the door was so strong now that it nearly choked him. Miss Agnes's eyes looked like someone had smeared charcoal around them, and her cheeks were red like it was winter time. Her had been released from its tight bun and hung down past her shoulders.

She turned her back to him and said, "I need you to help me unbutton the back of my dress. I can't seem to reach it."

The only time she had ever touched him was with either the belt or the wooden spoon, and she had never invited him to touch her. *It's just buttons, so hurry up and get it done so that you can leave.*

As he began unbuttoning the dress, she said, "I'm sorry I hit you with the spoon this morning. I didn't aim to hurt you."

An apology? Israel was certain he misheard her, but he was not about to ask her to repeat it. He finished the last button and said, "That's all of them, Miss Agnes. May I go now?"

Shock shot through him as she pulled her dress off her shoulders and stepped out of it, standing there naked. When she turned around to face him, he staggered backward. He wanted to cover his eyes, to run out the door, to do *something*, but all he could do was stand there, frozen in horror.

Holding her arms out to her sides, she said, "Why did you sneak in here to see me like this, you naughty boy?"

He felt his tongue moving, but he couldn't open his mouth.

"I suppose I'm going to have to tell the headmaster about this. What do you think will happen to you then?"

Finally Israel found his voice. "But, Miss Agnes, you asked me to come here. You told me—"

"And who do you think is going to believe that story?" she said, cutting him off. "You're nothing but a dirty little boy who's going to grow up to be a dirty old man."

He began to cry. "Please don't tell on me. Please."

She reached down and picked up her dress. "I'll tell you what I'll do. If you don't tell about me hitting you in the head with the spoon, I'll not tell what you tried to do to me tonight."

He could make no sense of what she was asking. "But I didn't try to do anything."

She grabbed the phone receiver and said, "Then I guess I better call Mr. Tilley to come here right now."

"No! Please don't!"

"Then you must promise me as I asked. Do we have a deal?"

Even though he felt like he was making a deal with the devil, Israel nodded his head and said, "I promise."

Chapter Three

MAGGIE—TEN YEARS OLD

Although she had been in bed for a few hours, Maggie remained wide awake, with all of her senses in a state of hyperarousal, alert to any warnings that her father was coming to her again. From the direction of her closed bedroom door, she heard the tiniest squeak—the doorknob was turning. She rolled over, turning her back to the door, jerked the covers over her head, and pulled her knees to her belly, making herself into the smallest ball she could.

There was a click as the door latch passed through the strike plate. In her mind, Maggie could see his large, rough hand pushing the door open as the floor creaked underneath his heavy footfall. As he got closer, she held her breath until her lungs burned; then she let the stale air out and gasped for a breath of fresh air. Her heart was beating as fast as a rabbit's when running from the hounds.

The seconds ticked by as she waited to feel the edge of her bed sag underneath him as he sat down beside her, but it never happened. An extra load of dread filled her as she realized he was going to toy with her, much the same way her cat played with a mouse when he caught it.

Moving an inch at a time, she eased the covers down to her chin and took a peek. In the corner of her room where a chair sat, there was the red glow of a burning cigarette. In the next second, the smell of its smoke filled her nostrils, and she felt like she was going to throw up.

For the next several minutes, the only sound was of him drawing on his cigarette and blowing out the smoke. Part of her wished he would come to her and get it over with because the longer he waited, the greater her terror became.

Eventually, she got her wish; the cigarette was extinguished, and he lay with her.

The first time it had happened, it hurt so badly she started to scream, but he clapped his hand over her mouth and nearly smothered her to death. Now, amazingly, she felt nothing because she was no longer in her body. Some time ago, she had learned somewhat of a mental trick and went somewhere else in her mind when he was with her and didn't return until sometime after he had left. She heard neither his threats as to what he would do if she told what was happening nor his grunts of satisfaction.

Later, when she came to herself, she turned her head and looked in the direction of her younger sister's twin bed but could only see the shadowy form of someone under the covers. It was Maggie's belief that as long as she didn't tell what was happening or fight against it, he would leave Rachel alone. *I will protect you, Rachel. As long as I am here, you have nothing to worry about.*

Getting out of bed, she went to the bathroom and used a wet washcloth to clean herself up, then returned to her covers and waited for the whimpers of her baby brother, Teddy, when he woke up. As she lay there, anger welled up inside her, not toward her father but toward God. *I hate you! Where's the God that's supposed to protect me? What kind of God creates people like him? I don't care what Mimi says— you can't be real, or this wouldn't be happening to me.*

Fatigue settled in, and she was just about to fall asleep when she heard the cry she'd been expecting. She crawled out of bed and walked into the hallway to the baby bed. Originally, both bed and baby had been in her parents' bedroom, but her father would not tolerate having his sleep interrupted by Teddy's cries, so he moved the bed into the only available space in their small two-bedroom house, the hallway.

Maggie looked over the rail, and in the gray light of dawn, she saw her brother smiling up at her. She smiled back at him and reached down to pull the rubber pants off his urine-soaked cloth diaper. "Shooo-wee," she said in a quiet voice so as not to awaken anyone. "Somebody stinks this morning."

Teddy blew bubbles at her and kicked his legs.

She unfastened the large diaper pins, pulled the diaper off him, and laid it across the end of the bed frame. Then she slipped a dry diaper under him and sprinkled him with a cloud of baby powder. After pinning the diaper, she lifted him out of the bed and set him on her hip. "Does that feel better?"

Teddy responded by kicking and bucking like he was a cowboy on a bronco.

"Let's go get you a bottle," Maggie said as she headed toward the kitchen. Glancing in the kitchen sink, she noticed the pot with burned SpaghettiOs in the bottom from when she had fixed supper for herself and Rachel last night. From the refrigerator, she took a baby bottle filled with milk, carried it to the sink, and let hot water run over it for a minute.

Teddy began fussing and crying.

"I know you're hungry, but I've got to get this warmed up a bit first." Turning off the hot water, she shook the bottle to mix the warmer and colder milk together in hopes it would produce a bottle with lukewarm milk, and then she popped it into Teddy's bawling mouth.

Like putting a stopper in a sink, his cries immediately stopped, and he sucked hungrily.

Just then, seven-year-old Rachel came into the kitchen, rubbing the sleep out of her eyes. "I'm hungry," she whined.

Feeling irritated, Maggie said, "Then fix yourself some cereal."

"I can't reach the bowls or the milk. Please help me."

It was true, Maggie knew—she just wished it wasn't—so she laid Teddy on the floor, jumped up on the counter, and handed Rachel a bowl out of the cabinet. From another cabinet, she took out a box of cereal, then jumped down and got the milk out of the refrigerator. After fixing a bowl of cereal for her sister and herself, she was about to sit down and eat when her mother entered the kitchen.

"Can you fix me some breakfast, Maggie? I feel like I might could eat something this morning."

Maggie looked at her with a mixture of agitation, sympathy, and sadness. Her mother used to be the prettiest woman she knew, but now she was stooped, thin as a pencil, with bald spots on her head where her hair was falling out. The dark circles under her eyes were made darker by the yellowish complexion of her skin. Her mother told her she was sick with cancer, but Maggie didn't know what that meant, except that the social worker, who had been coming to the house periodically, had told her that her mother was dying.

Her mother folded herself into one of the chairs at the table and said, "Can you hand Teddy to me so I can hold him?"

Maggie obliged, and although her own stomach was growling, she went to the stove and placed a skillet on the eye to fry some bacon for her mother. As she did so, she said to herself for what seemed like the thousandth time, *It won't always be like this. One day things will be better.*

Chapter Four

ISRAEL—ELEVEN YEARS OLD

Tears made silver tracks down Israel's cheeks as he sat on a bench in the woodshop and said to Darnell, "I want to stay, but I want to go, too."

Darnell limped over to the bench and sat down beside him. Putting his arm around him, he said, "It's a confusing time for you, I know. You've lived here your whole life, so this is all you know. That's why you want to stay. But this family that's going to adopt you will give you a brand-new home and life. You'll finally have a mother and father that you can call your own and who will call you theirs. It's what every kid at the orphans' home wants."

Israel leaned the side of his head against him. "I'm going to miss you most of all. You're the one who's been like a father to me. Nobody will ever take your place."

When Darnell didn't say anything, Israel looked up at him and saw he was crying, too. Israel had heard people speak of having a broken heart, but he never knew what that felt like until that moment.

Darnell pulled a red bandana out of his back pocket and blew his nose. "Tell you what you do; you write me and let me know how things are going for you, and I'll write you back. We can keep in touch that way. But I suspect that your new life is going to be so wonderful that you'll hardly give me a thought after a while. And that'll be okay because it'll mean you are happy and doing good." He pulled on a gold chain that disappeared into a pocket on the front of his overalls, and a pocket watch appeared. Opening it, he said, "It's time for you to go."

Israel looked at the watch and watched as Darnell unfastened the chain from his overalls and handed the watch and chain to him. "Here, I want you to take this with you, so you'll remember me and all the good times we had in the shop here. You're special, Israel. Life is hard for you right now, but it won't always be that way. One day you'll be able to breathe easy and enjoy your life."

Israel took the watch and closed his hand around it, then threw his arms around Darnell.

With a choked voice, Darnell told him, "Time for you to run along now."

With a reluctant heart, Israel released his hold on him and walked to the door. Turning around, he said, "I love you, Darnell."

"And I love you, too, Israel."

And with that, Israel stepped through the door and into a new life.

*****

After a four-hour drive sitting between his new mother and father, during which time neither of them said a word, even when they stopped for gas and to use the bathroom, Israel followed them inside their house, the first time he ever remembered being in any building other than the buildings at the orphanage, at school, and at church.

Standing between the parents in the living room, Israel looked at five other children who were standing at attention. Their eyes seemed to be glued to some distant object and gave no indication anyone else was present in the living room. He felt a chill on the back of his neck.

The father said, "Begin."

Like obedient soldiers, all the children took a step forward and recited together:

Thou shalt have no other gods before me. Thou shalt not make unto thee any graven image. Thou shalt not take the name of the Lord thy God in vain. Remember the Sabbath day, to keep it holy. Honor thy father and thy mother. Thou shalt not kill. Thou shalt not commit adultery. Thou shalt not steal. Thou shalt not bear false witness against thy neighbor. Thou shalt not covet.

Then they took a step backward, maintaining their glazed stares.

"Very good," the father said. "Now it's your turn, Israel."

Confused, Israel said, "I don't know what you mean."

The father struck him so hard on the back of the head that he stumbled forward. "You will address me as Sir. 'I don't know what you mean, *Sir*.'"

Rubbing the back of his head, Israel looked up at him, feeling both angry and scared.

"Do not look at me! Return to your position between us and keep your eyes forward."

Israel moved back into position.

"Now, repeat yourself."

With a trembling voice, he said, "I don't know what you mean, Sir."

"That's better. You just heard the children recite God's Ten Commandments, the commandments that are to govern every aspect of our life, the commandments that will be enforced in this house. I want to hear you recite them."

Israel searched the faces of the children and saw signs of tension and fear creeping in at the edges of their mouths and eyes. The oldest one gave him the quickest of furtive glances, and in it, Israel read a warning.

"I'm sorry, Sir, but I don't know them."

"Sir," the wife said, "he's just arrived and hasn't even gotten settled in. Would it be possible to give him some time to learn our ways, please, Sir?"

The father's voice thundered, "And give an opportunity for this spawn of Satan to corrupt our precious children? I think not! All it takes is one bad seed to ruin everything we've instilled in them. He'll learn the Ten Commandments right here, right now. He will learn that we have rules and that things will be done my way in this house. Abraham, step forward and recite the first commandment."

The oldest child took a step and said, "Thou shalt have no other gods before me."

"Israel, repeat it."

Israel began, "Thou shall not have any—"

Another slap on the back of his head stopped him. "Thou shalt," the father said. "There's a *t* on the end of the word. It's the King James Version, the only version of the Bible that can be trusted. All other versions are nothing more than perversions. Say it again, Abraham."

Abraham obeyed.

Knowing what was expected of him this time, Israel repeated it perfectly and exhaled a sigh of relief.

"Excellent. Isaac, step forward and repeat the second command."

The next child in line obeyed, saying, "Thou shalt not make unto thee any graven image."

Israel tried to listen closely to every word, but the phrase made no sense to him, and his increasing anxiety caused it to get all jumbled up in his mind. He knew he was not going to get it right but knew he was expected to try. "I will try it, Sir. Thou shalt not make any—"

Israel was looking at Abraham when the blow to his head came, and he saw the boy flinch just before stars filled his own field of vision.

"Repeat it for this slow-witted creature, Isaac."

After Isaac repeated it, Israel said, "Thou shalt not make unto thee any . . . any . . ." Try as he might, he could not find the last words Isaac said.

This time he was kicked in the back of his knees, causing them to slam onto the hard floor as he fell down.

"Sir," the wife said.

"Do not interrupt, woman. The Bible says, 'Let a woman be in subjection to her husband.' Keep quiet, or you'll get yours. Say it for him again, Isaac."

This time Isaac said the commandment slowly and deliberately, enunciating each word clearly.

Israel felt like hugging his neck for this help and was able to recite the commandment correctly.

"Rebekah, you who conspired to deceive your own husband and cause him to choose the wrong son for the blessing, which has caused the havoc that has been in the Middle East ever since, recite the third commandment."

The girl in the middle stepped forward and said, "Thou shalt not take the name of the Lord thy God in vain—unless you are Father."

There was an audible gasp from the mother.

A collective and noticeable shudder ran through the other four children, but Rebekah remained stoic.

The father growled, "You cheap, no good, lying little bitch. I'll show you—" He took a step toward her when the mother jumped in between them.

"She didn't mean it, Sir," she pleaded. "She wasn't really thinking clearly, were you, Rebekah?" She looked beseechingly at the girl.

Israel felt as if he had been dropped into the middle of some horrible nightmare. Even though Rebekah didn't move or make a sound, to him, she looked like she was about to give a smirk. Part of him wanted to join the mother and prevent whatever was going to happen next because he was certain it was going to be awful, and he didn't want to watch it. But fear had his shoes nailed to the floor, so all he could do was grit his teeth and squeeze his fists.

"She knew exactly what she was saying," the father said. "I'll teach her a lesson she'll not soon forget."

The mother went to her knees and bowed her head. Clutching her hands together and lifting them up as if praying, she said, "Let me take her punishment. Do to me whatever you were going to do to her."

He looked surprised. "You want to be the girl's scapegoat and carry her sins outside the tent of meeting like the Israelites did on the Day of Atonement? Are you children watching and listening to this? It's a Christ-like act she proposes, taking Rebekah's iniquities on herself and allowing herself to be crucified."

Israel stared in disbelief as the father unbuckled his belt and jerked it out of its belt loops. When it cleared the last belt loop, it made an ominous sound like the cracking of a whip.

"Stand up," the father said. His close-set eyes looked like they were on fire, and his lantern jaw stuck out.

The mother stood facing him with an expression that was a mixture of fear, resignation, and anger.

"Now, bend over, lift your dress, and pull down your panties."

This proved to be too much for the children as they simultaneously burst into pleas for forbearance and huddled protectively around their mother.

Israel found himself standing on an island of uncertainty. Part of him wanted to run and try to escape, where to he didn't know, but anywhere would be better than this terrifying scene. Another part of him wanted to attack this monster. Despite the fact he didn't know any of these people, the injustice of it all filled him with rancor. Another part of him wanted to join the protective shield of children, but again, his feet remained frozen to the floor, and he found it impossible to look away.

The father lifted his hand into the air and swung the belt like a whip, left, then right, against the children, striking them randomly, some on their backs, others on their arms, and some across the face.

Howls of pain filled the room.

"Get away from her, you vermin, and return to your positions. Follow the example of Israel, here."

Israel felt his face turning crimson as he stood in a pool of shame.

The mother started pushing the children away from her. "Do as Sir says. It will be okay. Let me do this."

The youngest two boys readily returned to where they were standing, but the oldest two boys dragged their feet as they obeyed. Only Rebekah remained glued to her mother's side. Her long, dark hair covered one side of her face, while a red mark was appearing on her other cheek where the belt struck her, but there was no look of fear or pain in her eyes, only a cold look that made Israel shudder. The mother had to forcibly peel Rebekah loose, one limb at a time, and put her in place between her brothers.

"Now, woman," the father said, "do as I instructed you to do."

When she stood up and raised her dress, Israel was finally able to squeeze his eyes shut. The rest of the macabre scene was absorbed only through his ears.

"For on that day," the father intoned, "shall the priest make an atonement for you, to cleanse you that ye may be clean from all your sins before the Lord."

The belt whistled as it flew through the air and smacked against her buttocks. It was the only sound in the room as he struck her over and over.

Finally he said, "That is sufficient. Return to your place beside Israel."

Israel opens his eyes and saw a trickle of blood running down the back of her legs.

An hour passed before this Spanish Inquisition of reciting the Ten Commandments mercifully came to an end. By that time, Israel's nose was bloodied, as was the oldest boy's, and the two youngest boys' faces were stained with tears, but Rebekah's demeanor remained unchanged.

Chapter Five

MAGGIE—ELEVEN YEARS OLD

"Maggie," her mother's thin voice called from the bedroom.

Maggie sighed. *What now?* She got up off the couch, where she had just lain down after washing the supper dishes, a supper whose highlight was fried bologna and cheese sandwiches. Speaking to Rachel, who was watching *My Favorite Martian* on their black-and-white TV, she said, "You stay here. I'll be back in a minute."

As she passed by Teddy's baby bed, she noticed his pacifier had popped out of his sleeping mouth. She picked it up and eased it past his lips, where his eager tongue began sucking on it.

In her mother's bedroom, the only light was a small lamp by her bed. She had become so thin that the only evidence that there was someone under the covers was her bald head resting on the pillow. Maggie's feelings about her mother kept changing from feeling sorry for her for being so sick, to anger at her for not taking care of them and for not protecting her from her father, to being afraid of what was going to happen after she died. "What do you want, Mama?"

"Will you bring Teddy to me so I can hold him for a little while?"

Without a word, Maggie walked out and returned with the still-sleeping Teddy. She eased him onto the bed and pulled her mother's arm out from under the covers and positioned it around him.

A faint smile creased her mother's features. "You're a good girl, Maggie. I don't deserve someone like you. I don't know what would have happened to Teddy and Rachel if you hadn't been here to take care of them." Her face contorted as she began crying. "I'm sorry I've been such a miserable mother to you."

Maggie's tough exterior cracked, and her feelings of sadness and loneliness swept over her. Patting her mother's hand, she said, "It's okay, Mama. I love you."

"Will you get the guitar and sing to me?"

Thankful to have something to do that she actually enjoyed, Maggie went to her room and pulled the beat-up Kay guitar, which her mother had been teaching her how to play, from under her bed.

Sitting in a chair beside her mother, she began playing and singing the Hank Williams songs that her mother loved. When she sang "I'm So Lonesome I Could Cry," she lost herself in the song, forgetting about her mother, and infused it with her own feelings of loneliness and sadness. Her cheeks were damp when she finished, and she noticed that her mother appeared to be sleeping, so she slipped quietly from the room, leaving Teddy in the bed.

*****

The next morning, Maggie awakened and immediately smelled cigarette smoke, which told her that her father had come home sometime during the night. She made her way to the kitchen to begin fixing breakfast. She was somewhat surprised to notice that Teddy was not in his bed because normally her father never let him sleep in their bed with them. Realizing that the cigarette smell was stronger the closer she got to the kitchen, she stopped. *I don't want to have to deal with him first thing in the morning.* So she went to her mother's room to spend some time with her and Teddy.

When she entered the room, she was stunned to see that the bed was empty, and all the sheets and bedding had been stripped from the mattress. She was mystified as to where her mother and Teddy could be because her mother hadn't been out of bed in weeks. *They couldn't be in the kitchen or living room, could they?*

She made her way there and spotted her father sitting in his chair, puffing on his cigarette. There were no signs or sounds of her mother or of Teddy.

He rubbed one hand across his high forehead and removed the cigarette from his thin lips with the other. In a matter-of-fact tone, he said, "Your mama died last night. People from the funeral home came and got her."

Maggie felt as if he just slapped her across the face. She stood there dumbfounded, unable to put a coherent thought together.

"Don't look so surprised," he said. "You knew this was going to happen. I just can't believe it took so long. Now fix me some breakfast. I'm hungry."

Maggie knew she needed to do as he said, but she couldn't make her body move. "But I talked to her just last night," she finally managed to say.

"I can't help that. That's just the way things happen sometimes. Don't start feeling sorry for yourself. Life's hard; you just have to deal with it."

Then it struck her. "Where is Teddy?"

"He's gone, too."

"Gone? Gone where?"

"I mean he's gone. I gave him to the social worker who's been coming by here while your mother was sick."

"Why did you do that?" she cried.

"The social worker told me we couldn't keep him here—that she was only letting him stay until your mother died. Said we couldn't properly take care of him, especially when you and Rachel start back to school."

Maggie clenched her fists and took a step toward him. "But I was taking care of him! He was mine!"

"You better stop right there," he said in a sinister tone, "or I'll knock you back into last Tuesday. Look here, your mother's dead and gone, and Teddy's gone, too. That's the end of it. Turn the page and move on." His voice got louder until he banged his fist on the table. "Now fix my breakfast like I told you to!"

Maggie was more than willing to take whatever he wanted to dish out if it would just bring her mother and Teddy back, but she knew that would never happen, so she turned to the stove. *One day, I'm going to kill him. I don't know how, but I'm going to do it.* When she cracked his eggs in the skillet, she surreptitiously spat on them, then smiled.

All of a sudden, she remembered Rachel and that she didn't know what had transpired. *I'm not about to let him tell her.* So after setting his plate of food in front of him, she went to their bedroom, where she found her sister still sleeping peacefully. She sat on the edge of the bed and thought about how she was going to tell her.

As she was looking at her, Rachel's eyes slowly opened. Pushing her tangled red hair out of her face, she asked, "Sissy? What's wrong?"

"Something bad's happened. It's Mama."

Rachel sat up and rubbed her eyes. "What about Mama? Has she gotten sicker?"

Shaking her head, Maggie said, "Mama died last night.'"

"Died? Mama's dead? Will she be coming back?"

"No, don't you remember we talked about it one time? Once a person dies, that's it; they're gone forever."

"Where's she gone to?"

"How should I know?"

"The man at church says people go to heaven and that it's a good place. Is that where Mama is?"

"You can believe that if you want to, but I think it's a story some grown-ups made so their kids won't be so afraid. I don't believe there's such a thing as God, or Mama wouldn't have died and left us, and Daddy wouldn't be—" She barely caught herself before blurting out what her father had been doing to her. "Anyway, life wouldn't be so hard if there was this God who was taking care of children like us."

"I like heaven," Rachel said. "It sounds really pretty. I bet Mama's happy there."

Maggie decided to drop any efforts to dissuade her. "There's more I have to tell you about what happened last night."

"More?"

"Teddy is gone."

Giant tears sprung up in Rachel's eyes. "Teddy died, too?"

"No, he didn't die. He's just gone."

"Gone where? Is he with Mama?"

Feeling exasperated, Maggie said, "No! Mama's dead, but Teddy's not. That woman who's been coming to check on all of us took him."

"Where did she take him?"

"I don't know—I guess to another family that has a mother and a father and who will take care of him."

"Will he be coming back?"

This time it was Maggie's eyes that filled with tears. She blinked, and they dropped onto the covers. "No. We'll probably never see him again."

Chapter Six

ISRAEL—FIFTEEN YEARS OLD

"You little whore!" Sir roared at Rebekah. "You've probably screwed the entire football team. What a disgusting disgrace you are." He ended his last sentence by spitting at her.

"Cherry and I were working on a school project and lost track of time," Rachel said calmly. "That's why I came home late. You can believe me or not; that's up to you."

Israel stood at attention with his other siblings and their mother, watching this oft-repeated drama between Rebekah, who was tall for her age, and Sir. He felt his chest getting tighter and realized his fists were balled up.

Sir said, "You're a liar, just like your namesake and just like Eve in the Garden of Eden." He turned and looked at the boys. "Always remember, you cannot trust a woman. They are deceivers and will drag you into the pits of hell after them." He unbuckled his belt and started pulling it through the belt loops.

Israel turned his eyes toward his mother and believed she was about to, once again, step in and take the punishment intended for one of them. There had never been a woman he admired and despised more. His admiration was for her willingness to sacrifice her own well-being for the sake of her children, but he despised her for not doing something to stop the abuse that was going on in their house.

Why doesn't she call the police or load us up and take us away from here? Or why doesn't she kill him in his sleep? This last question was one that he'd been asking of himself lately. Even Rebekah, whom he viewed as the strongest person in the house because of her unyielding attitude toward Sir, wouldn't actually kill him, he believed. But her nonviolent approach was exacting a toll on Sir. Israel saw it in his eyes, how he sometimes looked at her with confusion and uncertainty, not knowing what to do with someone who refused to bow and scrape to him.

Israel's own heart vacillated between rage and terror in these situations. He knew all too well that the physical pain from Sir's beatings was real enough, but it was getting harder to tamp down his rage and desire to fight back.

He stood there suspended between action and freezing up until he saw his mother make the slightest move, then he broke ranks with his brothers and said, "Stop it!"

In that moment, it felt like all the air had been sucked out of the room and at the same time like the room was so full of air it was going to explode.

Sir wound the belt around his hand and slowly turned toward Israel.

Rebekah looked over her shoulder at him, and for the first time that Israel had ever seen, a tear descended from the corner of her eye.

Even though Israel was nearly as tall as Sir, his bulk was less than half his father's. Despite this, he took a step toward Sir. "It's enough, Sir. It's time for all this to stop." His voice sounded hollow in his own ears, and he almost felt as if he was dreaming. He didn't look at his mother or his brothers. He knew he was on an island with this.

A malevolent smile spread across Sir's face, and he pounded his belt-wrapped fist into the palm of his other hand. "Do you want to take her punishment?"

"No, Sir. I'm saying all of this needs to stop. What you do to us is wrong."

"'Children obey your parents.' 'Wives be in subjection to your husbands.' That's what my Bible says. Nowhere does it say I should listen to what any of you have to say about it. The Bible is the rule for this house, and anyone who doesn't want to live by that rule can leave. Do you want to leave, Israel?"

Israel had thought about leaving a hundred times, but he had always been held back by worry over what would happen to his mother and siblings if he did. Not that he'd ever done anything to protect them, but that was before today.

Sir closed the distance between them until their faces were inches apart.

Israel felt his resolve and anger draining away, but he refused to back down. "Sometimes I do want to leave, Sir. But I stay here for my brothers, sister, and mother."

Sir laughed. "You're a bigger fool than I took you for. None of you have a brother or sister or mother or father. You're all a bunch of orphans that we took in off the street. You owe everything to us. But you are an ungrateful lot. Not a one of you has the decency to appreciate what we've done for you." Without warning, he delivered a backhand blow with his belt-wrapped fist to the side of Israel's face, nearly knocking him off his feet.

Israel staggered backward and went down on one knee. White-hot rage coursed through his veins. Lifting his head, he looked at Sir, then raced toward him like a defensive tackle. He hit him in the midsection with his shoulder and kept driving with his legs, just like he'd learned in football.

Somewhere far away he heard a voice that sounded like Rebekah's calling his name.

A heavy blow hit the back of his head, filling his vision with stars; then everything went black.

*****

Israel stood surrounded by a thick fog, trying to figure out where he was. In the distance, he heard voices, but he was uncertain from which direction they were coming or whose voices they were. When he turned around, everything started spinning, and he felt like he was falling off a cliff. He opened his mouth to cry for help, but nothing came out.

Gradually the fog began thinning, and he recognized the voices of Rebekah and Abraham. Something cool and damp was laid across his forehead.

"Wake up, Israel," Rebekah's voice said. "Please wake up."

"I think he's coming around," Abraham said.

Finally, Israel opened his eyes. He was in his bed, and Abraham and Rebekah were peering down at him with furrowed brows. Confused, he tried to push himself up, but searing pain shot through his head, and he fell back onto his pillow. "What happened?"

"You protected me from Sir," Rebekah said with a tremor in her voice.

"You charged him like a bull or something," Abraham added. "It was amazing!"

The scene and his actions slowly came back to him. "I remember now. What happened after I hit him?"

They both looked away. "He knocked you unconscious," Rebekah said. Turning back to him, she took his hand. "I'm sorry he did that to you. It was my fault. You shouldn't have gotten involved."

Israel tried to shake his head no, but the pain made it impossible. "That's not true. It wasn't your fault. I just couldn't stand it anymore. We've got to tell someone what's going on here."

"No," Abraham said. "If we tell, and nobody does anything about it, he'll make it even worse on us. He might even kill one of us."

"We're just supposed to keep taking it?" Israel asks. "He's already killing us little by little. To do nothing is insane."

"He's right," Rebekah agreed. "We've got to do something."

"Listen to me," Abraham said, "I've lived in this hell the longest of any of you. You just have to hang in there. It will be over soon. I'm about to graduate from high school and leave for college, and I'm never coming back. That's the way out for you, too."

Israel locked eyes with Rebekah and in them read that she thought very little of Abraham's idea. "You do what you think you need to do," he said to Abraham, "and I'll do what I think I need to do."

Abraham looked from him to Rebekah. "What are you going to do?"

"What I'm going to do is none of your concern. Don't worry about me; you never have anyway."

Even though the comment wasn't meant for Israel, he could still feel the sting in her accusation.

Abraham appeared to shrivel under the heat of her withering look. Giving them a disdainful wave of his hand, he said, "You both are crazy," and walked out of the room.

In the silence left behind, Rebekah asked, "What's your plan?"

Israel said, "Abraham makes a good point when he asks what will happen if we call the police and they come and then don't do anything. I can't imagine what Sir would do."

Rebekah started pacing back and forth and waving her hands in the air. "But how can they not do anything about it? I mean, he's been abusing everyone for years. Even if they don't believe us, surely Mother's word will be enough to convince them."

He shook his head. "I don't believe she'll back our story. She'll be too scared of what's going to happen to her if she does. He's got her beat down so far that she can't think for herself. Sometimes I feel sorry for her, and other times I hate her for it."

"Me too. So if we're not going to call anyone and make a report, what are we going to do to stop him?"

"I'll think of something."

"I think we're going to have to kill him; that's the only way this is going to stop."

Israel had already come to the same conclusion, but to hear Rebekah say it out loud in her calm, matter-of-fact way made it seem even more dramatic than he'd imagined. He just couldn't come up with a way of killing him that he thought he could pull off. He'd thought about making a garrote out of one of his guitar strings like he'd seen portrayed in the Godfather movies, but he wasn't sure he was strong enough to fend off Sir's attempts to fight him off. *Maybe rat poison . . .*

"I've got an idea," she cut in on his musings. "Mother has been getting nerve pills from her doctor. What if we put some in Sir's iced tea that he drinks while watching TV after supper?"

"You think that would kill him? How many would it take?"

"I'm not sure, but we could put the whole bottle in there, I guess. I've been reading up on the medicine, and people do die from overdosing on it. They just sort of stop breathing, I think."

It wasn't an idea Israel had even considered, but Rebekah seemed so sure of it that it made sense to him, too.

The silence in the room deepened.

After a moment, he said, "Sounds like we have a plan."

*****

Late that night, Israel wrote:

Dear Darnell,

I'm sorry I haven't been very good about writing you regularly, but I do think about you just about every day. I don't know if you remember or not, but I've told you what kind of crazy place this is that I'm living in. The father of the house is insane. He beats all of us all the time.

Well, I've finally had enough. I've made a decision to do something about it. I can't tell you what it is because you might have to tell someone. I'm just letting you know so that if you ever hear something about me that shocks you, it's probably true. I'm sorry if it makes you ashamed of me, and I wish there was another way out. But there's not.

Don't write me back because I probably won't be here anymore. I'll let you know how things turn out, when and if I can.

—Israel

Chapter Seven

MAGGIE—FOURTEEN YEARS OLD

With Rachel sitting beside her on the floor, Maggie opened the edge-worn cigar box she'd pilfered from the trash and converted into a treasure box of sorts three years ago.

Rachel pointed and asked, "What's that?"

Picking it up, Maggie answered, "It's a brooch Mama used to wear before you were born. She called it a cameo."

"Is that her?"

"No. It's just a figure of a woman. All cameos look sort of the same."

"It doesn't look like Mama."

"That's because it isn't. That's what I just told you." She picked up a tortoise-shell-colored comb. "And she wore this in her hair before it all fell out."

"I can't remember Mama not being sick. Didn't she used to be pretty?"

Maggie took out a folded photograph and unfolded it, revealing a dark-haired woman with dark features and a sharp nose, which was the exact point at which the horizontal and vertical creases of the folds intersected. "She was beautiful, with long, flowing hair that she fixed lots of different ways using this comb. Turn around and I'll show you." Rachel turned her back to Maggie, who then shaped her hair into a bun and held it in place with the comb. "Go look in the mirror."

It troubled Maggie that Rachel still seemed so simpleminded and childlike about lots of things. She had to repeat first grade and was in danger of having to repeat fourth grade, too, which made Maggie wonder if her sister was retarded and needed to be in special classes.

It didn't help that their father called Rachel "stupid" and "dummy," although Rachel didn't act like it bothered her. It was Maggie who would get livid about it. One time she yelled at him to stop it, but that resulted in a bruise on the side of her face that caused him to keep her home from school for a week, "In case people start getting nosey and asking questions."

Rachel reached into the cigar box and pulled out a tiny shoe. "This was Teddy's, wasn't it?"

"Yes," Maggie answered, taking it from her. She turned it over in her hand, then sat it on her palm. "Look how tiny he was."

"I don't remember what he looked like."

Maggie felt ashamed because she, too, had difficulty remembering details of what he looked like. While there were maybe a dozen photographs that had her and Rachel in them, there were none of Teddy. *Just one more reason to hate my father.*

"Teddy didn't have much hair," she said to Rachel, trying to paint a portrait from her limited memory. "His eyes were kind of dark. He was really cute. And he used to blow bubbles when he wanted you to pick him up."

Rachel smiled. "And you raised him because Mama was so sick, right?"

Maggie cocked her head to one side, puzzled over why Rachel asked questions she knew the answer to. *Maybe she's afraid she'll forget things, just like I've forgotten what Teddy looked like.* "Yes, Mama was sick."

"And you raised me, too."

"Not at first. When you were a baby, Mama took care of you."

"I don't remember that. I only remember you taking care of me. Why doesn't our daddy ever take care of us?"

Finally, this oft-repeated conversation took a new turn as Rachel asked a question she'd never asked before. But it was a question Maggie had no simple answer for. *Because he's an asshole*—that's what she wanted to say, but she knew that wouldn't satisfy Rachel. "It's hard to explain, Rachel," she told her little sister.

A few moments of silence passed before Rachel said, "Why doesn't he ever lie in bed with me like he does with you sometimes? Does he not like me?"

Maggie's heart stopped, and she could not breathe. She'd always believed Rachel was asleep whenever he came to her. *How long has she noticed? What has she actually seen?* She was horrified that her sister thought her father came to her bed because he liked her and that Rachel wanted him to come to her bed, too.

She grabbed both of Rachel's shoulders. "What have you seen going on in my bed? And how long have you been watching?"

"Ow! You're hurting me," Rachel said as she tried to wriggle out of her grasp. "Why are you so mad?"

Maggie only gripped her tighter. "Shut up and answer me! What have you seen?"

"He gets in bed with you and lies on top of you. He starts breathing really heavy, and after a while, he leaves. He looks happy when he leaves."

Maggie wondered how to have the kind of conversation with her sister that should never have to happen. Releasing her grip on Maggie, she said, "I'm sorry I hurt you and that I got so upset. I'm going to tell you something that I don't know if you're going to understand, but you've got to try." She took a deep breath. "Father doesn't come to my bed at night because he likes me and definitely not because he loves me. What he does to me when he gets there is wrong, very wrong. He could probably go to jail for it."

Rachel screwed her face into a frown, and Maggie was certain she wasn't doing a good job of explaining things to her. "Okay, it's like this," she said to her. "He has sex with me. He enjoys it, but I despise it. You do know what sex is, don't you?"

"Sort of . . ."

"Do you know what a man's dick is?"

"You're not supposed to say that. Teacher says it's wrong."

"It's okay if you and I talk about it in our house."

"It's what they use the bathroom with, isn't it?"

"Yes. Well, he puts his dick inside of me, right here." She pointed toward her own vagina.

Rachel's expression morphed into one of disgust. "Why does he do that?"

"Because he wants to. But fathers should never do that to their children. No adult should ever do that to a child. Only evil people do that kind of thing. And if Father ever tries to do that to you, you must promise me that you will tell me. This is very important; you have to promise it." Panic rose in her throat at the very thought of him trying to rape her sister. At the same time, she got the feeling of being trapped. *How can I ever leave home and leave Rachel behind?*

Rachel looked at her and said in a tiny voice, "I think he tried to do it."

Maggie felt her blood run cold. She stared, unblinking, at her sister. She had the odd sensation that she was caught in an episode of *The Twilight Zone* that kept getting more and more twisted, and she couldn't escape from it. It was several seconds before she found her voice. "Tell me . . . tell me what . . . happened."

"You're going to get mad at me."

"No, I won't; I promise. Because whatever happened wasn't your fault. Just tell me exactly what happened."

"Well, I was sitting on Daddy's lap watching TV, and I felt something pushing on my bottom that felt uncomfortable. When I jumped out of his lap and turned around to look, his thing was sticking up out of his pants."

A wave of nausea hit Maggie so strongly that she almost threw up. She reached for Rachel, pulled her onto her lap, rocked her, and began to cry. "I'm so, so, so sorry, Rachel. It was never supposed to happen to you. I thought if I let him do it to me, he would leave you alone. God, what a fool I am! I should have known better."

Rachel pushed herself back and wiped Maggie's tears with the palms of her hands. "It's okay, Maggie. But what are we going to do?"

"I'm not sure yet, but I'll think of something." *I'm going to make him regret ever touching her.*

Chapter Eight

ISRAEL—FIFTEEN YEARS OLD

"Is he dead?" Israel looked from Rebekah to Sir, then back to her, as his heart galloped.

Sir was sitting in his recliner, with his chin resting on his chest. Israel could detect no signs of his chest rising or falling.

Rebekah laid her hand on his chest and kept it there for several seconds. "Yes, I think he's dead."

Israel relaxed his grip on his homemade garrote and stuffed it in his jeans' pocket. "I can't believe how easy that was by using Mother's pills. I didn't even need this garrote."

"What do we do now?" Rebekah asked.

"I say just leave him here and let Mother find him when she and the others get home from going to the movie. You and I can pretend to be asleep in our beds. She'll think he died of a heart attack or something."

"Yeah, but what if she calls the police or something, and they come and send his body for an autopsy? They'll discover those pills in his blood; then what will happen?"

"I hadn't thought about that." Israel felt his anxiety returning after it had subsided in the face of how easily Sir died. "It's stupid that we never really talked about what to do after we killed him. What do you think we should do?"

"We need to get rid of the body," Rebekah said simply. "We'll load him in the bed of his pickup truck and haul him off somewhere."

Shaking his head, Israel said, "That'll never work. You can't just dump him in a ditch somewhere. He'll be found for certain, and then there will definitely be an investigation."

"That's okay. Let them investigate. There won't be any evidence that points a finger in our direction. What possible motive would we have to kill him? Nobody knows what's been going on here all these years."

As usual, Rebekah sounded so calm and logical about things that Israel found it hard to argue with her or to find a flaw in her plan. "It sounds too easy," he commented.

"All we have to do is not panic. That's why killers get caught—because they panic and make mistakes."

"But how do we explain to Mother that he's not here?"

She shrugged. "We'll say he never came home from work."

"But his truck will be here."

This slowed Rebekah down, and she didn't say anything for a minute. "What about this? We put him in the cab of the truck and leave him and the truck on the side of the road, and we walk back home."

"That might work."

"Do you have a better idea?"

He detected irritation in her tone. "No. I just want whatever we do to be foolproof."

"You grab one of his feet, and I'll grab the other, and we'll drag him out to the truck."

Israel was shocked at how difficult it was to move Sir. *It never looks this hard on TV.*

As they passed through the front door and headed down the steps into the dark, he was thankful they lived in a rural area of the county with no neighbors close by to witness what was happening.

Suddenly, he stopped pulling. "Shhh! What was that?"

"What?"

"That sound. I thought I heard something."

"You're just scared. Calm down, and let's get this over with."

When they started dragging the body again, there was a groaning sound from Sir. Immediately, they dropped his legs and jumped back.

"See? I told you I heard something. He's not dead!"

"But I checked his heartbeat and didn't feel—"

Another groan from Sir swallowed whatever she was about to say.

"Damn, Rebekah, he's still alive! What are we going to do?" This time he saw panic in her eyes, too. When she didn't reply, he remembered his garrote and took it out of his pocket.

She looked at it as if she'd never seen it before. "Are you going to . . ." she trailed off.

"We've got no choice!" he yelled. He rushed to Sir's head, got down on his knees, slipped the guitar string around Sir's throat, and pulled on the two handles with all his might.

Israel had no idea how long he'd been pulling on the garrote when he felt Rebekah's hand on his arm. "That's enough, Israel," she said. "You can let go now. It's definitely over."

When he let go, his cramped fingers remained curled, as if still gripping the handles. He stood up and staggered a little.

Rebekah steadied him and said, "Are you okay?"

"Yeah, I'll be fine. I just . . ." He looked down at Sir and saw a pool of blood shining in the moonlight. Pointing he said, "How'd that happen?"

"You pulled so hard on the garrote that it cut into his throat and jugular vein."

He stared at her.

"It's true," she said. "I'm going to go get a shovel from the shed so that we can cover the blood with some dirt and gravel."

This was going to be so simple—easy. What's going to happen next?

When Rebekah returned with the shovel, he took it from her and began covering the damning liquid evidence. "We're never going to get everything taken care of before Mother returns. What are we going to tell her?"

"We'll tell her we decided to go for a walk and look at the stars. She won't care."

Israel was amazed at how quickly she could come up with a lie and wondered if there were other lies in her life no one knew about. "Okay, then, let's just get this over with."

With much more difficulty than Israel had imagined, they finally shoved Sir into the bed of the pickup, then got in the cab and drove off, with Rebekah driving.

He looked at the East Ridge Cemetery entrance as they drove past and yelled, "Stop the truck!"

She slammed on the brakes, which caused him to slide off his seat and crack his knees against the dashboard.

"Ow!" he cried.

"Why did you want me to stop?" she asked.

Pointing at the cemetery he said, "Look over there."

"What?"

"See that funeral tent? They must be having a burial there in the morning."

"So what?"

"So they've already dug the grave, or they wouldn't have the tent up."

"And?"

"Let's put Sir in the grave." He watched Rebekah mull over his idea. "It's perfect. No one will ever find him."

"But won't that mess up how far down they can lower the vault? I mean, what if it makes it stick out of the ground?"

"I guess what we need to do is dig the grave lower, put Sir in it, then cover him up to the original level the grave is."

"Do you think you can do it?"

"How hard can it be?"

An hour later, with sweat stinging his eyes and his breathing labored, he called up to Rebekah. "Shine that flashlight in here again. I think I've hit another tree root."

From the darkness above came a shaft of yellow light that lit the bottom of the grave. "How are you doing?" Rebekah called down.

"Except for the fact that I have blisters on my hands, I'm covered in mud, it's hard to breathe down here, and I'm exhausted, I'm fine." He leaned back against the cool wall of the grave and inspected the bottom. He spotted the skinned edge of a tree root. "There it is," he said to no one in particular. Picking up the ax, he chopped the root in two and pitched the piece up to Rebekah. "Catch!"

The light from the flashlight danced wildly, then steadied. "Got it," Rebekah called to him.

Israel rubbed his back muscles that were screaming in pain. *I'd give anything for something to drink. Just a little farther down and I'll be finished.*

Thirty minutes later, he tossed the shovel out. "I'm done. Lower him down here."

Several minutes passed, and then Rebekah called down to him, "He's too heavy for me. There's no way I'll be able to lower him down. You'll have to come up, help lower him down, then go back down there and lay him flat."

Tired and fed up with all of it, he said, "Just roll him to the edge and push him off in here."

"You sure?"

"Yes," he said angrily.

A couple more minutes passed, and suddenly there was a gust of wind immediately followed by a resounding thud at the other end of the grave. Working completely in the dark, Israel had to figure out by feeling where Sir's head and feet were so that he could stretch him out. After he got him situated, he called, "Okay, tie one end of the rope to the bumper of the truck and toss the other end down here; I'll climb up it."

As he waited for the rope, he thought of the irony of the situation. *All the times I've thought about killing him and how good it would feel to do it, and now I really don't feel anything . . . except exhaustion.*

Finally, he heard what he assumed was the end of the rope landing close by. Grabbing hold of it, he climbed up and out of the grave and collapsed on his back beside it, enjoying the fresh air. After he caught his breath, he said, "The first thing we're going to do is find me something to drink. I'm dying of thirst."

When Rebekah didn't answer, he said, "Hey, did you hear me? Are you all right?" The only answer to his question was the rhythmic cadence of tree frogs singing close by.

He sat up and looked around. "Rebekah?"

There were no sights nor sounds of her. He went and looked in the cab of the truck and found it empty. "Rebekah," he called more loudly. Then in a half whisper, he said, "Have you gone away?"

Chapter Nine

MAGGIE—SIXTEEN YEARS OLD

"You in the market for a used car?"

Maggie straightened up from looking through the window of a car and turned around. What she saw caused her to feel like she'd been struck through the heart by the proverbial cupid's arrow. A man she guessed to be in his late thirties, with jet black hair, flashed her a smile that she was certain could still be seen on a moonless night and looked at her with eyes that nearly danced out of their sockets. He was dressed in a plaid suit, with a white belt and white shoes that had stacked heels.

Sticking out his hand to her, he said, "I'm Jackson Wallace, owner of Honest John's Used Cars. If you don't see a car you like, I'll find you one. Everything on the lot is in top-notch shape, dependable as the day is long. You like the looks of that Buick?"

Maggie shook his hand and felt a charge of electricity shoot through her. With her heart thumping against her chest, she found her voice and said, "I'm needing something dependable, but I'm also needing something sort of cheap."

Jackson frowned and shook his head. "No, no, that won't do. We can't have a pretty young lady with dazzling green eyes like yours driving around in a piece of junk. Won't your old man cough up any of his money to help you buy a car? What's the matter with the old codger?"

You don't have time for me to tell you what all is wrong with him. She'd thought about this aspect of buying a car and had decided she'd work the sympathy angle in hopes the dealer would feel sorry for her and cut her a good deal. "The truth is my mama died when I was a little girl. It's just been me and my papa ever since, and he's gotten in really bad health and can't work. I got me a job after school and on weekends. We use it to pay some of our bills, but I've got to get a car, or I won't be able to keep my job." She pulled her eyes away from his and looked down at the ground. "We're in a bad way."

Jackson moved beside her, slipped his arm around her shoulder, and squeezed her close to him, giving her an immediate thrill. "Hey, don't you worry. If Honest John can't help you, then nobody can."

"So if your name is Jackson Wallace, how come the name of the business is Honest John's?"

"It's all about marketing, honey. Everybody thinks car lots are filled with shysters bent on stealing their money. Even if they don't completely believe the sign on my business, it might make them think better of me than other car dealers."

He walked slowly around the car but kept his eyes on her.

She noticed he was taking in all of her, not just her face, which made her a little uncomfortable but also made her proud of the way she looked.

As he came back around to where she was standing, he said, "We might be able to work out a sweet deal here, one that would help us both out. My wife is my secretary, but she had a baby last week and is going to be off for a while. I'm needing somebody I can depend on to answer the phone and do a little paperwork for me. Can you type?"

"Sure. I'm taking typing now and doing really well at it."

"Good, that's good. What if I let you have this car, and in turn, you started working for me?"

Maggie stared at him, dumbfounded. "You mean like a trade? I give you work, and you give me this car?"

"I knew you were a sharp one the minute I saw you. You're exactly right."

"Is that legal?"

"Sure, honey, people do that kind of thing all the time."

"How long would I have to work before the car was actually mine?"

"It'll be yours right from the get-go. We'll put it in your name and everything."

Maggie could not believe how easy this second step in leaving home was turning out to be. She'd managed to achieve the first step six months ago when she convinced her father's sister to take Rachel and raise her. Her aunt had asked her why, and Maggie told her the truth about the abuse. "Oh, honey," her aunt had said, "that sort of thing goes on all the time. It's just the way things are. You'll get over it. I did." That attitude almost made Maggie change her mind about letting Rachel go, but the aunt was single and didn't date, so she figured it had to be better than staying with her.

Selling the idea to her father of letting Rachel go had been prickly at first, but when she'd appealed to his Scrooge-like attitude toward money and pointed out to him that it was going to become increasingly expensive to feed and clothe two girls, he'd acquiesced.

Sticking out her hand toward the used-car dealer, she said, "We've got a deal, Mr. Wallace."

He clasped her hand between both of his and winked at her. "You don't have to call me Mr. Wallace. You can call me Jackson." Releasing his hold on her, he said, "Turn around for me."

Maggie obliged.

"What size clothes do you wear?"

"What size clothes? I don't understand."

"I'm going to buy you some things that'll catch people's eyes when they come by looking for a car. It's all part of marketing. There's lots of tricks of the trade that I'll teach you while you're working for me."

Maggie had never had someone give her such individual attention and make her feel special like Jackson was. And he was so good-looking! *All I've got to do now is save up some money after I pay this car off, and I'll be able to run away.*

*****

When she arrived for work after school the next day, Maggie walked into the office.

Jackson was on the phone but still managed to give her a smile. After ending the call, he asked, "So what did your old man say when you drove home a new car yesterday?"

"He accused me of stealing it. Then when I told him about the deal you gave me, he said I was swapping sex for the car. He makes me so mad!"

"What a prick! Don't pay any attention to him. He's probably from the old school that says anything that looks too good to be true probably is. You just trust ol' Jackson Wallace to treat you right. The deal I gave you works for both of us." He reached down beside his desk and handed her a sack. "Here's the clothes I promised you. Why don't you go try them on and see what you think?"

She took the sack and went into the bathroom. She felt a little weird about a man she didn't know buying her clothes but found it a little exciting at the same time. Her shock came when she opened the sack and found bras and panties in there along with the expected clothes.

She'd never been allowed to buy lacy, bright-colored underwear because her father said only sluts wore those kinds of things. But after her initial shock, she quickly stripped and tried them on. Twisting and turning to see herself in the mirror, she smiled at what she saw. *It makes me look so much older!*

Next, she put on a silky paisley print top that scooped low on her neck and pulled on a skirt with a hem that was halfway up her thighs. She loved how slick they felt against her skin. Looking back in the sack, she spotted a pair of high heels, which she slipped on. It took her several moments to be able to stand straight without her ankles buckling, so when she finally exited the bathroom to model the apparel, she moved very slowly and cautiously.

As she entered Jackson's office, his jaw dropped, and his eyes scanned her slowly from top to bottom; then he gave a whistle. "Oh wow, Maggie, you look incredible. You look like you're twenty-one years old."

Maggie felt her face grow warm as she blushed at his praise.

"Have a seat here at this desk, and let me show you what you'll be doing for me."

As the afternoon wore on, Maggie found Jackson had a sense of humor much like hers, and they liked the same kind of music. She wasn't sure what the name of his cologne was, but she found it intoxicating and enjoyed him leaning over her shoulder to point out details he wanted her to manage. The fact that no customers came by didn't seem to matter to him, and she was pleased, too, because it meant all his attention was focused on her.

Before she left to go back home, she changed back into her other clothes that now looked even more drab than before. As she did so, she felt her mood descending into that place of darkness, hopelessness, and dread. *But now I have something to look forward to each day, a place where I can be someone else.*

The last thing on her mind as she went to sleep that night was the handsome face of Jackson Wallace.

Chapter Ten

ISRAEL—SEVENTEEN YEARS OLD

Standing in a circle of jeering and cheering boys, Israel crouched low while holding his boxing gloves in front of his face. It was the annual "prove yourself" tradition that the football coach put the boys through at the end of spring practice. Boys were chosen randomly and put in the "ring" of players to face a teammate and were to fight until someone gave up. Sometimes it turned out that best friends faced each other, with neither wanting to throw the first punch, but the coach and a chorus of voices around them teased them about being chicken and a sissy until they finally fought.

Israel was pleased that his opponent today was Hal Stoudemeyer. He hated Hal, who was arrogant, strutted around like he was better than everyone else, and had a smart mouth, all of which were Israel's pet peeves. He and Hal had started some shoving matches in the past because Israel refused to kowtow to him, but people had always broken it up before it turned into a real fight. *Now's my chance. I'm going to smash his face, bloody his nose, and black his eyes. He'll find out he's not as tough as he thinks he is.*

Suddenly the coach's whistle sounded for the fighting to start. For the first little bit, Hal kept dancing just out of reach of Israel's punches, while at the same time he laughed and sneered at Israel. Then Israel feigned with his right, which caused Hal to flinch and be struck by a perfectly thrown left hook. Israel felt the blow land solidly and saw Hal's head snap. It thrilled him to see a look of fear and uncertainty appear on Hal's face. Adrenaline coursed through Israel's veins, and he could no longer hear anything around him.

Like a tiger stalking its prey, he circled left, then right, landing blows to Hal's ribs, midsection, and jaw. Finally, he landed a blow square in his face. Bright blood poured out of Hal's nose, and he gave the coach a pleading look for help.

The grizzled coach only laughed and yelled, "What are you made of, Hal? Fight it out!"

Israel moved in for the kill, raining blows to the side of Hal's head until Hal fell onto his back. Israel pounced on his chest and flung the loosely tied boxing gloves off his hands and began pummeling Hal's face with his bare fists. Blood splattered across the floor and onto Israel's arms. Never had he felt such a mixture of rage and power. A loud roar exploded from his mouth, "I'm going to kill you!" Then everything went black.

*****

The next thing Israel remembered was sitting in the coach's office with the coach and a police officer asking him questions.

"So you're saying you weren't trying to kill Hal even though everyone heard you say you were going to kill him, is that right?" the policeman asked.

Confused, Israel looked back and forth at the two men. "What are you talking about?"

Looking at the coach, the policeman said, "Are you sure he didn't get hit in the head and suffer a concussion or something? He acts like he doesn't know where he is."

"Stoudemeyer never landed a blow. Do you remember the fight, McKenzie?" he asked Israel.

"I remember we started fighting, and I landed a couple of lucky blows, but then I blacked out, I guess, because I don't remember anything else until I came to in here with you two. Why are the police here? What happened?"

The two men shared a look, and then the policeman said, "You may have killed Hal. He's in the hospital right now, and they're not sure he's going to make it. How do you feel about that?"

Without warning, Israel vomited in the middle of the floor. Fear spread through him like a virulent virus, and he began shaking uncontrollably.

The coach jumped up and grabbed a bucket and towel. "He's not saying you did kill Hal. It just doesn't look good right now." Glancing at the officer, he said, "Why don't you let me take him home? Can't you see the boy's tore up about it?"

*****

Several hours later, Israel sat up in his bed quietly strumming his guitar with his thumb. The clock radio read 12:37 a.m.

What's the point? I'm screwed no matter what happens. He stripped the pillowcase off his pillow, walked over to his chest of drawers, and began stuffing clothes in it. Before walking out of his bedroom, he placed his guitar in its tattered guitar case and carried it with him.

Passing through the kitchen, he grabbed three apples, a banana, and a couple of cans of Spam and dropped them into the pillowcase. With his hand on the doorknob of the back door, he looked back at the darkened house. *Goodbye, everybody, maybe we'll meet again down the line.*

Making sure he kept to the dusky edge of the light cast by the streetlights, he made his way through the silent streets toward the railyard a mile away. In history class, he had read about hobos during the Depression making their way from place to place by hiding in freight cars, and he'd been fascinated by it. *No one to answer to. Go anywhere you want to. See the country.* It sounded better than any other situation he'd lived in.

Suddenly the silence was torn by the blaring sound of a train engine's horn. Israel nearly jumped out of his shoes. The hitches on the heavy freight cars banged against each other as the engine stretched the line of cars taut. Israel broke into a run, ducking between stationary cars, trying to find the train that was leaving the yard.

Another blast from the engine's horn helped him find his destination just as the cars began inching forward. *I've just got to find a car with its door slid open.*

Car after car crept past him, but they were picking up speed, and he began to panic that he might not find an open car. *Then what am I going to do?*

At that moment, a car appeared with its door yawning open, an inky black unknown beckoning Israel inside. He trotted alongside it, pitched his loaded pillowcase inside, then sent his guitar case sliding after it. Timing his jump perfectly, he landed with his foot on the rung of a step, grabbed the side of the door, pulled himself inside, and collapsed on the floor.

As if congratulating him on his accomplishment, the engine gave a long blast on its horn.

Once he caught his breath, he sat up and watched the receding lights of the city until he could see them no more, then gathered his belongings, curled up in a corner of the car, and let the rhythmic clickety-clack of the tracks and rocking of the car lull him to sleep.

Chapter Eleven

MAGGIE—SEVENTEEN YEARS OLD

Maggie watched as Jackson ushered a customer back into his car, smiling all the while. *Another customer without making a sale.* The used-car business had not been what she expected when Jackson hired her last year. She thought there would be multiple sales every day, with satisfied customers spreading the word to their friends about the good deal they got. The reality turned out to be that sometimes Jackson would only sell one car in a week, which meant she often sat around with nothing to do. She hated being bored.

What she looked forward to nowadays was when the business closed, and she and Jackson would do what he referred to as "after-hours work." He had first introduced the idea to her as a game they could play to help him unwind from the stress of the day. Her role was a sexy woman looking to buy a car, but she had no money. The goal was to tease Jackson by crossing her legs, subtly inching her skirt a little higher, or leaning over his desk so that he could see her breasts. It gave her a sneaky thrill to have the kind of power over a grown man that could make him so aroused, like he was wrapped around her little finger.

At first, the game had been all looking and no touching, until the day he begged her to let him kiss her. "You look so delicious—I just can't stand it! Just one kiss," he'd said. She'd fantasized about what it would be like to kiss him but never thought he would be interested in carrying the game that far.

When she agreed to let him kiss her, he caressed her face between his hands, leaned down, and gently touched his lips to hers. Maggie felt a spark of electricity pass between them. She tingled all the way to her toes. She put her arms around his neck and pressed her lips harder against his until he opened his mouth and ran his tongue over her lips. Fire coursed through her veins, and she felt her face flushing as she opened her mouth and their tongues danced against each other.

What she hadn't known then was that that kiss opened a door from which she could not return. She couldn't get enough of Jackson, couldn't wait for the close of the business day, ached to feel his warm breath on her face, to smell his rich cologne and to taste his mouth.

It wasn't long before Jackson placed his hand on her breast during one of their make-out sessions. At first, she had reflexively flinched and pulled away but then found that it was a pleasurable thing to be touched that way by someone she loved.

As she watched him heading across the car lot and toward the office, she thought, *I can't believe I'm in love. I doubted that I could ever love a man, but he is so much more than I ever dreamed of. And he loves me, too.*

The fact that he was married never really bothered her. *If she can't keep her man satisfied, that's her problem.* Besides, Jackson referred to his wife as "a nag" and "a fat cow."

She ignored the few friends she had who told her she was completely crazy for messing around with a man more than twice her age. She always countered, "You girls don't know what you're missing."

Jackson entered the office looking downcast. "I can't believe how slow business is. This is supposed to be a busy time of year, but these stupid people around here are too ignorant to recognize a good deal when they see one." He plopped down in his desk chair and ran his fingers through his thick hair.

Maggie reluctantly handed him an envelope. "This came in the mail today. It's from the electric company warning that they are going to shut off the electricity if the bill isn't paid in ten days."

Like water spewing out of an open fire hydrant, Jackson let out a stream of profanity as he swept his arm across his desk, sending the phone, ink pens, and papers flying across the room.

Maggie froze in shock. She'd never seen him act this way and was uncertain what to do. She thought about hurrying out the door and leaving, but her heart went out to him. Stepping behind him, she started gently combing his hair with her fingers. "It's okay, baby. Things are going to work out; you'll see. You're just going through a dry spell."

He sat back in his chair and rested the back of his head against her breasts.

She felt him let out a big sigh. Letting her hands slide down to his shoulders, she began massaging them. "Just relax. Everything's going to be fine."

"You're the best thing that's ever happened to me," Jackson said. "If I didn't have you, I think I'd kill myself."

She swiveled his chair around to face her. "Don't ever say that! You're better than that. As long as we've got each other, we can face anything." She leaned in and kissed him.

"That's what I need," he said hoarsely as he stood up and lifted her off the floor.

She threw her arms around his neck and laughed. "Gosh! You're so strong! She looked into his eyes and saw they were filled with desire.

"I want you," he said.

"You've got me," she smiled.

"No, I mean I want you, all of you."

This was the moment she'd been expecting for weeks now. She knew he wanted to have sex with her but was probably thinking she wasn't ready. But she'd been ready; just waiting for him to make a move. She whispered in his ear, "And I want you to take all of me."

He laid her down on top of his desk and unfastened his belt.

*****

During the sex, Maggie thought about how it was different from and similar to the times her father raped her. There was the same grunting, strained sounds; a taking from her what he wanted. But she felt joy that she was able to give pleasure to the one she loved, even if it wasn't pleasurable for her. When he finished, she went to the bathroom and performed her same ritual.

As she came out, he was fastening his pants and looking much happier. "Listen to me, Maggie. Let's me and you leave this one-horse town."

She smiled cautiously. "What do you mean?"

"I mean let's leave. We'll set up business in another city. Anywhere is better than here."

Uncertainty crept up on Maggie. "You mean, like running away? I haven't finished school yet."

"Screw school. I can teach you everything you need to know. You could actually start selling cars like me. You'd probably be dynamite at it, as good-looking as you are."

"Where will we go?"

"Let's get out of Tennessee. What about Little Rock? I hear things are really starting to boom over there. I bet we can make a mint."

"I've dreamed of leaving home forever, but not quite like this."

"You scared to go with me?"

She rushed to him and hugged him. "No, no, never. It's not that. It's just you've surprised me with the idea. When do you think we should try to leave?"

"Why not tonight? I've been thinking about it a long time and should have been talking to you about it, but I've got it all planned out. You're eighteen, and you can do and go wherever you want to. Your old man can't do a thing about it."

Maggie's mind swung to her father and her promise that she'd make him regret ever laying a hand on her. She wasn't going to leave without fulfilling that bitter promise. "Okay," she said, excitement growing with the prospects of achieving two of her life goals on the same night. "Whose car are we going to take, mine or yours?"

"We need to take yours because all I have are dealer's tags. I don't want the police or anyone to have any excuse for stopping us."

"Then I'll come pick you up a little after midnight."

*****

Maggie sat on the edge of her bed, staring at her small suitcase and her guitar. In one hand, she held a lighter, and in the other hand, a can of lighter fluid. Her clock read 11:43 p.m. Through her closed door, she could hear the muffled sounds of the TV, which always put her father to sleep.

Walking to the door, she cracked it and saw the empty beer cans lying next to his chair and heard his snoring. She carried her suitcase and guitar and sat them at the front door, then walked back to her father's chair.

I've dreamed of doing all sorts of things to you, none of which were painful enough. But this seems fitting because it will prepare you to burn in hell. She soaked the crotch of his pants with lighter fluid, then squirted it on his shirt and lastly on his face.

The cold liquid stirred him from his drunken slumber, and he cracked open his bloodshot eyes. "Whass goin' on?" he slurred.

"Welcome to hell," Maggie said as she lit the lighter and pitched it into his lap.

Immediately flames started leaping up, and he tried to stand but was so drunk he collapsed back into his chair that was now on fire, too. "Help!" he finally cried.

Through gritted teeth, she said, "That's what I wanted to hear. I wanted to hear you crying for help and to know that no one is going to save you."

With her father's cries for help coming from behind her, she headed out the door.

Chapter Twelve

ISRAEL—EIGHTEEN YEARS OLD

On his eighteenth birthday, Israel awoke to the screeching sounds of the wheel bearings of the freight train he had hopped onto three days earlier. Rolling to a sitting position, he wiped the sleep out of his eyes and walked over to the open door of the freight car that had been his escape and refuge.

As the train eased to a stop, he read signs on buildings that let him know he was in Wheeling, West Virginia. Down a steep embankment below him, the Ohio River snaked its way between the railway and the buildings.

Spurred by his empty stomach, he said to himself, *I guess this is as good a place as any.* Walking back to the corner where he had been sleeping, he grabbed his pillowcase, which was much lighter than when he first snuck onboard, now that he'd eaten all of the food that was in it. Carrying it and his guitar case to the door, he stuck his head out and looked both ways for any signs of railroad employees. Convinced that the coast was clear, he jumped and landed on the loose gravel at the edge of the railroad ties. Gravel scattered underneath his scrambling feet, and fear gripped him as he realized he couldn't keep his balance and still hold on to his guitar and pillowcase. He somersaulted down the embankment, losing his grip on his guitar case, until he splashed face first into the edge of the river.

Pushing himself out of the water, he wiped the mud and water off his face, quickly grabbed his guitar case that was floating in the water, then found his pillowcase a quarter of the way back up the bank. He sat down and inspected his stinging elbows and knees. There was a ninety-degree tear in one knee of his jeans, from which a bloody wound stared at him. The elbows of his blue jean jacket somehow managed to remain intact, but he was certain there would be bruises on his elbows tomorrow.

He stood and gazed at the rows of industrial plants and warehouses, then climbed up the embankment and followed the rail line. *I just hope this leads me downtown and to someplace I can find something to eat.*

His throbbing knee gave him a slight limp as he walked several hundred yards until he spotted a sign: "Centre Market." As he got closer he was thrilled to discover a farmer's market with a variety of locally grown vegetables and fruits. *I should be able to slip in and steal at least enough to make my stomach stop growling.* Unfortunately for him, the crowd was small, so slipping around undetected was not going to be easy.

When he spotted an apple stand, his mouth started watering. *I love apples!* Easing toward it, he watched a man, who he suspected was the proprietor of the stand, talking to a customer. Israel stood at the opposite end of the stand and turned his back toward the two men so that they couldn't see his hands. He held his pillowcase waist-high in front of him, slowly reached for an apple, and dropped it into his pillowcase, then stood still and held his breath to see if he was noticed.

When he heard no word of challenge from behind him, he decided to try to get another apple. This time, as he dropped it into his pillowcase, he looked across the way and saw a young woman, perhaps his same age, standing behind a booth of vegetables, watching him.

Crap! He started to bolt but stopped when he saw neither shock nor alarm on her face nor any hint she was about to alert the proprietor of the apple stand. Israel wondered if he was mistaken about the direction she was looking and thought that perhaps she was looking at someone close to him and not directly at him. He turned his head around slowly, looking in every direction, but saw no one other than the two men at the other end of the apple stand.

Curious, he looked back at the young woman. When their eyes met, she motioned with her index finger for him to come to her. Pointing at his chest, he mouthed, "Me?"

She nodded.

Uncertain of her motives but willing to take a chance on finding them out, he moved casually away from the apple stand and made his way to her.

The closer he got, the better he could see how pretty she was. Her thick, chestnut hair framed the small features of her face, and her eyes were so dark brown they looked nearly black. When he was standing in front of her with the vegetable stand between them, he said, "Thank you."

"For what?" she asked.

Her voice was deeper than he expected it would be. "For not calling me out for stealing."

"Is that what you were doing? I thought you were going to test the merchandise before buying a bushel of apples to take home to your mother so she could make apple butter to sell."

He was about to explain his situation more truthfully when he thought he saw a hint of a smile playing across her thin lips and her twinkling eyes. "You're just messing with me, aren't you?"

A warm smile spread across her face, revealing rows of perfect teeth. "Maybe."

Relieved, he smiled back. "Okay, here's the truth. I just jumped off a train and haven't eaten in about a day." Looking serious, he added, "Look, I hope you don't think stealing is something I do all the time. I'm really not that kind of guy. It's just that—"

"You're out of money and don't have a job," she said, finishing his sentence.

Israel felt defensive. "It's the truth! I guess maybe you hear that from people a lot around here, but I promise you, it's the truth."

"They always say that, too," she replied, keeping her voice calm.

He was having difficulty reading her and found himself getting defensive. "If you think I'm lying, then why not tell that man I stole his apples?"

"Because those are my apples."

He frowned, looked at the apple stand, and then looked back at her. "What do you mean?"

"That's my father over there. He mans the apple stand, and I man the vegetable stand. We grow both on our farm."

A sick feeling came over Israel. *I'm sunk.* "He's your dad?" Lifting one of the stolen apples out of his pillowcase, he asked, "And this is your apple?"

"That's what I said."

Nervously, he handed the apple to her. "Here, take them back. I'm sorry. I—"

"Keep it. And here's a couple of tomatoes and a piece of squash you can take, too." She pointed to the vegetables in front of her.

He hung his head. "But I don't have any money."

"Exactly. I'm trying to make you feel beholden to me."

Israel could hardly keep up with his wildly swinging emotions: embarrassment, guilt, fear, confusion, anger. And he was now more confused than ever. "I'm not sure what you mean."

"Do you have a name?" she asked.

"Yes, it's Israel McKenzie."

She offered to shake his hand. "Nice to meet you, Israel McKenzie. My name's Ada Lane."

He shook her hand. It felt warm and solid, like the hand of someone who meant what they said.

"We need a hired hand on our place," Ada said. "The man who used to help us fell and broke his leg. We can't do all the work ourselves. You're hungry. You need a job. We've got food, and we need to hire someone. Sounds like a perfect match to me. What do you think?"

Israel felt as if he needed to put both hands on the sides of his head to stop it from spinning. Instead, he shook it as if clearing cobwebs. "I'm not sure this is where I want to stay. Maybe I want to get back on the train and go farther."

"No, you don't," she said with a certainty that he found unnerving. "You don't know where you want to be or where you want to go. You really don't know anything except that you didn't want to be wherever you ran away from."

To have this woman who had known him less than five minutes sum up his life in two sentences was amazing. And the longer he gazed into her face and especially those deep, mysterious eyes, he found her captivating as well.

"Well, make up your mind," Ada said.

"But I don't know anything about you, or what kind of work you want me to do, or what you're going to pay me."

"Boy, you sure are particular for a starving hobo. I don't know anything about you or what kind of worker you'll be or if you're some kind of mass murderer." Again, there was that playful smile that tugged at the corners of her mouth but never actually broke into a full smile.

But the mention of the word *murderer* sent a chill through Israel and made him think about running back to board the train.

Ada interrupted his thoughts. "I'm just going to tell him you stole the apples. Hey, Dad!" she called.

"Shhh! Don't tell him!" Israel looked over his shoulder and saw her father looking at them.

"What's up, Ada?" her dad answered her.

Israel gave her a pleading look.

She smiled and said to her dad, "I've hired us a new hand for the farm."

Chapter Thirteen

MAGGIE—TWENTY-EIGHT YEARS OLD

With pain shooting through every part of her body, Maggie lay in bed, trying to be certain Jackson was sound asleep. Moving as slowly as a sloth, she inched her way toward the edge of the bed, then rose. She made certain to avoid stepping on the part of the floor that squeaked and made her way into the bathroom. Silently closing the door, she turned on the light.

The gruesome visage that stared back at her from the mirror was not an unfamiliar one to her. Using the crooked index finger that had been broken in a previous beating, she carefully touched her left eye, which was red and swollen shut. Her bottom lip was split, and a thin line of blood ran down her chin and her neck. Her hand trembled as she turned on the cold water, soaked a washcloth, then gingerly wiped the blood off.

Long past were the days of feeling terror and horror like she had the first few times Jackson beat her. The very first time it had happened, she was so stunned she questioned if what happened was real and blamed herself for doing something wrong that set him off. But it wasn't long before her days were filled with dread because of the uncertainty of when the volcano would erupt. During those years, the tension was so great that she was almost relieved when he finally did start hitting her because at least it was finally over with. Of course, there were his empty promises that it would never happen again and that he was sorry, but she learned not to put any trust or hope in those.

Now, though, she was numb to the emotion of it all, living like a disembodied spirit, sleepwalking through her days with a silent resignation that all this would never end.

The only feeling she allowed herself was a seething hatred toward God for cursing her life and never being there for her.

Suddenly, she heard the bedsprings squeak from the other side of the bathroom door. She switched off the light and held her breath, listening for any sounds that Jackson was walking across the floor toward her. Seconds ticked away until she finally let her breath out, having concluded that he was only turning over in bed.

Switching the light back on, she gently placed the cool washcloth on her swollen eye and winced. Step by step, she began retracing the evening's events to try to figure out what she'd done that had made Jackson so angry.

Unbeknownst to her, he had come to the diner where she worked and spotted her waiting on a young man, Tanner, who had become a regular and always asked to sit in her section. He was a pleasant man, but what she liked the most about him was that he was a great tipper, sometimes tipping her more than his meal cost. She was laughing at something he'd said when she saw Jackson out of the corner of her eye, looking through the window of the diner and glowering at her. She immediately knew she was in trouble.

The funny thing was that when they'd first moved to Little Rock, Jackson had told her she needed to flirt and "show a little skin" so that she'd get good tips from the male customers. And he was right—it worked. But after a year or so, he started becoming increasingly jealous and obsessed with the idea that she was cheating on him. She tried to explain to him that she was just being friendly; that was when he slapped her face and swore at her.

When she got home after Jackson saw her laughing with Tanner, their apartment looked like a cyclone had blown through it. Broken dishes were lying on the floor, the TV screen was smashed, the couch was overturned, and pieces of newspapers and magazines were scattered around like confetti. Jackson was in a drunken rage—a rage like she'd never seen before.

As soon as she walked through the door, he grabbed her arm and slung her against the wall, pinning her there with his hands around her throat. "I saw you flirting with that same guy again! Did you take him in the back and give him a blowjob? Or did you strip and give him a lap dance? You're nothing but a whore!"

"I can't breathe," she said hoarsely. "You're choking me."

He eased his grip but didn't release her. "So what's your story?"

Maggie coughed and said, "I swear to you there's nothing going on between us. I was just being friendly like you used to tell me to be. He always gives me a big tip."

He let go with one hand and backhanded her across the mouth. Immediately the taste of blood was on her tongue.

"Don't you try and blame this on me!" he yelled. "You sure that he gives you a big *tip*, or is it a big something else he gives you? You disgust me." He slammed his fist into the side of her face.

Stars appeared, and everything started going black. She felt herself sliding down to the floor. The last thing she was conscious of was his wicked, maniacal laugh.

She had awakened on the bed with Jackson asleep beside her. What happened while she was passed out and how she ended up on the bed, she did not know. But from the pain she was feeling between her legs and from her rectum, she was certain he'd raped her yet again. She could only manage to take tiny breaths because anything more than that caused a knifing pain in her side.

Touching her closed, swollen eye again, she said to herself, *I better go have that seen about tonight.* She looked at the bathroom door, wishing she had X-ray vision and could be certain what Jackson was doing.

Nervously, she turned out the light, slowly opened the door, and eased into the bedroom. Besides the ticking clock on the wall, the only sound she heard was Jackson's heavy snoring. As she tiptoed across the room, the clapper of the clock struck the chime, nearly causing her to jump out of her skin.

She stood at the edge of the living room, trying to remember where she'd left the car keys. An image came to her of the keys sliding across the kitchen floor after they'd flown out of her hand when Jackson grabbed her and slammed her against the wall.

While on her hands and knees searching for them in the dark, she thought she heard Jackson's voice and froze. Seconds ticked by as she strained to hear if he was coming her way. The seconds turned into minutes before she finally trusted the thought that he was talking in his sleep, and she continued her search.

In the next instant, her hand fell upon the lost keys. Gripping them, she slipped out the door, got in her car, and headed for the hospital.

*****

Sitting on the exam table that was separated by pale green curtains from the other exam tables in the emergency room, Maggie watched as Dr. Collins put the finishing touches on the cast he'd placed on her hand and forearm. It was odd to her that she'd not even noticed the pain from the broken wrist but supposed it was because of the knifing pain of her broken ribs, four of them according to the doctor, and her concern about her eye.

He walked over to a sink, washed his hands, then slipped the wheeled stool underneath him and rolled to a stop in front of her. "Maggie."

She kept her head down.

"Maggie, look at me," he insisted.

Reluctantly, she lifted her head.

"I don't know how many times I've seen you in here over the last seven or eight years, but it's too many, and it's always for the same reason. One of these days he's going to kill you, and you know it. You've got to quit making excuses for him. He's nothing but a monster. I get tired of having to put you back together after he's treated you like a punching bag. You need to leave while you can."

"You've told me all this before, and everyone at work tells me the same thing, too, but you all think it's just as simple as walking out the door. It's not. What am I supposed to do then? 'Start over,' you say. But start over with what? I don't have anything, and I don't make enough money to support myself. You want me to go live in a homeless shelter?" She could see some of the intensity leave his eyes as he took in the weight of what she was saying.

A nurse stuck her head through the curtain. "Dr. Collins, we really need you in Exam 8, stat."

Keeping his eyes on Maggie, he answered, "I'll be right there." Alone again, he said, "I don't have the answers, Maggie. But I have someone that I want you to talk to. She's a social worker the hospital recently hired, and I've asked her to come in. She's waiting in her office. I hope maybe she can help."

Maggie frowned. "Is she going to get the police involved? I don't want any police coming to our apartment."

"I really don't know. Let me bring her in here, and you can ask her about that." He patted her hand and left.

A social worker. What does she think she's going to do for me? Give me a million dollars? She gave a small laugh at her hyperbole and was instantly reminded of her broken ribs. She waited a few minutes. *This is stupid. I'm going home.*

She eased off the table and was getting adjusted to the feel of the sling her broken arm was in when someone behind her said, "You must be Maggie."

Maggie turned and saw a rather tall, angular woman with dark hair that had silver threads scattered through it. Her hair said she was in her midforties, but her face was more youthful-looking than that. She had eyes that smiled and a face that had fewer wrinkles than her own. Although Maggie knew she must look like something out of a fright movie, the woman seemed unperturbed.

"I'm Charlene Chester," the woman said as she stepped up to Maggie. "But most folks just call me Charlie."

In a subtle move that Maggie appreciated, she reached out to shake Maggie's hand with her left hand since Maggie's right one was in the cast. Maggie accepted the handshake as she continued to examine the woman. *Nice pantsuit. Was probably a women's libber back in the day.*

"Nice to meet you," Charlie said. "Looks like you've had a bit of trouble, and according to Dr. Collins, it's not the first time. You want to tell me about it?"

Maggie shrugged. "What's the point?"

"I've got a feeling you might be a candidate for a new program that's been started in the city. It's specifically for battered women. A place they can live in safety and put their lives back together again."

Maggie perked up. "Really? I've never heard of something like that."

"It's a new idea, especially for this area. But we've learned a lot in recent years about the damaging effects of domestic violence and how women get trapped in it. Maybe that's you."

"It makes me nervous to think about leaving because it's not bad between me and my husband all the time. Sometimes it's really good. He can be funny and thoughtful."

"And he can be as mean as a junkyard dog, too, right?"

Maggie nodded.

"Here's the thing, Maggie, no relationship is bad all day, every day. They all have moments or even days when it's good. The danger, though, is that the bad days always get worse and more frequent."

"I never thought about it like that, but you're right."

"What kind of work do you do?"

"I'm a waitress." Maggie read Charlie's face. "Yeah, not much, huh. Certainly nothing I can support myself with. That's another reason I've never left."

"But that can be fixed. If you come to live in the shelter, we can work on getting you the training or schooling you need to become something else."

"I've always wished I'd gone to college."

"Great! There's no reason you still can't go."

In a dark corner of Maggie's heart, a door cracked open, and a shaft of hope shone through for the first time in years.

Chapter Fourteen

ISRAEL—NINETEEN YEARS OLD

Looking below at Ada's smiling face, Israel eased himself down the narrow top of the ladder that leaned against the apple tree and headed toward the wider bottom resting on the ground. His chest apron bulged with apples and bumped against the rails.

"You better not come down unless you have at least a bushel of apples in that apron," Ada called up at him.

"You know, I could lose my balance and fall on top of whoever might be underneath me," he called back.

"Ha! Even with these braces on my legs, I can move faster than you can fall."

It was one of the rare instances when she made a reference to the aftereffects of having polio as a child. She had always moved so fluidly that Israel didn't know she wore braces until several weeks after they'd met, when she had on a dress that let them show. "Yeah," she'd said when she noticed him looking, "a nice set of rails, don't you think? Pretty much a turnoff for guys."

But Israel had never felt that way. Actually, it endeared her to him even more because of the incredible way she accepted it and dealt with it. "I guess I learned that from my mom," she'd said; her mother had also had polio and had worn braces.

Stepping off the last rung of the ladder, he walked over to Ada, who was standing beside a bushel basket, and leaned over to let his trove of red apples topple into it.

She squealed with delight. "Look how big some of them are."

"Are we having a good harvest?" Israel was still trying to acclimate to farm life and the ebb and flow of it.

"It looks like it's going to be a bumper crop. God's been good to us." She picked up an apple and admired it like a jeweler would a diamond ring.

There were so many things about Ada that he loved, and this was one of them—that she got great joy out of simple things.

He was less convinced than she about always giving God the credit for things, although he knew this would displease his old friend, Darnell Williams. "Whatever happens to you," Darnell used to say, "don't never forget God's hand in things."

Ada started to lift the basket full of apples, but Israel stopped her. "I'll get it." He lifted it onto the waiting wagon, where it joined rows of other baskets brimming with apples.

He felt her hand on the small of his back. "I know you're strong and like to show it off, but I could have done that," she said.

Turning, he put his arm across her shoulders, and she slipped her arm around his waist. They gazed into the western sky where the sun was just touching the horizon, filling the sky with brilliant orange and lavender hues.

Israel felt his chest fill with emotions, and not for the first time since coming to work with Ada's family, his eyes brimmed with tears. Never had he known such peace and tranquility and something else, but he was afraid to name it out loud. He would only ask himself, *Is this what love feels like?*

They stood without speaking until the sun disappeared.

Taking his hand, Ada asked, "You ready to head in?"

"Sure." *Sure? That's the best you can come up with, "Sure"?* He wanted to kiss her but was afraid, uncertain whether he should, whether it would make her mad, or even if he knew how to kiss. Between never dating in high school, what he saw happening between Sir and his mother, and his experience with his dorm mother, Miss Agnes, and her twisted self, being physical with a female was fraught with confusion. The only girl he'd ever really liked was Rebekah, his adopted sister, and even though they weren't kin to each other, it just felt wrong, so he ended up feeling ashamed of how he felt.

From the first day he started working on the farm, Ada's mother and father had insisted he take his meals with them, even though the room he slept in was built onto the back of the house and had its own entrance. Most evening meals concluded with her dad pulling out his guitar and inviting Israel to get his and join him as they all sat around and sang songs. Sometimes they sang folk songs; other times, they sang songs that Israel used to sing in church when he was living at the orphanage. But when Ada's family sang church songs, they sounded like the lyrics really meant something to them, rather than the empty, hollow sound that he remembered from years ago. For the first few months Israel felt like he was a stranger in a Norman Rockwell painting, but he had grown to feel like he belonged to this family and that they truly embraced him.

That night, after the apple picking, when the songs had been sung and Ada's parents were looking sleepy, Ada said, "Israel and I are going to go for a walk if that's okay."

Israel was surprised because she hadn't mentioned it to him.

"Sure, sure," her mother said.

"Just don't keep the hired help up too late," her father said with a smile. "We want to get our money's worth out of him tomorrow."

"You can count on me, sir," Israel said.

"I know I can."

Outside, he said to Ada, "I didn't know we were going on a walk tonight."

"Neither did I," she said.

There was something mysterious about her tone and manner that Israel couldn't interpret. "What's going on?" he finally asked. "Where are we going?"

"Let's go sit underneath the big sycamore tree on the hill," she answered.

This pleased him because it was one of his favorite spots on the farm. From there, he could see the entire farm and the creek that ran through the middle of it.

Ada took his hand in one of hers, held his arm with her other hand, and rested the side of her face against his arm as they walked. It made him feel warm inside.

When they got to the tree, he helped her sit down on the ground and then joined her. Lightning bugs were busy sending out messages in hopes of attracting a paramour, while from below the hill came the sound of an owl hooting.

"Israel," Ada said, "I have something to say to you."

Her tone was so serious that it frightened him. Had she been assigned the unpleasant task of telling him that his services were no longer needed on the farm? Was she mad at him about something? Had he done or said something wrong? His heart thumped against his chest, and his throat felt tight. He turned and looked at her in the dim light.

With a touch as soft as the down of a chick, she placed her hands on the sides of his face. "Israel McKenzie, I love you."

Israel's heart leaped for joy. "This is what I've hoped for more than anything in the world because I love you like I've never loved anyone. You've helped me learn what love is." Emotions closed his throat off as he held her face in his hands. The night's ambient light sparkled in her dark eyes.

After a moment, she said, "Then why don't you kiss me?"

This was the moment he wanted but also feared. How to execute the perfect kiss? Something in him took over, and all thoughts left his head. He leaned in and pressed his lips against hers. Warmth spread through him like he'd been struck by a sunbeam.

She returned his kiss and put her arms around his neck, pulling him tight against her, and began leaning back toward the ground. He let her pull him on top of her and felt himself becoming aroused. That sparked a new fear as to what it might mean and what he should do about it.

When their lips parted, her breath felt hot against his face. She whispered, "I want you to make love to me."

"I want to do it," he replied, "but I'm scared. There are things you don't know about me, things I've seen, things I've done."

She put a finger on his lips. "Stop talking. Stop thinking. Just come to me." She reached for the zipper of his pants, and he lifted her skirt.

After a few minutes of white-hot passion and the most pleasure he'd ever felt, Israel collapsed on top of her, trying to catch his breath.

*****

Two months later, Israel was working in the barn, replacing some of the planks in the floor of the wagon, when Ada came in. He turned and smiled at her.

She smiled back at him and said, "I've got some big news."

He paused from working and brushed sawdust off himself. "What's up?"

Clutching his two hands, she said, "We're going to have a baby."

He frowned. "You mean your mom and dad are having another baby?"

She gave his hands a gentle tug. "No, silly. You and I are going to have a baby. I'm pregnant."

Israel felt as if someone had punched him in the stomach. Ever since the night they'd had sex, he'd been fighting feelings of guilt and shame. Words he'd heard echoed from the pulpit as a child about "all fornicators will end up in hell" constantly filled his head. And now came the damning consequences of what they'd done—pregnancy. His mouth went dry as he looked at Ada's face, which was filled with excitement.

"Well, say something, silly," Ada said. "Isn't it exciting?"

"How can you be excited? We're not married. What will your parents say? I'll never be able to face them again. What will your father do to me?"

Her smile sagged a bit. "I've already told them, and they are excited for us. Papa says we need to get married because that's the right thing to do, but they are happy for us. Aren't you happy about it? Don't you still love me?"

Her second question roused him. "It's not that, Ada. Of course I love you. I will always love you. It's just . . . I guess I didn't think that could happen by having sex just one time."

She laughed. "Mama said I must be built like she is because that's all it took for her to get pregnant with me."

He wanted to join her in her excitement but just couldn't muster any. All he felt was fear and confusion.

*****

That night, he stuffed all his belongings into a backpack, then sat down and wrote a note to Ada.

My dear Ada. I told you I will always love you, and I will. But you deserve better than me, and the baby sure deserves a better father than I will be. I'm damaged goods, Ada. That's all I know to say about the why of it. I'm running away so that you can move on with your life without me. The best thing you can do is forget about me.

—Israel

Chapter Fifteen

MAGGIE—THIRTY-TWO YEARS OLD

Maggie sat engrossed in Professor Reed's lecture—truthfully, more by Professor Reed himself than his topic, Milton Erickson's the family life cycle, even though she was certain some of the information would be included in the final exam. She was captivated by everything about Professor Reed, from his long salt-and-pepper ponytail that matched his goatee, to his seemingly ever-present tweed jacket that sometimes had chalk dust on its sleeves, to his long arms and large hands that punctuated his lectures—and of course, those cobalt-blue eyes of his.

Sometimes she had to pinch herself to believe that she was actually a sophomore at the University of Tennessee at Martin. The six months she'd spent at the women's shelter in Little Rock were transformative. The staff and other women who passed through there had made her start to believe in herself, to believe that it was possible to become someone other than who she'd always been. It was especially Charlie Chester who had helped her understand the cycle of domestic violence and why she'd stayed with Jackson so long.

Even though she was the oldest student in nearly all of her classes at college, she didn't care. She was soaking up everything about the experience. She was amazed at how confident and self-assured her professors were, especially Professor Reed, and she tried to sign up for his classes every semester. Last week it seemed to her that he actually noticed her and smiled as he looked at her. That smile—it was a cross between a knowing smile and a snicker, like he knew what she was thinking.

When the chime rang, ending the class period, Professor Reed was holding a sheaf of papers. "This is the study sheet for the test on Friday." He turned and looked at Maggie. "Ms. Stinson, would you please hand these out for me?"

Surprised to hear him call her name, Maggie cleared her throat and said, "Sir?"

"Will you hand these out to the class, please?" And he gave her that hidden smile of his.

She felt her face getting red as she rose and took the papers from him.

After all the students got one from her and had hurriedly exited the room, she took the remaining copies back to him. "These were left over." He took them from her while holding her with his eyes. She was spellbound.

"You know, Ms. Stinson, you are the kind of student that we professors enjoy more than any others. You're here because you know what you want, not because your parents sent you. I've recognized you in my other classes and noticed that your comments are always insightful, and the papers you turn in are actually interesting to read."

Maggie couldn't find her voice. She was floored to have such profuse praise heaped on her by the professor she admired the most. *Don't stand here like an idiot. Say something!* "Thank you, Professor Reed, that means a lot coming from you. I'm just trying to do the best I can."

There was a pause as he looked at her, and she wasn't sure if he was trying to think of what to say next, or if he was done with her and wanted her to leave.

"When's your next class?" he asked.

"I have an hour break between this class and my next."

"Have you got time to come to my office for a few minutes? I'd like to hear what your plans are for yourself."

Maggie was surprised that her chin didn't actually hit the floor. *He wants to hear my plans? Wants me to come to his office?* It all felt like a bit too much. She blurted, "I'd love to."

"Then walk with me."

On the way there, she chastised herself, *"Love to"? Did you have to use the word* love*? Did that sound stupid or juvenile? What's he thinking? Good God . . .*

He ushered her through the door to his office and shut it. As she glanced around, she felt as though she had stepped into the pages of an issue of *National Geographic* magazine. On one wall hung a Native American spear, bow, arrows, and shield. A set of bookshelves had tiny elephants carved from ivory; alongside them rested an African mask. There were scores of bookends scattered among the several bookshelves, all carved and painted or stained in exotic colors. She turned in a slow circle, fascinated. "It's amazing," she whispered.

"Thank you. I've had the opportunity to travel to many places and always like to bring back something as a reminder of my journeys." He pointed toward a pair of red leather armchairs sitting at one end of a similarly upholstered couch. "Let's have a seat."

Maggie walked carefully to the chairs. *Just don't do or say anything stupid.* She felt the rich leather embrace her as she took a seat and looked out the only window in the office. From this fifth-floor vantage point, she could see nearly all the campus, with its crisscrossing sidewalks loaded with hurrying students. "Nice view," she commented.

"Yes, I agree. Took me a while to acquire this spot, you know, working my way up the ladder until I became department chair. But I paid my dues and appreciate where it got me." He slipped off his jacket and folded himself into the chair beside her.

Maggie caught a whiff of Old Spice cologne and barely stopped herself from saying, "You smell good."

"So tell me about your plans for the future. I'm sure you have an advisor, but I'd like to give my input, too. I see lots of potential in you."

"Really?"

"Absolutely. I'll be honest with you: I get weary of these kids right out of high school who are so immature and childish and not even interested in doing the work it takes to make good grades. Students like you are a breath of fresh air."

Maggie felt like looking around to see if there was someone else in the room he was talking about. "I appreciate that, Professor Reed, but you make learning interesting."

He smiled and tented his fingers under his chin. "Thank you for saying that. Sometimes I can't tell if anyone is listening or not."

She'd never thought about what it might feel like to have the roles reversed in a classroom and see students sleeping in class or talking to each other and laughing. She suddenly felt a little sorry for him. "I guess I never thought about how hard it would be to do what you do."

"You have no idea," he said with a sigh, and his face sagged a little. But it immediately lifted as he said, "But it's students like you that make it all worthwhile. So why don't you tell me a little bit about yourself?" He rose and walked toward a credenza. "Would you like something to drink? A martini, perhaps?"

Afraid of how it would look if she said no, Maggie said, "Sure, that would be nice."

"Go ahead and talk. I'm listening."

What do I tell? How much do I tell? The truth? And sound like some kind of welfare case? Her head spun in search of a believable lie. "Well," she began as he walked toward her holding two glasses, "I used to live in Little Rock. My husband had a business, and I helped him with it. But he died unexpectedly in an accident, so I had to rethink my future. That's when someone suggested I attend college. I'd never heard of this school, but a friend I knew had graduated from here and suggested it."

"What was your friend's name? Perhaps I knew them."

Without thinking, she told the truth. "Charlene Chester." She immediately felt like clapping her hand over her mouth.

Professor Reed's eyes lit up. "Charlie? Of course I knew her. A really good student with a lot on the ball. She came through our social work program. What's she doing in Little Rock?"

Maggie felt trapped in the web of her lie. *If I tell him I met her in the hospital, he's going to want to know how and why. If I tell him she's involved in the women's shelter, will he add two and two together and figure out that I knew her because I was living there? What if I make something up, and he tries to contact her and finds out I lied?* She could feel sweat popping up on her upper lip. She took a sip of her martini, felt it go down smooth, and then took a large swallow of it. In an effort to stall her answer, she said, "This tastes nice and smooth."

He smiled. "I prefer using vodka to make mine."

She drained her glass.

"Would you like another one?"

Offering him her glass, she said, "Yes. That would be nice."

As he took her glass and headed back to the credenza, she sensed warmth spreading through her body and felt more relaxed.

He came back with another martini and said, "I hope you don't think this is inappropriate, but you have very pretty eyes."

His comment was unexpected, as her mind was still searching for a way to tell him about Charlie, but it still managed to make her heart flutter. *Professor Reed, the coolest professor on campus, thinks I have pretty eyes!* "Thank you," she said as she crossed her legs and took a swallow of her martini.

He took a seat and leaned toward her. "You know, Margaret, may I call you Margaret?"

"Most folks call me Maggie."

"You know, Maggie, I really have a need for a student assistant, and I think you would be perfect for the position."

"Student assistant? What would I be doing?"

"It's nothing very complicated. You would be typing up my class notes and tests and making copies of them. You might handle some of my phone calls." Looking at her hand, he said, "I notice you're not wearing a ring. You haven't remarried, have you?"

Maggie looked at her empty ring finger. The question puzzled her until she finally remembered that she'd said her husband had died. The truth was, she didn't know if she was married. Jackson might have divorced her by now. "No, I haven't. Why do you ask?"

"Well, there might be some evening hours involved in your position, and I wouldn't want it to cause any problems at home."

"No problems there." She found herself enjoying this conversation. He was easy to talk to and actually listened to what she said. "I would love to hear stories about the places you've been to."

He rose and walked over to the sofa and sat down, then lifted a photo album off the coffee table. Patting the cushion beside him, he said, "Then come over here—I'll show you the pictures I took in Gambia."

Chapter Sixteen

ISRAEL—NINETEEN YEARS OLD

With his faced covered in dirt and with flames where his pupils should have been, Sir approached Israel. "So you thought you'd killed me." He lifted his chin, revealing his bloody neck, then laughed. "Well, the joke's on you. I've killed Rebekah, and now I've come for you."

Like the talons of a hawk, terror seized Israel's heart. *This can't be happening!* "You were dead! I buried you!"

"You just thought I was dead. I came to and dug my way out." He reached into his pocket and pulled out a garrote.

Israel stared in disbelief. It was the garrote he'd used on Sir. "But . . . but . . . it can't be . . ."

"Oh, it's real, all right." Sir stepped close and grabbed Israel's arm.

Israel swung his fist in an effort to get loose.

"Hey, watch out!" called a woman's voice.

Israel looked around and realized he was on a bus.

The woman sitting beside him looked terrified. "You nearly hit me!"

He shook his head and rubbed his eyes. "I'm sorry. I guess I was having a nightmare."

"You told me to wake you when we got to Charleston, South Carolina."

"Yeah, yeah, uh, thanks. What time is it?"

"A little after midnight."

"I'm really sorry. Are you okay?"

She stepped into the aisle. "We're pulling into the station. You better step out."

Keeping his head down, he slipped past her, retrieved his guitar and bag from the storage area under the bus, and walked into the terminal. He squinted against the bright fluorescent lights and scanned the area for the closest men's room. His eyes briefly alit on a petite blonde woman sitting in a row of empty chairs and holding a child who was nearly as big as she was. To one side of her, there was a solitary suitcase. When he spotted the men's room, he forgot everything else and hurried toward it.

A few minutes later, he exited the restroom, wiping his hands on his jeans because there were no paper towels available. Feeling more relaxed now that his bladder wasn't about to burst, he looked around for a coffee machine. Again, he spotted the blonde woman and her child, but this time she was looking back at him.

Nice-looking. When she didn't avert her gaze from his, he decided to walk over to her. "Hi there."

"Hi." Her reply was accompanied by a tiny smile that quickly vanished.

Israel looked around to see if anyone was watching them, then looked back at her. "You with anyone?" He took in her lack of makeup, light blue eyes, the edge of a tattoo that disappeared underneath the neck of her shirt, pierced ears with no jewelry in them, blue jeans, and unidentifiable-brand tennis shoes that had holes in the toes.

She nodded at her sleeping daughter. "Just my little girl."

He felt a little odd talking to a woman he had never met, having just recently deserted Ada. "I was fixing to get me a cup of coffee. You want some?"

Her face brightened a little. "Yes, that would be nice. And maybe a bottle of juice for my girl?"

"Sure. I'll see if I can find a machine." *She's kind of cute.* He began trying to guess what her story was. *She's sitting in a bus station at midnight, so she's either about to start a trip, is at the end of a trip, or stopped in the middle of a trip. If someone was going to meet her here, she wouldn't have asked for juice for her daughter. She's not got much money, probably spent it all on the bus tickets. Dark circles around her eyes can either mean she's not slept much, or she's been doing drugs, or both. She's a little older than me, and the little girl is about eight, which means she got pregnant while in high school.*

At the coffee machine, he realized he had forgotten to ask her how she liked her coffee. He turned around and looked at her. He mouthed the words, "Black? Sugar? Cream?" while shrugging his shoulders.

She smiled and mouthed back, "Black."

As the cups were filling, he saw that one of the drink machines had apple juice, so he put in his money and pushed the button, but nothing happened. He pushed the button again, with the same result. Then he kicked the front of the machine. Prodded by his persistence, the machine decided to let go of the bottle, and it hurtled down the chute, where he retrieved it. Tapping the machine with the top of the bottle, he said, "Thank you very much."

With the two cups of coffee in one hand and the apple juice in the other, he returned to the woman. "Here you go."

She took the apple juice first and spoke to her daughter. "Hope, wake up. Here's some apple juice."

Hope made a mewing and stirred a bit but didn't sit up.

"Come on, Hope. Drink the juice this nice man bought you."

Hope finally roused herself, pushed her hair out of her face, and rubbed her eyes. Without so much as a glance at Israel, she grabbed the apple juice and guzzled the entire contents.

It was then that he got a full view of the side of the woman's face that had been hidden from him. It looked as if it were made of wax and had gotten too close to a heat source and began melting. Her eye drooped, and her skin sagged, pulling down the corner of her mouth. Thankfully, he managed to hide his surprise and shock. His heart went out to her. He knew what it was like to be self-conscious of how you looked. "How long has it been since you two ate?"

"We're fine," the mother said as she pulled her long hair over the front of her shoulder so that it hid that side of her face.

"I'm not," Hope said, now appearing more alert. She looked directly at him and said, "I'm hungry."

Israel noticed her round cheeks and tiny nose.

"Hope, that's not polite," her mother said.

"Let's start this all over," Israel said. "My name is Israel McKenzie." He extended his hand toward the woman.

She smiled and shook his hand. "My name is Christine Arnold."

"And my name is Hope. I'm seven," her daughter said with a smile. She slid off Christine's lap and grabbed Israel's hand. "Your teeth look funny. Let's go find something to eat."

"Hope!" Christine said.

Israel smiled. "It's okay. I don't mind a bit." Looking down at Hope, he said, "Okay, let's see what we can find."

As he walked across the lobby toward the vending machines, he enjoyed the feeling of her small hand in his, the feeling of being trusted, of being looked up to.

Hope stared wide-eyed at the vending machines, then started pointing and exclaimed, "I want that and that and that and that and that. And Mommy will like that and that and that."

Israel laughed out loud. "Well, I didn't keep up with you at all. How about we make selections one at a time?"

Eventually they returned to Christine with arms and hands full of their goodies. When he opened his arms over the chair beside her, Twinkies, Twix bars, Otis Spunkmeyer cookies, plain potato chips, barbeque potato chips, Oreo cookies, and Baby Ruth bars tumbled into a pile.

"Oh, good grief," Christine said. "Did you leave anything in the machine?"

Hope laid a honey bun, Reese's candy, and Starburst in her mother's lap. "These are for you."

Christine looked at the treasure of sweet treats and said, "I'm sure we'd be condemned by the surgeon general, but how's a girl to resist all her favorite decadent indulgences?" She tore open the wrapper on the honey bun and bit off a third of it.

Hope looked up at Israel. "See what I told you? She loves them." Using her teeth, she tore open the Twinkies and pushed half of one into her mouth, making her cheeks bulge out like a squirrel's as she chewed.

He pointed at the chair beside Christine and asked, "You care if I sit there?"

With her mouth still full of honey bun, she nodded and mumbled a welcome.

He sat down and pulled out a half-eaten stick of jerky and began eating it. The three of them ate in silence for several minutes before he asked, "Where are you guys headed?" He immediately saw a wary look come over Christine.

"We haven't decided yet. We're still looking at our options."

"Not true," Hope said. "We don't have any money to go anywhere."

Christine's face turned crimson, and she looked away.

Not wanting to make Christine feel any more embarrassed, Israel said, "Hey, who hasn't been out of money before? I know I have."

She looked back at him. "Where are you going?"

"This is as far as I planned to go. I hear they're hiring lots of construction workers for all the hotels and motels being built, so I thought I'd give it a try." He hesitated for a second about pushing her for more of an answer about herself, then decided he had nothing to lose. "What's going on with you two?"

Hope spoke up. "Mommy wrote letters to a man. He was supposed to meet us here, but he didn't show up."

Christine's shoulders slumped. "It's true. I found him through a personal ad in the newspaper. We've been writing back and forth for a year. More than once, he asked me to come to Charleston and marry him, but I told him he was moving too fast, that I wasn't ready. Finally, though, I decided he was who he said he was and that it was time to take our relationship further. We were supposed to meet here in the bus terminal at noon today."

"And he never showed?" Israel asked.

"My guess is he got a look at this." She pointed to the deformed side of her face. "That's enough to scare anybody off. I don't blame him. I wasn't honest with him. All the pictures that I sent him hid that side of my face, and I never told him about it."

Israel wondered what would make a woman spend her last red cent on a bus ticket that would take her to a man she'd never met face to face. *Whatever kind of situation she was in before she boarded that bus to come here must have been awfully bad.* "And you guys have been here since noon today with nothing to eat or drink? What are you going to do?"

"I . . . I really don't know what to do."

"We can go with you," Hope said with a smile. "I don't want to go to another one of those homeless shelters we've been in before."

Israel was taken aback by the precocious child's suggestion and shocked by this revelation. But even as he heard Christine scolding Hope and protesting such a suggestion, he couldn't figure out any other workable options for them, and he for sure wasn't going to abandon them here. "Look," he said, "I was going to rent a motel room for a couple of nights until I can find a job and then an apartment. I know we don't know each other, but I'm willing to share the room with you two. I'd get a separate room for you, but I don't have that kind of money." He held up both his hands. "I promise you that this is on the up and up. I'm not going to try anything weird."

Christine looked uncertain.

"Come on, Mommy," Hope said. "It'll be fun."

Christine sighed. "Okay, I don't think we have any other choice at the moment."

Chapter Seventeen

MAGGIE—THIRTY-THREE YEARS OLD

Maggie sat propped up in her bed in her apartment, sweating profusely and barely able to breathe. Her body felt like it was caught in a vise. *This is it. I'm going to have this baby.*

For the past three months, a part of her had accepted the reality of her situation, but another part of her kept denying it was true. *I can't be pregnant! It's going to ruin everything.* Professor Reed, Gary, as she called him by his first name now, would never tolerate the complication of her being pregnant. He'd said more than once that he had no time for children because he didn't want to be tied down by them. That was why he and his wife had divorced—she had wanted children.

Maggie's relationship with him had moved so fast that she could hardly keep her bearings. That first day in his office when they were looking at his photo album of Gambia, his knee had barely touched hers, but it triggered waves of excitement through her. Afterward, she'd decided some of what she felt was affected by the liquor and that she probably read too much into what happened.

But the next time she was in his office, he was pointing something out to her that he wanted transcribed, and his hand touched hers. It was a touch that wasn't necessary to get his explanation across, so she knew it was an intentional move by him. She'd looked up at him, and he stared directly into her eyes; then his gaze shifted to her lips. She'd felt her mouth go dry. *My God, does he want to kiss me? Am I dreaming, or am I drunk?* The moment passed without anything happening, but it planted a seed in her.

He was kind, thoughtful, and tender. The exact opposite of what Jackson had been. Gary was someone who would never hurt her.

The first time they had sex was on the couch in his office. He made her feel like a princess in a fairy tale who had finally found her Prince Charming. He was careful and considerate, wanting her to enjoy herself. It had been unlike any sexual experience she'd ever had. As she wrapped her legs around his waist, she'd felt her soul becoming entwined with his.

After that, their meetings in his office became less about schoolwork and more about having sex and drinking martinis, always drinking. At first, she'd gone along with the drinking because she knew that's what he liked, but it gradually became something she looked forward to as well. It sped up those warm feelings in her and made it easier to totally release herself in whatever position he wanted to take her.

But then she developed stomach problems, feeling nauseated all the time. And at the same time, she found herself wanting to eat more and at odd hours of the night. It wasn't until three months later when she caught a view of her profile after stepping out of the shower that the possibility of being pregnant dawned on her. She placed her hands on her abdomen and stared. *But I take my birth control pills every day. How . . . ?*

On that day and thereafter, she made a conscious effort to reduce the amount of food she ate. She could not let Gary find out lest he end things with her. When she was with him, she pretended that she wasn't pregnant, that she was just imagining things.

Then one day he said he thought she was putting on weight. She could hear the reprimand in his tone of voice, and it scared her to think he might figure out what was going on.

But what am I going to do with a baby? I'm getting close to graduating; I can't afford to stop going to school. She'd heard about places that did abortions, but she wasn't about to let someone she didn't know perform such a procedure on her, and she was terrified of trying to give herself an abortion. She was scared to go to an OB doctor for fear that someone she knew might be there and mention it to Gary. In the end, she had decided she would deliver the baby herself and give it to an adoption agency.

As she entered her ninth month, she wore loose-fitting dresses and extra-tight girdles to hide her swollen abdomen. She was finding it harder and harder to keep up with school and with the demands of satisfying Gary. And he seemed to be interested in seeing her less often. "That's okay," he'd said when she asked if they were to meet one night. "I've gotten caught up on things and am going to call it an early night. Maybe another night."

A little warning bell had gone off in the back of her mind at his comment. *Is he getting tired of me? Does he not love me anymore? It's because I've gotten fat; that's what it is.* She restricted her intake even more, yet still, the scale inched upward.

Then one day she stopped by his office in the middle of the day and walked in without knocking. The scene she saw made the world stop turning. He was sitting on the edge of his desk. Standing in front of him, a little too close, was a young and gorgeous woman. They both were holding what Maggie suspected were martinis. Gary looked surprised at first, then quickly regained his composure. "Hi, Maggie. This is Beverly. I'm her student advisor."

Beverly ran one hand down the side of her perfectly svelte body and batted her long-lashed eyelids at Maggie. "Hi, Maggie," she purred.

Unable to think, Maggie had turned and left without saying a word. In her mind, she heard the sound of breaking glass as her world began crashing down around her. *He's found someone else . . . or maybe he's always had someone else. Maybe I've been a fool to believe he was only interested in me.* She spent that night and the next day crying, uncertain what to do next.

Then came the night that she awoke to find her bed soaked. *My water broke!* Feeling scared and nervous, she waited for the first contraction to hit. She was surprised at how mild it was and thought, *Maybe I'll have an easy time of it.* But that only lasted for a couple of hours. After that, the contractions began in earnest, increasing in severity and frequency.

Nearing total exhaustion as the contractions took their toll on her, Maggie tried lifting her knees toward her as far as she could and pushed against the pain while screaming into a pillow she held over her face. As the contraction subsided, she panted, trying to catch her breath. Then another contraction slammed her, and she pushed again. This time she felt something release and slide between her legs.

Leaning up, she peered down at the glistening form of her baby. She lifted it and its trailing umbilical cord. Everything looked as it did in the books she'd read in the library, but the baby was making no sounds or movements. Panic set in, and she held it upside down by its feet and slapped its bottom three times. Still nothing happened.

"No, no, this can't happen. Come on—you have to start breathing," she said to the lifeless form. "Please breathe." She patted its tiny cheeks, held its chest in one hand, and tapped it on the back, hoping to coax a breath out of it. Tears began running down Maggie's face, and her heart felt as if it were a piece of paper being torn in two, leaving uneven and jagged edges.

Thirty minutes later, she lay in bed, dry-eyed, with her stillborn baby lying across her chest. *Of all the horrible days in my life, this may be the worst. I thought maybe the one good thing I could do in my life was to give life, but I can't even do that right.* She swaddled the baby with a receiving blanket she'd bought at the Dollar Store and laid it on the bed beside her, then got up and went into the bathroom to clean herself.

By the time she came back out, she had decided there was only one thing she could do with the baby. She got dressed, placed the wrapped baby into a grocery sack, and walked out to her car.

Her first stop was a Walmart, where she bought a shovel. After putting it on the back floorboard of her car, she drove out into the country, taking gravel roads she was unfamiliar with. She continued driving slowly until the first gray hint of dawn lightened the sky. Then, as she crossed a wooden bridge spanning a small creek, she spotted a tiny thicket.

She pulled over and stopped. Her hands dropped into her lap as if they had no feeling in them. Truth was, she felt mostly numb all over, even her mind, as if she wasn't thinking about anything. Picking up the sack with her baby in it, she got out, retrieved the shovel, and headed into the woods.

Digging the hole was more difficult than she expected, with vines and roots doing their best to prevent her from accomplishing the grisly task. But finally, she had a hole of sufficient size, and she got down on her knees. Taking her child out of the sack, she unwrapped it, kissed its cold face, and said, "I'm sorry I failed you. I promise I did love you. This is not what I wanted to happen."

She rewrapped it, placed in the sack, and laid it gently in the bottom of the makeshift grave.

By the time she refilled the hole and walked back out to her car, the sun's rays were filling the sky. Maggie pitched the shovel into the back seat and slammed the door shut. Before she stepped into the driver's seat, she looked up and yelled, "Once again, thank you, God, for nothing!"

Chapter Eighteen

ISRAEL—NINETEEN YEARS OLD

Israel held open the door to the apartment he'd found to rent, and Hope walked in, carrying a bag of groceries. Once she passed him, he followed her, toting three bags of groceries in each of his hands. They proceeded into the kitchen, where Christine was finishing washing some dishes.

"Did you guys empty the store?" Christine asked with a smile.

"I got paid yesterday, so I thought we needed to get stocked up on something more than the beans and ramen noodles we've been living on."

"I hope you got plenty of Hamburger Helper because that's about the extent of my cooking skills. Nobody ever showed me how to cook anything."

Not for the first time, Israel thought, *I can't believe I'm sharing an apartment with a woman and her child, especially since I left Ada because I was afraid of having a family.* He'd had a dream about Ada recently and woke from it feeling guilty and with his face wet with tears. He couldn't figure out why he'd left her and yet felt so much sympathy for Christine, someone he didn't even know, that he couldn't leave her to the streets. *Maybe that's it; maybe it's because I knew Ada would be okay, having her parents to help her, but Christine had no one to turn to.*

He set his groceries on the counter and started to ask Christine about her comment that nobody ever showed her how to cook, but he held his tongue. He'd decided not to pry into her past but instead let her tell him about it when and if she wanted to. Lord knew he had his own past he wasn't going to talk about.

Hope spoke up. "I told him you didn't know how to cook anything but Hamburger Helper, so we bought ten boxes of it."

Israel saw Christine wince a bit. Hope's straightforwardness kind of reminded him of how Rebekah had been. *Rebekah, whatever became of you?* "Has she always been so honest?" he asked Christine.

"Yes, painfully so. I try to get her to use a filter, but it doesn't work. It's like she's on a mission to know and to tell the truth and doesn't care who it might hurt." She paused, then added, "Maybe that's because she got tired of the lies she was told so often."

"I'm like one of the kids in the story 'The Emperor's New Clothes,'" Hope said. "Grown-ups act like they're scared of the truth."

"Like I said . . ." Christine commented with a shrug.

Israel took a seat at the kitchen table and watched them put away the groceries. When Hope asked to go with him to buy groceries, it had caught him by surprise, figuring she wouldn't want to go without her mother. But perhaps it shouldn't have because whenever he came home after work, Hope couldn't seem to get enough of him, always wanting to sit by him when they ate or when they watched TV in the evenings. She would pepper him with questions about what kind of work he did and what happened during his day. It reminded him of something he saw on TV about how young ducklings will imprint on whatever or whoever provides food and safety for them.

*****

After supper, Israel sat in a chair with Hope asleep in his lap while Christine sat on the couch.

Christine said, "I still can't thank you enough for what you are doing for me and Hope."

"You tell me that every day. You don't have to keep telling me. I'm doing it because I want to."

"It's just that I'm not used to people doing something for me without expecting something in return, especially sex. It's the only currency I've never run out of, and it has always gotten me what I wanted. But you've not even hinted that that's what you're looking for from me."

Israel blushed. *Does she think I'm weird because I haven't tried anything with her?*

Before he could think of how to respond, she said, "You're probably surprised that with a face like mine any man would want to have sex with me. But men can be like animals. They wouldn't care if the woman had a sack over her head as long as she spread her legs."

Her bluntness and coarseness felt like rough sandpaper against his heart. "I wasn't thinking anything like that. Sure, I noticed your face when we first met, but it's like I don't even see it now. What I was thinking about is how sad it makes me feel that you've had to use your body like currency." He hesitated, then added, "I've known men like you're describing, who treat women and children like property. I've seen unspeakable things done. Just so you know, sometimes those men get what's coming to them." As soon as the words left his mouth, he regretted turning loose this tiny fragment of his secret. Hoping that he could distract Christine, he stood up and said, "You want something to eat or drink?"

She looked at him steadily for several seconds.

In those seconds, he tried to make up his mind what he would say if she asked questions.

Finally, she said, "The world is full of sick SOBs. And out of the billions of people on the earth, you and I meet each other in a bus station. I don't know about you, but I don't think that was an accident. I think God made that happen. And I'm glad."

Israel took a few moments to let that sink in. He opened his mouth to say something, then stopped.

"Go ahead," she said. "Spit it out. Say what's on your mind."

He took a breath and said, "Being here, in this apartment, living with a woman and her daughter, is the last thing I ever expected to happen to me. No, that's not true. If it was the last thing I expected, that would mean it was on a list of expectations. Truth is, I *never* dreamed this would happen. What amazes me is that I'm not nervous or worried about it, about what we're doing or where we're going with this. It's just the way it is right now, and I'm okay with it."

Tears welled up in her eyes. "I'm afraid to think about or talk about the future for fear of messing up the present. When I was a little girl, I used to make up dreams about my future based on the crap I watched on TV, and none of those dreams came true. For the first time in my life, I'm content to just be, and that's because I met you. Even as I say that, I know it sounds crazy. I barely even know you, yet I feel safe with you—I trust you."

As she spoke, Israel's chest filled with emotions. He bit his tongue to try to keep from bursting into tears. He wanted to say something but feared his voice would get stuck in his throat or that it would tremble and give away how emotional he was feeling. When the wave of emotions passed, he swallowed, and said, "There's no better feeling than feeling safe with someone. I had someone like that in my life, but it scared me, and I ran away." Waves of shame and guilt flooded him, and he felt like someone was choking him.

Hope rolled over and said, "You can trust us."

Shocked that she'd been listening, he said, "I thought you were asleep."

Christine asked, "How much have you heard us say?"

As she sat up, Hope said, "Everything. I heard everything. I liked listening to it. All I've ever heard is grown-ups being angry and yelling at each other."

All Israel was able to do was look at both of them with tears running down his cheeks.

Chapter Nineteen

MAGGIE—THIRTY-THREE YEARS OLD

With tears dripping off the end of her nose and chin, Maggie sat on the edge of her bathtub and stared at the razor blade in her trembling hand. *Don't be such a chicken. Just do it!*

Unable to squeeze out from under the heavy weight of regret, shame, and depression, she hadn't left her apartment since her baby's birth—and death—four days ago. Wave after wave, the emotions battered her as if she were a ship marooned on sharp rocks.

She thought Professor Reed might call and check on her when she didn't show up to work, but when he didn't, she knew the truth. *He's moved on to another pitiful, naïve coed. How does he keep getting away with it? Somebody needs to do something about him!* But that momentary fire of anger was smothered by the wet blanket of loathing she felt toward herself.

She touched the razor blade to her wrist. *This is the only way out. I can't stand this anymore.* For some reason, she recalled images of her little sister, Rachel, and wondered where she was and how she was doing. One time, she called her aunt to see how things were, but a stranger answered the phone and said she didn't know Maggie's aunt nor anyone named Rachel.

Like making a right-hand turn at an intersection, she suddenly began traveling down memory lane. The journey took her directly to her father, then to Jackson Wallace, eventually stopping at Professor Reed.

Wiping her tears with the back of her hand, she thought, *Men! That's what has ruined my life—men!* She began thinking how the three of them would feel when they heard about her suicide. *My father, if he were alive, would be happy about it, and Jackson probably would, too, while Professor Reed wouldn't even care, though he'd put on a big act about it.* She simmered for a second, then boiled over in rage. *Why should I give them the satisfaction? Screw them all!*

She stood up and flung the razor blade into the trash can. Looking in the mirror she said aloud, "What would Charlie Chester say to you right now? She'd say, 'Get up and get over it. Quit feeling sorry for yourself. The only person who fails is the one who quits trying.'"

Maggie turned on the water and washed her face. *I refuse to be a quitter.*

After failing to find something on TV that interested her, she thought, *What would feel good right now is a drink.*

She drove to a bar downtown that she had heard kids on campus talking about. Music was blaring when she entered, and the lighting was dim. Taking a seat at the bar, she ordered a bloody Mary, drank it quickly, and ordered another one. A warm feeling began spreading through her, and she smiled.

"Let me pay for that one," a man said as he took the stool beside her. He looked to be ten years younger than her.

"I'll pay for my own drink," she said icily.

He smiled, and his eyes drifted slowly over her body. Smiling, he said, "I don't mind, really."

Maggie hit him so hard that she knocked him off his stool and onto the floor. "Keep your eyes to yourself!" she yelled. "I said I'd buy my own drinks. Are you deaf?"

Two muscle-bound men in tight T-shirts appeared out of nowhere. "Is there a problem here?" one of them asked.

The young man picked himself up off the floor. Pointing at Maggie, he said, "She's crazy; that's the problem."

"He bothering you?" the other man asked Maggie.

"Yes, and I took care of it. I don't need a man to save me from anything. You're all so disgusting. You think because you have testosterone that you can do whatever you want. Well, not with me!" She slapped some money on the bar and strode out to her car.

When she slid behind the wheel, her heart was still racing from the encounter inside. *I can't believe I just did that. But, boy, did it feel good!*

She decided she hadn't drunk enough to give her the feeling she wanted, so she drove to the next town over, where she knew they had a liquor store.

Forty minutes later, she walked into her apartment with a bottle of vodka in a brown paper sack. Before sitting down on the couch, she went to her bookshelf and pulled down a dog-eared copy of *Codependent No More* by Melody Beattie. *I need to remind myself of the things I learned while I was in the women's shelter about setting boundaries.*

Thirty minutes later, she was asleep.

*****

The next morning, Maggie awoke with her head feeling crushed by a headache. She squinted against the sun streaming through her window and saw in her lap the opened copy of Beattie's book and the empty vodka bottle resting against her thigh. It took her several moments to piece together the happenings from last night into an understandable picture. She gave a weak smile at the memory of the man at the bar sitting on the floor with a look of surprise on his face.

After starting the coffee maker, she went to take a shower. As she undressed, light glinted from the razor blade resting in the trash can. *I don't ever want to forget what that felt like, to be so desperate and hopeless that killing myself seemed like the best solution.* She shuddered at how close she had come to ending her life.

While standing under the warm spray of the shower, she heard Charlie Chester's voice, "You need to make a plan; that's the only way to know where you're going. Plan your work and work your plan." *She was right then, and that's what I need to do now.*

Feeling a little refreshed from her shower, she toweled off, dressed, then poured herself a cup of coffee and sat down at her dinette table with a pen and notepad.

One hour and several cups of coffee later, she read over her completed list:

SHORT-TERM GOALS

1. Go to the dean's office and file a complaint on Professor Reed.

2. Pass out flyers warning females to avoid being alone with him.

3. Go to Professor Reed's office and confront him.

4. Return to classes and make up work missed.

LONG-TERM GOALS

1. Complete degree.

2. Establish a women's shelter in this area.

3. Establish a career helping those who are less fortunate.

She paused for a moment, then added:

4. Stop drinking.

She immediately felt focused and ready to move forward, so she got dressed and went to the dean's office. Thirty minutes later, she stormed out, fuming over what was said: "All we have is your word against his." *What a sorry excuse to do nothing about a problem they know has been going on for years.*

But she was also furious with herself because she couldn't truthfully say that she'd been coerced, threatened academically, or promised special favors as a way to explain why she became involved with the professor. On the surface, it appeared she was complicit in her affair with him. She had found it hard to articulate how he'd seduced her with his charm and covertly controlled her with his position of power and prestige on campus.

Striding across campus like a storm trooper, she headed straight for Professor Reed's office. Once in the building, though, she remembered that he had class during that hour. *Perfect!*

She walked down the corridor to the classroom and flung open the door. All heads turned her way with startled expressions. Professor Reed's hand stopped halfway through writing a word on the chalkboard. He raised his eyebrows at her. "Is there a problem, Ms. Stinson?"

His smug tone of voice made her want to throw up. *I wish I could make myself throw up all over his precious herringbone jacket.* While walking deliberately toward him, in a loud voice, she said, "Yes, there is a problem, Professor Reed, and it is you. You are the problem. Why don't you tell the class how many years you have been seducing your female students?"

She turned and faced the class and noticed three girls' faces turn crimson as their mouths flew open in surprise, and one of them was the girl she'd seen him with the other day. "I can see that I was not the only one out of this class."

Professor Reed said, "I have no idea what—"

Maggie whirled on him. "Don't you dare try to lie! Do you deny that you've been having sex with me on the couch in your office? Because I don't deny it." She'd decided on this tactic, knowing it would place him on the horns of a dilemma—to deny it invited her to reveal details about his anatomy that he couldn't deny, but to admit it would mean that all the other students he was seeing would know he was a philanderer, and that word would spread like wildfire.

Color rose on his cheekbones, and he gave a nervous laugh. Looking at the class, he said, "Clearly, Ms. Stinson is suffering from some sort of psychotic episode and has lost touch with reality. I believe it would be best if we end class now. You may leave, and I'll take care of getting her the help she needs."

She spun around and fixed the students with a stare. "Don't even one of you dare leave this room, not until you know the truth."

No one made a move, apparently mesmerized by what was happening.

Facing the class confidently, she said, "Let me ask a simple question; are any of you having an affair with the professor?"

The lecture hall became as silent as a funeral parlor.

She pointed at the professor. "This man thinks he is Don Juan, but he is nothing more than a degenerate. He's only interested in himself, though he makes you believe he's interested in you. He tells you all sorts of fascinating stories about his travels around the world, though I'm beginning to wonder if any of them are true. And he can't tell a story unless you and he are drinking alcohol. The school isn't going to do anything about him unless there's an outcry from more people than just me. Will you join me in destroying this monster?"

A young girl in the front row stood up. In a voice trembling with emotion, she said, "I'll join you. Your story is the same as mine. He made me think I was special to him."

The girl Maggie had recently seen him with stepped into the aisle and walked down front. She went straight to the professor and slapped him across the face. "I hate you! Wait till my father hears about this. He'll probably try to kill you."

Another girl stood and said, "There's no telling how many there are just like us and for how many years he's been doing this. I'll join you."

Suddenly the class broke into applause, and Maggie turned to see the professor scurrying out the door.

Chapter Twenty

ISRAEL—NINETEEN YEARS OLD

Three months after moving into the apartment with Christine and Hope, Israel was getting ready to go to a jobsite where he was to work on taking some concrete forms off a sidewalk he and the crew he was with had poured two days ago. It would be a solitary job, and he was looking forward to the quietness of it.

As he picked up his canvas bag of tools, Hope asked, "Can I go with you today?"

More and more, she was becoming like his shadow. He'd even taken her to work with him a couple of times when he was only going to be there for a few hours.

Although he was looking forward to working alone that day, he couldn't resist the pleading expression on her face. "Sure," he said. "Go put your work clothes on."

He'd barely finished fixing himself a cup of coffee to take with him when she came running into the kitchen wearing her denim overalls. Her eyes sparkled with excitement. "This is going to be fun, isn't it?"

"We'll make it as fun as we can, but we've got a job to do, and it has to be completed today."

"That's not a problem. With my help, you can get it done."

Israel chuckled as they headed out the door and got in the dilapidated pickup truck he'd scraped enough money together to buy. He would never chance taking it for a long trip, but it was good enough to shuttle back and forth to work.

As he eased into the morning traffic, Hope asked, "Why doesn't Mommy have a job?"

He'd wondered the same thing because she'd applied for several. His conclusion was that it was her face that stopped people from hiring her. She pretty much told him as much and that it was nothing new to her. That reality angered him, but he was powerless to do anything about it. "She just hasn't found the right job yet," he answered Hope.

"Are you and Mommy going to get married?"

He nearly spat out the mouthful of coffee he'd just sipped. "What makes you ask that?" *Gee whiz, this girl and her questions!*

"Well, we're all living together, and we like each other, so I figured you all would get married someday."

Truthfully, he'd been thinking lately about where things were going with Christine. *I like her and all, but she's awfully moody and can be hard to get along with sometimes. I think what I like the most about our situation is the feeling of having a family, of having someone to come home to, especially to see Hope's eager face.* Whenever he had those kinds of thoughts, he winced inwardly at how badly he had treated Ada, especially now that he knew he could have been a good father to their baby.

"Are you going to answer me?" Hope intruded on his musings.

"Marriage is a really serious step for people to make, Hope. We need more time before we think about doing anything like that." His answer seemed to satisfy her, but it didn't satisfy him. All that day, he pondered over what he should do, and by the day's end, he concluded, *I've got to go back and find Ada. But how in the world do I explain that to Christine and Hope?*

His heart was full and heavy when he got home that evening, and one look at Christine told him she was in a bad mood.

"Where have you been? I thought you said it was a small job and wouldn't take long."

"Sorry. I took some time with Hope and showed her how to use some of the tools. Time just kind of got away from me."

Christine knelt down in front of Hope. "Are you okay, honey? Did he hurt you or bother you?"

Israel was immediately confused. "Why are you asking her that? You know I'd never hurt her."

She ignored him. "Tell me the truth, Hope. Are you okay?"

Hope, who had fallen asleep on the way home and still wasn't fully awake, jerked away from her mother. "I'm tired and want to go lay down."

Christine turned on Israel, shoving her finger in his face. "You've done something to her. That's not normal for her to want to go lay down. If you've laid a hand on her, I swear I will kill you."

He shook his head to try to clear his bewilderment. At the same time, he felt his ire coming up at being accused of something he didn't do. "I don't know what's gotten into you, Christine, but you need to calm down. Look, I'm tired, too. I'm going to take a shower and get cleaned up. You and I can talk about whatever is going on after I get finished." He turned away from her before she could respond. *What is the matter with her? It's just confirmation that I need to get away from her. She's got more problems than I do, and that's saying a lot.*

He took an extra-long shower, letting the hot water and steam help him relax and put his mind in a better place. He began formulating how he was going to explain to Christine and Hope that he was going to be leaving and going back to West Virginia and that he was going alone.

As he finished drying off and getting dressed, he thought he heard men's voices. He zipped up his jeans and, frowning, stepped out of the bathroom. "Here he comes now," he heard Christine say. In the living room stood a middle-aged woman holding a legal pad and two burly police officers behind her, all three with grim expressions on their faces. Christine was standing off to one side, but Hope was nowhere to be seen.

"Are you Israel McKenzie?" the woman asked.

A sudden feeling of uncertainty and dread came over him. *Someone found out what I did to Sir.* Hanging his head, he said, "Yes, I am."

The woman pointed at him and said to the policemen, "Arrest him."

The men stepped to either side of him. "Put your hands behind you."

Israel obeyed and felt handcuffs being squeezed onto his wrists.

One of the policemen said, "Israel McKenzie, you are under arrest for sexual abuse of a minor . . ."

The policeman continued speaking, but Israel heard nothing else that he said. He stood there shocked and dazed.

The officer shook him. "I said, do you understand these rights as I've explained them to you?"

Israel finally found his voice. "What is going on? Why am I being accused of this? I've never touched a small child like that—never!" He looked at Christine. "What is this about?"

She gave him a hateful look. "You . . . you . . . predator! You took us in just so you could molest my daughter. I hope you burn in hell!"

"That's not right," he exclaimed. "Someone's got the wrong story here." He looked at the officers and woman. "Where is Hope? Ask her yourselves if I ever touched her." Nodding toward Christine, he said, "She's making this up. Why, I don't know, but she is."

The woman spoke up. "I've already spoken with Hope, and she corroborates her mother's story. We've taken her to a safe place until we could arrest you and remove you from the apartment."

This blow felt like a nail being hammered into his coffin. A sound resonated within him, like a Tibetan gong, telling him he was a condemned man. He could not explain why Hope said what she did. *I'm innocent of what they are charging me with, but the scales of justice are being balanced because of what I did to Sir.*

Chapter Twenty-One

ISRAEL—TWENTY-TWO YEARS OLD

Israel flinched as the iron-barred door banged shut behind him and a loud buzz indicated the door in front of him would be opening. He was so scared that he felt every organ in his body shaking. Sitting in the county jail during all the delays for his trial, the trial itself, and then waiting for the sentencing had been one thing, but now he was entering the federal prison where he would be living for the next twenty years. "Hard time," everyone in county jail had told him.

The guard beside him spoke gruffly, "Step through."

He shuffled through the opening, accompanied by the jingling and scraping sounds of the chains on his ankles. In another setting, the sound might trigger excitement in the hearts of boys and girls eager to see Santa Claus. But for Israel, it was like the tolling of bells for a condemned man.

When he'd first met his public defender, he'd told him he wanted to plead guilty—not because he'd done anything to Hope but because he felt like he deserved to be punished for things in the past, things he didn't reveal to the lawyer. But after his lawyer told him what happens to pedophiles in prison, fear compelled him to fight for his life.

The problem was the medical evidence was conclusive that Hope had been sexually abused, something Israel could not get his head wrapped around. There hadn't been any other men around her since he'd met her and Christine.

It wasn't until his lawyer had him talk with a psychologist he'd hired as an expert witness that a new possibility emerged. "I suspect the mother is the perpetrator," the psychologist had said. "It's a classic case of trauma bonding where the victim forms a close bond with the perpetrator. Hope would never point the finger at her mother for fear of losing her and being left all alone, in her mind anyway. Her mother convinced her to say that it was you who had done it."

That idea devastated Israel, and for a long time, he rejected it. But as time wore on, and he thought about his time with Christine, he began to accept that it was true.

Hope—he felt sorry for her and wished there was something he could do to save her. Coming to an understanding that he was powerless to do anything was a bitter pill to swallow.

The prison guard showed him to a room where another guard was pulling on blue exam gloves. "Strip," he said.

For the umpteenth time since the whole ordeal began, Israel was subjected to a strip search. *Open mouth, stick out tongue, raise tongue, bend over and grab your ankles, buttocks spread*—never had he felt so dehumanized.

The guard gave a cruel laugh. "Get used to it. Inmates have special treatments for scum like you who've molested little girls."

This was the terror that kept Israel awake at night. He'd seen movies that depicted the tortures child rapists were subjected to in prison. He started to protest his innocence to the guard but knew it was pointless. *They all probably say they are innocent.*

His first night there, nothing happened, although he lay awake all night waiting for it.

Every day his heart would be in his mouth as he got ready to turn a corner or enter a room, knowing that the inevitable might be waiting. And finally, it was.

During a shift in the laundry room, he suddenly realized everyone had disappeared, even the guard. His legs began trembling as he looked furtively around the room.

Out of a darkened corner, three inmates appeared, all with shaved heads and tattoos splattered across their arms, necks, and faces. The one in the middle grabbed his own crotch and said, "I've been waiting to take care of you."

Israel felt sick to his stomach.

When the two other men grabbed him, he tried to fight back, but it was useless; they treated his torso like a punching bag until he was bent double in pain and trying to catch his breath. As they folded him over a table, he felt his pants being jerked down. The one behind him said, "This is what happens to people like you."

Dear God in heaven, strike me dead. I'm begging you. Don't make me have to go through this. But his call into the night went unanswered.

After it was over, he waddled back to his cell, knowing it was pointless to report what happened or ask for help. He bit his lip in an effort to keep from crying, but an iron gate wouldn't have stopped his flood of tears, so he buried his face in his pillow.

Unfortunately, that was just the beginning . . .

Chapter Twenty-Two

MAGGIE—FIFTY YEARS OLD

Having been startled awake in the middle of the night, Maggie sat up in bed, trying to figure out what awakened her. All of her nerve endings were firing, making her feel as though electricity was running through her body. She strained to hear anything that was an aberration from the normal night sounds in her house. There was the hum of the air conditioner, the ticktock from the grandfather clock in the living room, and an occasional creak that was a natural part of her house settling.

Suddenly, there it was—a tiny baby crying!

Maggie couldn't believe her ears. *That's impossible!* But there it was again, unmistakable for anything except a baby's cry.

She switched on the lamp beside her bed, but nothing happened. Getting up, she walked cautiously toward the door of her room and flipped the light switch. Again, nothing happened. *Has the power gone off?*

Her hand bumped into the doorknob as she felt for it. Opening the door, she stepped into the dark hallway. A faint light shone from underneath the door of the bedroom at the end of the hallway, which seemed longer than it should be. *Optical illusion?*

Another cry came directly from that room. Maggie's heart raced, and the hair on the back of her neck stood on end. *This can't be real. Should I call the police?*

Although she wanted to go back to her bedroom, lock the door, and push her dresser up against it until dawn, she felt inexorably drawn toward the sound. Walking felt like she was trying to move through sludge, so much so that she was leaning forward and out of breath by the time she reached the door.

By now the baby's crying sounded more insistent or maybe panicked. "I'm coming," Maggie said. "Mama's coming."

She pushed open the door. Against the opposite wall was a baby bed lit by a small lamp on a nightstand beside it.

The baby was mewling now.

With tears running down her face, she approached the bed. "It's okay; I'm here."

Lying in the shadows on the mattress was a swaddled form.

With trembling hands, Maggie reached down and lifted the baby and brought it to her chest. Something hit the top of her feet. Looking down, she saw what looked like dirt clods all around. Confused, she pulled back the corner of the baby's blanket.

Looking up at her from the cradle of her arms was the flame-ringed, laughing face of her father.

She jumped back and cried out in horror. She looked around wide-eyed and realized she'd fallen asleep in her recliner. An old black-and-white movie was playing on the TV. Lowering the footrest of the recliner, she sat up, put her hand on her chest, and felt the thumping of her racing heart. *My God, what a nightmare.*

It wasn't the first time she'd had a nightmare about her baby. Through the years, her sleep had been disturbed by various macabre distortions of that fateful night. *Am I ever going to get over it?*

She switched on a light, got up, and poured herself some vodka, spilling some because her hands were still trembling from the dream.

After a couple of swallows, she began to feel calmer and walked over to the mantel above her fireplace. She picked up a yellowed pair of white infant shoes, part of the outfit she intended to dress her baby in when intending to give it up for adoption. They were the only possession she had as a keepsake of her baby. *I've told you thousands of times: I'm sorry for what I did. You didn't deserve that.*

Replacing the shoes on the mantel, she stepped over to a wall and looked at the frame holding her diploma from the University of Tennessee. Beside it hung a plaque engraved with the words, "To Margaret Stinson for helping to create the Reelfoot Women's Refuge, 1993." Underneath was a photograph of Maggie with a crowd of smiling women, trying to push their faces into the picture. On the glass covering the photo, someone had written in the corner with a permanent marker, "We love you, Maggie!"

The edges of the two frames weren't perfectly parallel, so she took a moment to bring them into alignment. Once she was satisfied, she took a sip of vodka from her glass and stepped to the right where she could read the inscription on another plaque: "To Margaret Stinson for her many year of service to the Carl Perkins Center, helping to improve the lives of children in northwest Tennessee." It never failed to irritate her that the *s* was left off the word *year*. No one apologized to her about it, apparently oblivious that there was an error. *Clearly none of them ever had Mrs. Shanklin for Senior English in high school.*

Walking over to her desk, she sat down and switched on the lamp. She pushed loose papers around until she pulled out a weathered page that had been torn from a legal pad. Smoothing it out, she looked at the goals list she had made for herself years ago on the night she almost committed suicide:

SHORT-TERM GOALS

1. Go to the dean's office and file a complaint on Professor Reed. *Took care of that one, though it did no good.*

2. Pass out flyers warning females to avoid being alone with him. *Hmmm, never did do that. Didn't have to once word spread across campus.*

3. Go to Professor Reed's office and confront him. *Now that was a moment in time!* She smiled at the memory of barging into his lecture hall and confronting him in front of the entire class. He was never seen on campus after that. She'd heard he'd moved to California.

4. Return to classes and make up work missed. *Check. Took care of that one, too.* School really changed for her then. First of all, she became famous on campus and a leading voice for women. She was convinced by others to run for student government president and surprised herself when she won. *Those were heady days for me.*

LONG-TERM GOALS

1. Complete degree. *Got it.*

2. Help create a women's shelter in this area. *Done, but not easily.* Not being familiar with northwest Tennessee, she hadn't been prepared for the dearth of social services in the area and how backward people were in their thinking. No one had ever said it, but it was clear by the tone of voice in the judges, lawyers, and law enforcement officials that violence committed by husbands against their wives was viewed as somehow the fault of the women—that if they didn't like being beat on, they should just leave. She had often suspected some of those she spoke to probably hit their wives, just like they had watched their fathers hit their mothers. But slowly, women began coming forward and telling their stories, eliciting donations from other women, and a shelter was finally built in a secluded area of Obion County.

She poured some more vodka into her glass and drank a swallow. *Nearly lost myself doing all that, plus working with all the victims of violence.* It had been Charlie Chester who'd told her during a visit that she was getting burned out and had better turn herself in a different direction.

3. Establish a career helping those who are less fortunate. *I guess I've done that, too. Went from helping battered women to helping battered children at Carl Perkins.*

4. Stop drinking. She looked at the drink in her hand. *Yeah . . . well . . .*

Laying the piece of paper down, she picked up a letter from Transitions Hospice Care. For three days, she'd been considering their offer of a position as a social worker with their agency. *From battered women, to battered children, to people whose bodies have been battered by disease? Hmmm, sounds like a pattern to me.* She gave a wry chuckle. *I guess if you grow up being abused and go straight into an abusive marriage, then you're drawn to what you're most familiar with.*

She reread the letter again and wondered what it would be like to escort people through their final stage of life. *Maybe it's time for me to take on a new challenge.*

Just before turning off the desk lamp, a hand-addressed envelope caught her eye. She didn't recognize the handwriting, nor did she remember seeing the envelope before tonight. There was no return address on it, and it was unopened. Picking up a plastic letter opener, she sliced open the envelope and pulled out a single sheet of paper. She unfolded it to find cutout letters of various sizes pasted on it, spelling out a message: "Be certain, your sins will find you out."

Chapter Twenty-Three

ISRAEL—THIRTY-EIGHT YEARS OLD

A loud tapping sound accompanied by a muffled voice interrupted Israel's dream. He opened his eyes, but it took him a moment to remember where he was. Rubbing his eyes, he sat up in the seat of his seriously used pickup truck and recognized the rest area he'd stopped at overnight. The grim face of a state trooper was looking at him and motioning him to roll down his window, causing Israel's heart to race.

Turning the hand crank to lower the cracked window, he asked, "May I help you, Officer?" He was scared to death, this being the first time he'd seen a law enforcement officer since getting out on parole a week ago. He tried to sound calm by telling himself, *You've done nothing wrong.*

"License and registration, please," the officer said without preamble.

Israel leaned over, retrieved the documents from the glove compartment, and handed them out the window. "Is there a problem, sir?"

"Stay right here while I go check this out."

From his rearview mirror, Israel watched the trooper return to the cruiser parked behind him and radio in to verify that everything was on the up and up. His stomach growled to remind him it had been several hours since he'd eaten, and his bladder strained for relief.

After what seemed an inordinately long period of time, the trooper walked back to Israel's window and handed him his papers. "You just got out of prison from over in Forrest City?"

"That's correct."

"Where are you headed?"

"Some place called Como, Tennessee. It's in the northwest corner of the state."

"These rest areas are for taking a nap in, not for camping out. You need to be on your way."

"Can I go pee first?"

"I'd rather you move on now." There was a veiled threat in the trooper's voice, so Israel agreed to leave.

At the next exit, he got off and pulled into a convenience store to get something to eat and drink but mostly to let the pressure off his bladder.

When he stepped to the cash register and placed his items on the counter, he asked, "What day is today?" While in prison, where every day is alike, he'd stopped trying to keep up with what day of the week it was.

The teenager paused in the middle of scanning his items and stared at him blankly. "Day?"

"Yeah, what day of the week is it?"

"Uh, it's . . . uh . . . Sunday. That's right—it's Sunday."

"Thanks. Is there a church anywhere around here?"

"Church?"

Beginning to wonder if the kid was slow-witted or if he was making fun of him, Israel felt agitation. "Church! You know, a building with a steeple, people inside, Bibles, singing, preaching. Ever been to one?" By now there were two people in line behind Israel, and he was uncomfortable with the amount of attention being focused on him.

The teenager called out to someone unseen behind him. "Hey, Tracie! Are there any churches around here?"

An older woman came through a set of swinging doors. "Who's asking?"

"This man here," the teenager said.

Israel felt like swearing at them both and bolting out of the store. As the woman got closer, he could see that her skin looked like it had been tanned by a taxidermist and pulled tight over her bones. Her bright red lipstick and heavy eye makeup gave the appearance of someone who was unwilling to acknowledge that Father Time was leading her over the hill.

With a voice that sounded like she had gravel in her throat, the woman said, "The closest one is three miles east of here. Head out of the parking lot and turn left. About a mile and a half up the road, you'll see a billboard for that car dealership in town." She looked at the teenager. "What's the name of that place?"

"Dillinger's," someone behind Israel answered.

"That's it," she agreed. "Dillinger's car dealership. Turn left at that billboard, go about two-thirds of a mile, and turn left again. The church will be down that road on your right."

Israel felt no confidence in the directions but wasn't about to question them further. He paid for his items and returned to his truck. He sat there and ate a granola bar and sipped on a Mello Yello. Then he reached in the glove compartment and took out an envelope. Pulling out the letter he'd read at least a dozen times since he received it from a lawyer who was waiting for him when he exited prison, he scanned it once again. It just didn't seem possible, one of those "too good to be true" kind of letters.

> *My dear young friend Israel,*
>
> *This will be my last letter to you. Cancer has finally defeated me—or at least worn me down so that I no longer want to fight. I'm ready to go be with God and my Savior in heaven.*
>
> *I'm so sorry that I never came to see you in prison. I don't have any good excuses for it. I just didn't think I could stand to see you in there.*
>
> *My memories are still filled with your young face when you used to come help me in the wood shop at the orphanage. That's the way I prefer to remember you.*
>
> *Your path hasn't been easy, I know. But eventually you will get out of prison, and you can begin a new life—a better life.*
>
> *Don't quit trying, Israel. Just focus on pleasing God and trusting him. That's the best advice I know to give anybody.*
>
> *When you get out of prison, my lawyer will give you this letter, and he'll give you a deed as well. It's to a piece of property and a house trailer that I'm leaving to you. I don't have any family to leave it to, so I want you to have it. It's a nice quiet place, the kind of place where you can heal and start over.*

The lawyer will give you a second letter that I'm suggesting you do not open, not right away. There are things in there that you need to know when you're ready to know them. You'll know when the time is right.

I'm counting on you living the kind of life so that you and I can meet again in heaven and catch up on everything.

Your friend,

Darnell Williams

Israel ran his fingers over Darnell's name. "Darnell," he said aloud. "You're the only true friend I've ever had." After returning the letter to the glove compartment, he cranked his truck and set out on the questionable directions to the church.

To his surprise, the directions led him straight to the parking lot of a small, white, wood-frame church. There were about a dozen or so cars in the parking lot, and a few people were just then entering through the front door. They were dressed casually, rather than in the fancy clothes he used to see some people wear when he went to church while living at the orphanage. He looked down at the shirt, jeans, and shoes he bought at a Goodwill store, then looked in the rearview mirror at his scraggly beard. *Wonder what those folks are going to think when they see me?*

He was on the verge of changing his mind about going in but remembered the promise he made to Chaplain Yardley, the chaplain at the prison, a thin man with graying hair, and the one kind person he met while serving time.

"Just remember," Yardley had said just before Israel was released, "God brought you through this difficult time, and now he's expecting you to do something with your life. Promise me you'll go to church after you leave here. Find a place that'll help you continue your spiritual journey."

Israel had no reason not to make the promise, so he agreed.

Opening the door to his truck and getting out, he mumbled aloud, "This is for you, Yardley, and for you, too, Darnell."

As he approached the door, he could hear the strains of "How Great Thou Art" and immediately was transported back in time to the first time he heard it in church at the age of five.

Inside the vestibule, he paused and listened, struck by the simple, unadorned a cappella singing of the congregation. There was no choir, no piano, no band—just the voices of the members. He wasn't sure why, but he felt his chest swell with unexpected emotions.

He slipped inside the auditorium and found a seat in the back row. A woman sitting in front of him turned and smiled, then pointed to the page in the hymnal that they were singing from. Israel retrieved a hymnal from the back of the pew, opened it up, and in a quiet voice, joined in the singing.

By the end of the song, tears were slipping from the corners of his eyes. Emotions had already choked off his voice. He blinked, and tears splashed onto the pages of the song, marking the place where a man's heart had been touched.

When the preacher got up to speak, he, too, was dressed in a way that reflected the congregation—no necktie or suit, just a chambray shirt and tan pants. The Bible story he told was one Israel had never heard. It was about a mighty warrior named Jephthah whose mother was a prostitute. His half brothers drove him from their home and land because of the kind of person his mother was. Banished, he lived in a foreign land for a number of years and became a renowned warrior.

The story resonated with Israel. *I know what it's like to be driven away from people through no fault of your own and to be ashamed to tell people about who your parents are, especially when you don't even know who they were.*

But it was the triumphant turn in Jephthah's life that gave Israel hope. A contingent of men from his homeland found him and begged him to return with them to help them defeat an army that was oppressing them. Feeling vindicated, he did return with them, and God gave him a mighty victory.

Israel felt like the preacher was looking at and speaking directly to him when he concluded his sermon. "Friend, are you a Jephthah? Ashamed of your past? Feeling like an outcast? Feeling like your life has no meaning? Then put your hand in God's hand, and let him lead you out of that place of darkness. Let him make your life meaningful again."

Overwhelmed by the entire experience at the church, Israel ducked out as everyone stood and started singing at the conclusion of the sermon. He sat in his truck with his forehead resting against the steering wheel. *Dear God in heaven, help me . . . help me find meaning and purpose. Help me find my way.*

Chapter Twenty-Four

MAGGIE—FIFTY YEARS OLD

Maggie stared at the envelope. The handwriting was exactly the same as that on the letters she'd received every day since the first one arrived six days ago. She braced herself for the message that awaited her.

After she received the second one, she considered going to the police about it, but then she would have had to explain what there was in her past that would cause her to feel like the letters were a legitimate threat of some kind.

Was it from setting her father on fire? Burying her baby? Or could it be that Jackson had found her and was wanting some kind of revenge for her running out on him? Or maybe a husband of one of the women she helped provide shelter for?

She sliced open the envelope and pulled out the letter. The message this time was, "His wrath will come upon you."

In spite of her best efforts to slough this off as the work of some kook, she still felt a chill run up her back. During the daytime, while she was getting settled into her new job at the hospice agency, she could push the situation to the back of her mind, but once she returned to the quietness of her house, fear began peeking in the windows, and shadows took on ominous shapes.

She looked over at the deadbolt on her front door. She was certain she'd already locked it and checked it, but "what if . . ." teased the edges of her thoughts. The only way she could satisfy the prompt was to get up and check the lock again.

Just as she put her hand on the lock, the door burst open, splintering the door facing and slamming into Maggie. She staggered backward; the only thing preventing her from falling was her last-second grabbing of the trim of the closet door.

It was a second before she saw a burly, bearded man with shaggy gray hair standing in front of her, his face a mask of rage. "You ruined my life!" he yelled. "You ruined my life, and now you're going to pay for it."

Maggie's brain flew in a thousand directions at once, trying to figure out if she knew this man, thinking about the path to her phone and if she could get past him to call the police, glancing around to see if there was anything close by she could use as a weapon, wondering if this was how her life was going to end.

The intruder grabbed the front of her shirt and jerked her within inches of his face. "You don't even remember me, do you? Your life went right ahead like nothing happened, while my life ended up in the toilet."

Suddenly, like the tumblers in a lock, Maggie recognized him. It was his cobalt-blue eyes, eyes like no one else she'd ever known. It was Professor Reed. But his eyes were the only thing recognizable as the man she once adored. Gone were the immaculately tailored clothes, the neat beard and mustache, and the professionally trimmed hair. Without thinking, she blurted out, "Man, you've let yourself go to pot." She knew it was a stupid thing to say to someone who was intent on harming her, but it was also true.

He struck her across the mouth, and she saw stars and tasted blood. "It's that smart mouth of yours," he said, "that's what your problem was and obviously still is."

Maggie said, "I thought you went to California and taught out there."

He dragged her across the living room and pushed her into a chair. "Ha! You make it sound so neat and simple. Just change locations and pick up where I left off, huh? The problem with that was that every time someone looked into my past, they found *you*." He pointed a long, damning finger in her face. In a sarcastic tone, he said, "And I don't know if you're aware of this or not, but it's next to impossible to live down a bad reputation. Prior to you, my life was perfect."

Maggie felt her fear being replaced by indignation. "Well, you know what? If you hadn't tried to be a Casanova and ruin the lives of countless innocent young girls, you would still have your job at UTM."

Maggie immediately regretted saying that as he slapped her hard across her face, producing another burst of stars.

"I didn't force anyone to do anything!" he screamed. "You liked it, and so did they. It fulfilled a fantasy for all of you. What's so bad about that?"

She felt the side of her face burning, and her lip was throbbing, but still, she was angrier than she was afraid. Jutting her chin toward him, she said, "You look at it that way to satisfy your conscience instead of seeing yourself as you really are—a predator. Just because those girls were legally adults doesn't mean you're any different than a child molester. You chose them, coaxed them, and groomed them to become your sexual playthings and to stroke your already-overinflated ego."

He laughed. "How long have you been practicing that speech? What about you? You were no teenager."

"Chronologically I wasn't, but as far as emotional maturity, I was still no more than fourteen." She felt herself standing up. "Men have taken advantage of me ever since I was a little girl. I've been molested, raped, and beat on; humiliated, shamed, and embarrassed." She stepped closer to him. "But you were the last one. You say your life was ruined by me? If that's true, then I could not be happier that I obliged." When she finished, she spat in his face.

She knew it was coming, but she didn't care. The first blow was to her stomach, which caused her to double over. The next blow was to the side of her head, which knocked her to the ground. Then he kicked her.

Gasping for air and with her teeth clenched in pain, she said, "Does it make you feel big and powerful to be hitting me? Feel more like a man?" She curled into a fetal position as blows and curse words rained upon her like a hailstorm.

*****

When Maggie came to, the first thing she noticed was how quiet it was. She could literally hear nothing. *Have I gone deaf? Did he burst my eardrums?*

In case the professor was sitting close by watching her, she opened her eyes into the tiniest slits possible. She was lying on her side on her kitchen floor. Through the doorway, she could see overturned furniture in the living room, and there were kitchen utensils scattered in front of her on the floor.

She took a breath and immediately regretted it. Pain, like a knife in her side, shot through her. *Broken ribs?*

She listened again for sounds of Professor Reed, and on hearing nothing, she turned her head to look in the opposite direction. A small cry escaped from her mouth as she spied him lying on the floor a few feet away. He was looking at her, and his mouth was open as if he wanted to say something. Then she saw that there was no life in his eyes. He would never be speaking to anyone again.

Groaning with pain, she managed to push herself into a sitting position. That's when she saw the large butcher knife buried to its handle in the professor's back. She tried to remember what happened, but she had no memory past the living room. How she ended up in the kitchen and how she managed to get the butcher knife were locked away in some corner of her mind.

She stumbled to her feet and surveyed the chaos. *I need to call the police and the coroner.* She picked up the receiver and was about to dial the familiar number when she paused. *What's going to happen after I call? The police will come, take my statement about what happened, take photos of the scene. The body will be taken away, and eventually, somewhere, there will be a funeral with glowing eulogies given by people who don't know the real Professor Reed.*

With the receiver still in her hand, she turned around, looked at the dead body, and had a thought. She hung up the phone and headed toward the back door. As she passed through the kitchen, she spoke to the corpse. "If there's one person who is not worthy of being eulogized, it's you, asshole."

Passing through her garage, she picked up a shovel and headed to the flowerbed in her backyard. Bright stars stared down from a moonless sky, curious to learn what Maggie's mission was.

Two hours later, soaked with sweat and panting, she stood chest deep in a grave. She climbed out, went inside, and grabbed the legs of Professor Reed and drug him out, eventually rolling him into the grave.

The eastern sky was turning gray by the time she finished filling the grave and placing flowers and shrubs on top. "An unmarked grave. That's what you deserve."

Once inside the house, she used bleach to clean the blood off the kitchen linoleum, and then she called the police. "Yes, this is Maggie Stinson. Someone broke into my house and attacked me, knocking me out. When I came to, he was gone." She paused to listen. "No, I didn't recognize him; he had a ski mask on. Can you send someone over here right away?"

Chapter Twenty-Five

ISRAEL—FORTY YEARS OLD

As he often did over the last two years, since coming to live in the trailer Darnell had left him, Israel drove slowly through the winding country roads, trying to take his mind off his troubles. And as had become his practice, he had a running dialogue with God while driving. "Lord, you know I've been trying to find me a job ever since I got here, well at least after I rested for a few weeks and got settled into Darnell's place. Problem is, my prison record keeps getting in the way. Won't nobody see their way around it to give me a chance to prove myself. If it wasn't for that money Darnell left me, I'd have already starved to death. But that money's about to dry up. What am I going to do then?"

He paused and listened. "Yes, I know things don't always happen according to man's timing and that you know what's best and give us what we need when we need it. But I thought I was going to be a Jephthah for you, that you were going to make me strong and powerful, and I would do mighty things for you.

"Sir? Yes, sir. I'm not trying to tell you how to do your business. And I don't mean to sound ungrateful, either. You lead Darnell to leave me this place, and I've had a roof over my head and food in my belly, which is more than I expected when you delivered me from prison. I just want the chance to make a difference in somebody's life, just one person. If I can do that, then I'll be able to say my goodbyes to this world."

He cocked his head so that his ear was pointing up. "I *have* been looking for someone I can do that for. I just can't find them. You're going to have to give me a clearer sign."

Just then he saw the Olive Branch Cemetery up ahead. Not really thinking about it, he turned into the entrance, where he spotted a funeral tent and a pickup truck toward the back of the cemetery. His mind returned to the last time he saw a funeral tent and how he had dug a grave inside a grave.

He eased forward, toward the truck and tent, and finally let his pickup roll to a stop behind the other truck.

A wheelbarrow lay on its side inside the bed of the pickup, as if it was taking a nap. There was a faded "Vote for Jimmy Carter" bumper sticker on the rusty bumper and the side mirror on the passenger door was broken off.

Switching off his engine, Israel stepped out of his truck and walked over to the grave. On one side was a tall pile of dirt, and on the other side were several shovels and a pickaxe.

A black man with broad shoulders and a thick neck leaned back against the side of the grave and wiped his face with a red bandana. Dark eyes looked up at Israel from underneath white eyebrows. "Afternoon," he said.

"Afternoon," Israel said, returning the greeting. "I've never seen a grave when it was being dug." This was a partial truth.

With a wave of his hand, the man said, "Well, this is what it looks like, at least when I dig one."

"My name's Israel."

"Everybody calls me Big John." He gave Israel a toothless grin.

"Do you always use a shovel when you dig a grave?"

Big John looked insulted. "Absolutely. You know, the shovel is one of the oldest tools known to man. I read that cavemen used the shoulder blades of animals to dig with. And most people don't stop to think about how many kinds of shovels there are. There's round-point shovels, like this one here, square-point shovels, like that one lying by the wheelbarrow, sharpshooters, corn scoops, snow shovels, even a hand trowel is a type of shovel. But none of them are any good if you don't keep them clean and sharp. A shovel is the only decent way to dig a grave. It's quiet and respectful of all those dead folks lying beside it. Bringing in a backhoe, like some folks do, disturbs the spirits. When a spirit gets woke up like that, it wanders around for a while until it can settle back down and go back where it come from."

Israel expected him to laugh at his joke, but Big John continued in a serious tone.

"After I finish digging a grave and filling it in, you can't tell anybody's been there because I peel back the grass and set it aside before I start digging. Then I lay it back down exactly like it was. Of course, any hole you dig and fill in is going to settle some, but I don't leave all those ugly tire marks like a backhoe does. I take pride in what I do."

A thought struck Israel. "You make a living doing this?"

"It's according to what making a living means to you. I've always made enough to get by—never gone hungry, always had a dry place to sleep. That's all a person really needs. Everything else is just wants."

"And you stay plenty busy?"

"I turn down folks all the time because I can't get to them when they need me. When a body's got to go into the ground, it's got to go."

"How long you been doing it?"

"Probably thirty years or so. I've wore out my share of shovels and broke more than my share of handles until I learned how to dig the right way."

"What do you mean?"

"People think you need to bury your shovel as deep as you can and then push down on the handle until the dirt comes up. If the dirt's right, that can work, but most often, dirt don't let go that easy, and you break your handle. You got to know what kind of dirt you're digging in and how much pressure your handle can take—that's the key." He looked at Israel thoughtfully. "You sure have lots of questions. Don't recall ever seeing you around these parts. You from around here?"

"Yes. I live on what used to be the Williamses' place. Moved here two years ago."

"That's over there where Newberg Cemetery is, isn't it?"

"Yes. It's a rock's throw from where I live."

"Now that there is a fine cemetery, even if it is just a family cemetery. The descendants take pride in how it looks. You're also not far from where Mount Carmel church used to be. There were slaves buried there, you know."

"Really?"

"That's what I was told. They put them on the north side of the church, and the white folks was buried on the south side. But all of that's gone now. The church has been tore down, and there's corn growing where all that used to be."

"What about the graves?"

"Some of the white folks were moved by family, but the slave graves were unmarked, and nobody did anything with them. And that's why that area around there is haunted."

Seeing no hint of a smile on the man's face, Israel asked, "You really believe it's haunted?"

"It has to be. All those graves being disturbed by tractors has made the spirits unsettled. If you go out that way at night and sit there in the dark, you'll see green lights moving around."

"You've seen it?"

"Yes, back when I was young and foolish. It's not wise to be hanging around spirits like that. They're mad and looking for someone to take it out on. There was a time when this young couple went parking out there one night, not really knowing where they were. The next day, they were found dead inside the car without a mark on them."

"What killed them?"

"Nobody knows. Autopsy didn't show anything. I think the coroner put natural causes."

Israel gave a low whistle. "Man, that's crazy."

"Ain't it, though."

Israel looked up at the sky. *Is this the one?* Then he looked at John and said, "Listen, I know you don't know me from Adam, but would you let me work for you?"

"You mean dig graves with me?"

"Yes."

"Well, digging a grave is sort of a one-man job. There's not enough room in here but for one person."

"Maybe I could fill the graves back in for you, which would free you up to dig another grave. Or you could teach me how to dig a grave, and then you wouldn't have to turn down work."

Big John gave him a long look. "You not touched in the head, are you?"

Israel laughed. "I suppose some people might say I am, but I think I'm as sane as the next man."

"Why do you want to do this kind of work?"

"It's solitary work. I've had enough of working with bunches of people. You can't trust people. They'll always take advantage of you and do you dirty. I'd rather be left alone to do my job. Don't worry—I'm a hard worker. You tell me something to do, and I'll get it done, without you having to stand over me. And what kinder thing is there to do than to create a resting place for a body that's wore out."

"Death don't scare you?" John asked.

"Trust me—there's a lot of things that are worse than death."

Chapter Twenty-Six

MAGGIE—PRESENT DAY

Maggie begins wrapping up her first visit with Israel. "Because you're now in hospice, that means you have access to the nurses or myself anytime you need us. I suppose you have family that checks in on you occasionally?"

He purses his lips. "Ain't got no family. It's just me, myself, and I. What about you? You got family?"

She's taken aback a bit by his assertion that he has no family. *Everybody has family; they just may not like to be associated with them.* And she doesn't like his personal questions directed toward her; it feels pushy. "This is about you, Israel, not about me. I'm here to help you in any way I can."

"Well, all right, then. Have it your way. I guess I shouldn't have asked. It's just that I'm not used to being around people that much, leastwise for the past ten years. Most of my time's been spent around dead folks."

Maggie senses both an openness and a wariness in Israel, making it clear to her that there's much more to this odd man than might be thought at first glance.

His next question stuns her. "How long you been an alcoholic?"

She thinks about the bottle of vodka hiding under her car seat. Though her stomach lurches, she tries to retain a calm exterior. "What makes you ask that question?"

"Don't know. Guess God put it on my heart to ask it. That happens with me sometimes. I'll do or say something that surprises even me. The only way I can explain it is that it comes from God." He looks up at the ceiling. "Is she the one, Lord?"

Maggie keeps feeling off-balance with this patient, like she can't get any traction with him because of how scattered and odd his thoughts and comments are. *I wonder if he has schizophrenia? Certainly was no mention of it in his record. But he definitely is hearing voices—at least he says he is.* "Am I the one what?" she asks him.

"It's sort of an odd story."

That's no surprise.

"You ever heard of a man in the Bible name Jephthah?"

"I'm afraid not." *Truth is, I don't know much about anyone in the Bible.*

Israel launches into the story, telling it with more energy than she would have expected from someone in his condition. After he finishes the story, he says, "I'm a lot like Jephthah. There's nothing about my childhood that makes me special. As a matter of fact, there's lots about it that I'm ashamed of and have never told anyone about."

Deep inside her, Maggie feels a sympathetic chord resonating as she thinks about her own childhood.

"Here's the deal," Israel says. "I think God saved me from some situations so that he could help me save someone else. I've been looking for that person for quite a while now. I'm wondering if it might be you. The Lord told me you might be."

"Might be?"

"That's the way it is with me and him. He nudges me but don't always come right out and make things crystal clear. It's like he wants me to figure it out for myself." He turns the conversation on a dime. "Hey, would you mind getting my guitar out from under the bed?"

Thankful to be released from the uncomfortable topic of God, Maggie answers, "Sure." Ignoring the pain in her knee, she gets down on all fours and peers into the darkness under the bed. *I'm not about to stick my hand under there without looking first. If he keeps a snake in the bathroom, what does he keep under his bed? Where's a good flashlight when you need one?* All she can see is the handle on what she supposes is a guitar case. Reaching for it without much trouble, she slides it out from under the bed. She's mildly surprised that a cigar box is lying in the crook of the neck and slides out, too. Time and use have left the edges of both containers dented and scarred. Holding up the cigar box, she asks, "What do you want me to do with this?"

"Just stick it back under there. That's my keepsake box. I might let you look at it with me before I die."

Her curiosity is piqued by the box, but she returns it as she asks, "You want me to take your guitar out of its case for you?"

"Please. And hand me a pick, too."

She unsnaps the rusty latches and raises the lid, exposing a blond-body guitar lying in a bed of royal blue crushed velvet. There are worn places on the dark neck where particular frets have been used more than others, and there are scratches below the pickguard where an enthusiastic strummer could not contain himself within the confines of the protective plastic piece. Maggie lifts it out of the case and says, "Have you always played Martin guitars?"

"I guess so because that guitar there is the only guitar I've ever played. Had it now for, let's see, over forty years. You know something about guitars?"

"I used to play. But I prefer Gibsons."

"What do you mean, you used to play?"

Maggie lets a private truth slip past her walls. "It's been years since I've had it out of its case." She swears silently for revealing more about her private life.

"Were you any good at it?"

"I'd say I was fair at playing rhythm. Never tried my hand at playing lead."

Israel shifts to a sitting position on his bed and takes his guitar from her. It's then that she sees the back of the guitar. There are scores of handwritten signatures scrolled all across it. Pointing toward it, she says, "Any famous signatures back there?"

He turns it over, slowly rubs his hand across the back, and points at one. "Just this one. Ned Ray McWherter. Used to be the governor of Tennessee. He was a good man. He heard about me and had me come to his house and play some tunes for him. It was just me and him. He smiled and hummed along with me. When I finished, he asked me if I'd dig his grave for him. Said he'd sign my guitar if I'd do it."

"That's pretty special," Maggie comments.

He begins lightly strumming the brass and silver strings of the guitar as he runs through a few chords. There is a far-off look in his eyes.

As he strums, Maggie unexpectedly feels her heartstrings being strummed as a childhood memory of her mother playing the guitar drifts forward, but Maggie quickly sweeps it back under the rug where she keeps it. Her eyes mist for a second, but she blinks the tears away.

Because he's not stopping to tune the guitar, it's clear to her that he plays regularly and that he owns a well-made instrument. *I really didn't figure he'd sound this good, considering how sick and weak he is.*

He stops playing and looks at her. "I tell you what I believe, anybody that's got a talent and isn't using it is just tempting God to take it away from them. When you get home tonight, you need to get your guitar out and apologize to it."

Maggie is stung by his words because she's told people the same sort of thing through the years, although without the God part. Israel's comment resurrects the guilt she's often felt and tried to keep pushed down about not playing her guitar more often.

He begins playing an introduction to a song that sounds familiar to her, but she can't quite place it, not until he begins singing—"The Long and Winding Road."

The plaintive song, combined with Israel's tremulous singing voice, the cluttered surroundings, and the fact that this is his deathbed, almost overwhelm Maggie's nerves of steel. It's only by biting her lip that she's able to keep from bursting into tears. *What a long and winding road it has been for me. And who will be sitting by my bedside when the end finally comes?*

When Israel reaches the end of the song, his last notes hang in the air like Spanish moss on the limbs of a live oak tree. "That's my theme song," he says. "My whole life has been a long and winding road in search of something."

That his thoughts mirror hers catches Maggie off guard and creates another wave of emotions. She barely manages to choke out her question, "In search of what?"

He looks at her with sad and tired eyes. "I really don't know. Maybe it's you."

Chapter Twenty-Seven

The first thing Maggie does after leaving Israel's trailer and sitting down in her car is to crank it, turn the air conditioner on high, and adjust the vents so that they are blowing on her face and chest. Tugging at the neck of her shirt, she lets some cool air race inside.

After she cools for a moment, she reaches under the driver's seat and pulls out her bottle of vodka. *What the heck just happened in there? I feel like I'm the one who's been in some kind of therapy session. What a strange little man.* She looks in the rearview mirror and sees her mascara has been trying to slip outside its prescribed boundaries. Using a Kleenex, she cleans up the black smudges.

And is it karma that the last patient of my career is known as the Gravedigger? Talk about irony! Fleeting memories of her own experience digging graves come to her mind, but she quickly shuts the door on them.

She looks at the vodka. *And he thinks I'm an alcoholic or something, ha!* Unscrewing the cap, she lifts the bottle in a symbolic gesture toward the trailer, then puts it to her lips and takes a gulp. Almost immediately she feels herself calming; the prickly feeling that was dancing just under her skin disappears, and she breathes a sigh of relief.

One thing's for certain: I'm dragging out my guitar tonight and practicing. It'll surprise him when I bring it with me tomorrow.

Secreting the bottle away, she puts her car in reverse, turns around in the driveway, and heads back to her office. On the way, she counts every third telephone pole, something she's done for as long as she can remember. She mentioned it to Charlie Chesterton one time, who told her as long as it doesn't interfere with her overall functioning in life, then don't worry about it. "You just have OCD tendencies. Lots of people do. It's neither a good thing nor a bad thing."

But as she's gotten older, Maggie has noticed more and more "tendencies." She divides random things by three, sometimes brushes her teeth three times or checks the locks on her doors three times, and always looks for the number three in any set of figures.

When she arrives at the parking lot of her agency, she sits and watches the second hand of her watch as it sweeps past twelve. As it approaches three after the hour, she reaches for the handle of her car door. Just then someone taps on her window and startles her. She jumps and stares.

"You okay, Maggie?"

It's Sheila, the agency's new director. Maggie likes Sheila's heart for helping people and believes she's a good director in spite of how young she is. *But hey, everybody's younger than me.* She rolls down her window. "Hi, Sheila."

"Hi, Maggie. Is everything all right? I was just coming back from lunch and saw you sitting there with a frown on your face, like you were thinking hard about something. Any problems I can help with?"

Well, you see, Sheila, your social worker is obsessive-compulsive and has to do things on threes. Yes, I'm a nut case, but it's not a big deal because I always get my work done. She smiles up at Sheila, and says, "No, no problems. I was just making some mental notes. Have you had a good morning?"

Sheila looks at her ever-present cell phone while answering. "I've got to hire another nurse. I'm going to have to let Delores Jones go. Too many complaints from patients and patient families. I did everything I could to help her and warn her about her attitude, but nothing worked."

Maggie's used to supervisors and administrators talking to her about personnel issues when they shouldn't. She's concluded that having the title of social worker attached to your name makes people think you are a good listener and that you know how to keep things to yourself. "You should have let her go long ago," Maggie comments.

"You really think so? I hate firing people."

"You can't help some people, Sheila. You better learn that lesson, or you'll burn out." *I should know.*

Sheila smiles. "Thanks. That makes me feel somewhat better. Are you going inside the office?"

"Yes."

"Let's walk in together. I wanted to ask you about one of our patients."

Maggie looks at her watch to see if either the minute hand or second hand is approaching a three. It's two minutes to one, so she missed the three-till mark. The second hand has passed both three till and three after and is just now passing nine after. She can't sit here, with Sheila waiting on her, until the second hand reaches thirty after. But a solution jumps out at her. When the second hand reaches fifteen after, it will be on the number three. She feels a sense of relief, and while keeping her eyes on her watch, she reaches for her purse and says, "Sure. Let me get my things, and I'll walk with you." She times the opening of her door perfectly with the instant the second hand touches the three and feels both pride and relief.

As they walk across the small parking lot, Sheila says, "Did you have a chance to make it out to see our new patient today?"

"Israel McKenzie?"

"Yes, that one."

"I did. We had a good first visit, just sort of breaking the ice."

"Do you think he's crazy?"

Maggie hates it when people ask her that question or throw around the word *crazy* like it's a mental diagnosis. She gives Sheila her pat answer: "You have to be a little crazy to live in this crazy world, don't you think?"

Sheila chuckles. "I suppose there's a lot of truth to that. I guess I didn't ask a very good question."

They step into the building, and Maggie follows Sheila to her office.

As Sheila sets her things on her desk and checks her phone, she says, "Do you think Mr. McKenzie is dangerous?"

"Dangerous? Of course not. Why do you ask that?"

"Well, some of our nurses are complaining about having to go out there and take care of him. They say it's not safe out there."

"And I'll bet the initials of one of those nurses are D. J.," Maggie says, feeling agitated. "Delores has never met a person she couldn't find a reason not to like."

"Is it true that he's a hoarder, and his house has all kinds of safety hazards in it?"

"Yes, on both accounts. But I'm confident there's not a person who works here that I couldn't find a safety hazard in their house, based on the criteria in our manual. As a matter of fact, I would enjoy going into Delores's house and seeing what all I could find that would classify it as unsafe."

Sheila, ever the politician, says, "Let's not make this personal. There's no point in attacking another employee, even if I did fire her. Just tell me what you're going to do about Mr. McKenzie's place."

Maggie feels her agitation shifting toward Sheila. "Do about it? I'm not going to do anything about it."

"It's going to be hard to convince our nurses to go out there. What about finding him another place to live, a place that's safer and more sanitary?"

"Why do that? Why disrupt this patient by taking him out of the place he calls home and moving him somewhere completely unfamiliar? All that will do is make him depressed and his anxiety worse. The man is dying, Sheila. If he wasn't, I might—and I emphasize *might*—see if I could talk him into moving. But as it is, based on what I've been told and have read in his record, he's not going to be around much longer. Why can't we let him die undisturbed?"

Sheila says, "I'm sorry, but I just don't understand how people can live like that. I hear there are bags of garbage with mice in them and a snake that runs loose. There's no running water or toilet." She shudders. "That's disgusting."

Maggie searches for a way to explain the situation to Sheila in a way that will make her feel how Israel feels. She points to Sheila's engagement ring. "Would you let me throw that in the garbage?"

Sheila clutches her hand to her chest. "Of course not!"

"Why not?"

"It's my engagement ring. It was Donald's mother's engagement ring, which makes it just that much more special. Nobody would throw away their wedding ring."

Nodding, Maggie says, "Most people would agree with you. They wouldn't throw it away because of all the emotions attached to it. I, on the other hand, traded my engagement ring and wedding ring in at the pawn shop as soon as I got away from my husband. Why? Because I didn't want any reminders of a painful period in my life. Here's the deal: the way you feel about your wedding ring is the way hoarders feel about everything. They attach meaning to a receipt, a hamburger wrapper, an empty milk carton, and everything else they come in contact with. That's why hoarding is so difficult to treat. You could forcibly remove everything from a hoarder's house, but it will be right back in the same shape, given enough time."

Sheila sighs. "Okay, I hear what you're saying, and I readily admit you've been at this longer than I have. So we'll try it your way. But if the situation becomes a threat to the health of our workers, we'll have to try something else."

Maggie smiles. "Good for you."

Later, sitting in her office writing progress notes about her visit with Israel that morning, she pauses to take a sip of coffee. *Maybe I should volunteer to do an in-service for the nurses on how to deal with and accept patients with a mental illness. And maybe I'll use myself as an example of how there are people around us every day who function effectively in spite of having a mental illness.* She chuckles to herself as she thinks about Sheila. *I wonder if checking your cell phone incessantly is a symptom of OCD.*

Chapter Twenty-Eight

Israel leans over, pulls back the corner of the curtain covering his bedroom window, and watches Maggie drive away. *Now that's an interesting woman. Careful and cautious, that's what she is. Lots of secrets locked up in that heart of hers. If she's the one, Lord, I'm going to need lots of help from you.*

He lets the curtain fall back in place, reaches under his pillow, and pulls out a spiral notebook with an ink pen fastened to the metal coil. He opens to a blank page and begins writing:

Dear Rebekah, my lost sister,

It's been forty years since I last saw you that night at the cemetery, but I have thought about you many times through those years. I wonder where you are now, what you are doing, and if you are happy. Above all, I hope you are happy.

When I was taken out of the orphan's home and came to live with you all, I thought it was the answer to a prayer. And even though Sir made our lives hell, it was still the closest thing to a family I've ever had. I loved you so much and was so in awe of you. You were and still are the bravest, toughest person, male or female, I've ever known. You never let Sir break you. I think it was your example that helped me survive my years in prison.

Yeah, I had to go to prison, but it was for something I didn't do. I know that's what all cons say, but in my case, you have to believe me that it's true. Horrible things were done to me there, but I survived.

I wish I could sit down and talk with you and let you tell me what happened to you that night in the cemetery. Where did you go? Why did you leave me? I'm not asking that to try and make you feel guilty. I just want to understand. And if you do feel guilty about it, please let it go. I don't have any hard feelings toward you about it.

I also hope you don't feel guilty about us killing Sir. I'm convinced we did the right thing. It had to be done, just like putting down a dog with rabies; they're too dangerous to let live. Do you have dreams about that night? I do. Sometimes I dream about him coming back to life and coming after me. I guess that's normal.

I know you won't ever read this letter because I have no idea where to send it, but I just had to write it anyway. The reason is, I'm dying with cancer. I'm real close to the end, probably just a matter of weeks. But I'm okay with dying. You see, I found God along the way, and I know he's going to be waiting for me on the other side. Even in spite of all the bad things I've done, I'm convinced he loves me and forgives me. I spent many a night on my knees beside my bed begging him to forgive me until one night I felt my heart open up like big barn doors, and a warm feeling came over me like I'd never felt before. I heard him tell me that I didn't need to keep asking forgiveness for the same thing over and over because he already forgave that some time ago.

I guess that all sounds crazy, like I'm touched in the head or something. If I am, I don't care because he and I still talk to each other.

What I'm hoping and praying is that you've found him, too, and that when it's your time to leave the earth, that'll I see you on the other side. Won't we have some catching up to do and some tales to tell?

Wherever you are at this exact moment, I hope you feel something in your heart and that, somehow, you'll know that it's me reaching out to you to let you know I love you.

Your long-lost brother,

Israel

Closing the notebook and slipping the ink pen in place, he lies down and closes his eyes. He lies still for several minutes, thinking about Rebekah, Sir, the other children whose names he's forgotten over time, and Mother. A tear leaks out of the corner of his eye and disappears in his sideburn.

With his eyes still shut, he begins singing:

> *I'm just a poor wayfaring stranger*
> *Traveling through this world of woe*
> *But there's no sickness, toil nor danger*
> *In that fair land to which I go*
> *I'm going there to see my father*
> *I'm going there no more to roam*
> *I am just going over Jordan*
> *I am just going over home*
>
> *I know dark clouds will gather round me*
> *I know my way is rough and steep*
> *But beauteous fields lie just before me*
> *Where God's redeemed their vigils keep*
> *I'm going home to see my mother*
> *She said she'd meet me when I come*
> *I'm only going over Jordan*
> *I'm only going over home*

I'm just a going over home

He barely squeezes out the final lyrics before emotion cuts off his voice. *Is that how it's going to be, Lord? Will I finally see who my real father and mother are? Or will it even matter to me when I'm in heaven with you?*

Chapter Twenty-Nine

The next day, Maggie pulls to a stop in front of Israel's trailer and gets out. She scans the yard with all its discarded refuse. *If I could get him to come outside, I bet he would have a story to tell about each and every piece—where he got it, who gave it to him, where he was when he got it, how long he's had it, and what it means to him. Hmmm. Maybe I can get him to do just that.* Opening the back door of her car, she grabs the handle of her guitar case and lifts it out.

She knocks on the front door of Israel's trailer, steps inside, and calls out, "Israel, it's Maggie, the social worker." When he doesn't reply, she makes her way through the living room and pauses. "Israel, this is Maggie. I don't want to sneak up on you and surprise you. Can I come on back?"

Immediately, Israel responds. "Come on back. Don't worry about surprising me. I like surprises."

As she heads down the hall, she keeps a wary eye out for Lucifer, the snake.

This time, she finds Israel sitting up in bed with his guitar in his lap. "Have you been enjoying your guitar this morning?"

Looking at his guitar, he replies, "Played it all night long. You woke up my muse yesterday, and she wouldn't leave me alone. It might surprise you to know that I know nearly all the Beatles' songs. They're the greatest band of all time. Changed music forever."

She smiles at how animated he is. "Play me something."

"Did you play your guitar last night like I told you to?"

"I tried."

"Tried? What do you mean *tried*?"

"It's been a long time since I played. My fingers are stiffer than they used to be, and I don't have any callouses. It just didn't sound very good."

"Of course it didn't. Your poor guitar has been in hibernation, neglected. That's a sad thing. I guarantee you it needs a new set of strings. I think I've got a set in my case. Look and see. And take your guitar out. I want to see it."

For every protest that Maggie serves up, Israel returns it right back to her. But when he says to her, "Let it touch your soul again," she has no defense. For the second time since meeting this unusual man, she feels like he has plucked her heartstrings because he's right—playing her guitar helped her through some dark passages of her life by speaking to her soul. "Okay, okay," she says.

As she restrings her guitar, he says, "I'm going to make an exception with you."

Keeping her attention on threading a string through a peg, she asks, "What kind of exception?"

"I'm going to let you call me Israel, instead of the Gravedigger."

Maggie smiles.

Fifteen minutes later, with new strings strung and tuned, her guitar sounds like it did ages ago. She smiles in spite of herself.

"See there?" Israel says. "It needed to be woke up, sort of like Rip Van Winkle. And from the looks of that smile on your face, you needed woke up, too. Maybe that guitar can take the place of your liquor bottle. Both of them can help put your mind in a better place, but one of them will kill you."

Before she can think, Maggie fires back. "My drinking is none of your business!" She immediately feels embarrassed for letting her temper get the best of her. To apologize wouldn't be honest because it truly isn't any of his business. And to try to deny she drinks would now be pointless.

Apparently unfazed by her sharp reply, he says, "I know it's not. Now let's play a song together." He suddenly starts playing and singing, in a very British accent, "When I'm Sixty-Four."

In spite of her irritation at him, Maggie can't help but laugh and tries to do her best to keep up with him.

Twenty minutes and five songs later, she can see him struggling to get a breath, and his strumming has slowed. She says, "Why don't we take a break? My fingers are so sore from last night, I don't think I can play anymore." She doesn't mind offering the excuse because it's true.

He closes his eyes and nods as he pants for air.

She takes his guitar from him and sets it beside the bed. "Can I get you something to drink?"

He whispers, "There's some Coke in the other bedroom."

Maggie steps back into the hallway and wonders how she missed seeing another bedroom. She eases past the bathroom, keeping her eyes peeled for the snake, past where a washer and dryer would be if there were a pair, and arrives back in the living room. Straight ahead is what she supposes is the kitchen area, filled with plastic garbage bags. She moves a little closer and sees a narrow opening filled with books that leads to the kitchen. *There's no way I can get through that without knocking things over.*

She decides to place her hands on each side of a stack and then pushes the bottom of it with her foot. It inches over. Working both sides of the opening, she repeats the action with each stack, gradually making her way through the columns. Finally, she reaches the kitchen and discovers a path through the garbage bags, leading to another room on the other side. *What is this,* Mission: Impossible *or something?*

When she arrives at the other room, she is faced with two sides of a coin—on one side are stacks of twenty-four-packs of Bubba Cola, neatly held by their plastic yokes, while on the other side are stacks of empty Bubba Cola cans, also held by plastic yokes. Maggie does a quick count and estimates there are at least eight hundred full cans of cola in the room. She mutters aloud, "Just when you think you've seen everything." Shaking her head, she pulls a can free from its yoke and heads back to Israel's room.

He appears to be asleep when she enters, but his eyes open at the squeaking in the subflooring. "You did find it, didn't you? Most people won't even try to look." He takes the can, which gives off a familiar *chooosh* sound when he opens it.

How he is able to drink a room-temperature cola is beyond Maggie. "How have you been feeling?"

"Feel pretty good. Certainly don't feel like I'm dying. Maybe the doctors made a mistake, and I'm not dying. They don't know everything, you know."

It's the kind of thinking Maggie has heard from other hospice patients and their families. Oftentimes, acceptance of the reality of their loved one's impending death has difficulty navigating through the sea of denial that families would rather live in. And at other times, the patient rallies just before death, seeming to have thwarted the death angel's efforts to wield its sickle to cut them off from the land of the living. It's a cruel trick because death is waiting just around the corner.

Learning to respect people's wall of denial is something Maggie struggles with because she would prefer to knock down that wall and force them to face the truth of impending death. "And what are you going to do if they aren't prepared to deal with the truth?" her supervisor had asked her years ago. When Maggie didn't have an answer, her supervisor suggested she try taking down that wall one brick at a time and doing it gently and respectfully.

So she says to Israel, "You're right—doctors don't know everything. Anything is possible."

"Don't BS me," he says sharply. "I know I'm going to die soon. I just wanted to see if you would be honest with me. You should know by now that life's too short to tiptoe around the truth."

"I didn't know I was being tested. Why do you feel you need to do that with me?"

"Because I want to know if I can trust you to be honest with me about how you feel about me after hearing my story. And can I trust you to keep it all to yourself?"

"I can tell you that everything you share with me is strictly confidential. If there's something I think needs to be shared with others, I'll ask your permission first."

He keeps looking at her with an expectant expression. When she doesn't carry on, he says, "And the honesty thing, what about that? Are you going to be honest with me from now on?"

"Yes, Israel, I'll be honest with you from now on."

"No matter what?"

"No matter what."

"Then I am going to die pretty soon, aren't I?"

Maggie nods. "Yes. Barring a miraculous healing, which I can't rule out, you won't be here much longer."

"You're not one of those, are you?"

"One of those what?"

"One of those who orders these prayer cloth things from a televangelist and thinks that by laying it on a sick person, it will heal them."

"I can honestly say I've never done that."

"Then what do you believe?"

"About what?"

"About God."

"What I think is not important, but what you think is. Why don't you tell me what you believe?"

He waves dismissively at her. "You are one careful woman. Afraid of people finding out the truth about you?"

Never has Maggie had someone ask her such pointed questions and give her so much difficulty in having a conversation. *It's like he knows what my secrets are and is trying to see if I'll tell them.* She decides to try one of his techniques and changes the direction of the conversation. "I was wondering if you felt like getting outside for a bit this morning and sitting in the yard. You have a beautiful golden rain tree I'd like you to tell me about."

Israel's face brightens. "If you'll help me, that sounds like something I might enjoy."

Maggie had not thought about how difficult it would be to walk backward through the maze inside Israel's house while holding on to him as he teetered along. It reminds her of when she used to roller skate backward with friends, except she weighed significantly less back then, and her hips weren't nearly as wide.

As they pass through the living room, Israel tells her, "Be careful. I don't want anything moved or knocked out of place."

"I'm trying to be careful," she replies. "It's interesting how nurses who come in here see chaos, but you see order."

"Chaos would be if I didn't know where anything was. But I know exactly what's in every stack of books and magazines." He nods toward his left. "Those in that area are from 2004. There's a *National Geographic* magazine in there that tells about the Southern Patagonian Ice Field, which is the largest expanse of glaciers outside of Antarctica and Greenland. It's located in southern Chile and Argentina."

Maggie smiles inside at how certain he is about the location of the magazine and at how specific he is about its content.

They finally arrive outside, where he points to a pair of 1950s-era metal lawn chairs that are sitting facing each other. "Let's sit over there."

By the time she gets him situated in one of the chairs, Israel is quite winded. "Give me a minute," he gasps as he tries to catch his breath.

Maggie eyes the other chair with suspicion. "You think that'll hold me?" she asks.

He nods his head and motions her to sit down.

She tries to lower herself into the chair slowly, but her bad knee can't tolerate that kind of pressure, so she collapses onto the chair. It responds by catching her and bending toward the ground, then springing up a couple of times. Grateful that it didn't bend double and break, she breathes a sigh of relief.

After a few minutes, Israel points to a stack of four bald tires. "You see those tires? Those tires were on the truck I drove here for the very first time, and that's the way they looked when I got here. I was riding more on air than on rubber because they were so worn out. One of the first things I did was buy me a new set. They wanted to charge me four dollars apiece to dispose of the old tires. I said heck no, I'd take them with me. You can't get rid of something like that that reminds you of your journey to freedom. No, sir. Those tires remind me of where I came from and how close I was to being worn out like those old tires when I got here. Everybody needs to remember where they came from, don't you think?"

Maggie finds herself being more careful when answering Israel due to a feeling that he's fishing for something from her. Exactly what, she's yet to figure out. "I hear a lot of people say that." Pointing, she says, "Tell me about that golden rain tree. You rarely see them around here. I love how the fruit looks like miniature Japanese lanterns."

Looking at the tree, Israel says, "The last place I worked before moving to Tennessee was a nursery. They let me bring a seedling with me."

She raises her eyebrows. "So you worked in a nursery? Where was that?"

"It was in the prison where I was an inmate."

Chapter Thirty

The single light bulb in Israel's bedroom tries its best to chase away the darkness that night has brought on but only succeeds in pushing it into corners and under his bed. Drifting between sleep and awake, dreams and consciousness, Israel remembers and relives events from his years in prison.

As soon as he told Maggie about having been in prison, he knew she'd want to question him about it. So he told her all of it—the good and bad, the humorous and horrific. *I'm surprised she took it as well as she did—hardly blinked, never squirmed or blushed. She's a tough woman. I'll bet anything she's been through her own hell, just don't know that she'll ever tell it.*

He tries to focus on pleasant memories of Chuck Paisley, who oversaw the greenhouse program at the prison. A retired high school agriculture teacher, with a worried look, there wasn't much Chuck didn't know about growing things. He taught inmates how to raise and care for vegetables, flowers, and plants. One thing Israel always remembered was Chuck telling him, "Working with plants is lots easier than dealing with people. Even though plants are needy, they don't whine and complain about it. They'll simply die a slow, quiet death if you ignore them."

Because the greenhouse was a stark contrast from the chaos and cacophony of the penitentiary, Israel spent all his spare time there during his last two years in prison. It was where he was introduced to the golden rain tree. Besides those tiny Japanese lanterns Maggie had mentioned, he loved how, in the fall, the leaves became the color of the sun—simply beautiful. "They were my favorites," he'd told Maggie. "That's why Chuck let me take that one there with me when I was released. Took it with me in a coffee can.

Wasn't hardly ten inches tall. Every time I see it now, I think about Chuck. He'd be proud of how well it's done."

Israel slips into a dream. He's lying in a field, looking up into a sky that is filled with golden rain tree leaves floating toward the earth. The sun is like a strobe light, flashing between the leaves. A scent wafts through the air, a scent he recognizes but can't name. It is a fragrance that makes him feel warm . . . and loved . . . and sad . . . and ashamed.

Turning his head, he sees Ada sitting beside him, smiling and offering him a glass of apple cider. She looks just as she did the last time he saw her. With tears filling his eyes, he sits up. "Oh, Ada, I'm so sorry for what I did. Will you ever forgive me?"

Her expression doesn't change. She's facing him but not really looking at him, and she doesn't answer his question.

He tries to take hold of her hand, but it is like trying to grasp a handful of fog—it's there, but it's not there. Leaves pass through her and settle on the quilt she is sitting on, and her image begins to fade.

"No!" Israel cries in desperation. "Don't leave me. I want to make things right with you." He grabs for her, but his hands fill with leaves, and she is gone.

Awaking from the dream, his cheeks are damp with tears, and his heart feels as if someone is squeezing it. He surprises himself with the thought, *I wish Maggie was here.* He tries to scoff at the idea because it makes no sense. He doesn't know her, has barely even met her. *Then why do I wish she was here?* He puzzles over the question, turning things over in search of an explanation. *Is it because God wants her to be here with me, and he's putting this in my heart? Is it because I enjoy the way she really listens to me and acts interested when I talk? Is it because, for some reason, I think she'll understand the regret I'm feeling over my past? Or maybe I just want to get to know her.*

He sighs from the exertion of thinking about it. *Are you going to tell her about Ada?* he asks himself. *What about Sir? How much are you going to tell her about yourself? Why would you want to tell her anything?*

Without any intent to do so, he drifts back to sleep again.

Chapter Thirty-One

Normally, Maggie wouldn't go to a patient's home every day—unless, of course, the patient or family asked her to—but here she is driving through the cedar thicket to Israel's trailer even though he didn't ask her to return today. *So why am I doing it?* It's the question she's considered since she awoke, but she can't find a logical answer.

Light reflects off her vodka bottle in the passenger seat. She glances at it. *Yes, I know you're there, waiting, wanting me to take a drink. And why don't I? Because I don't like Israel accusing me of being an alcoholic. How stupid is that? Why should I care what he thinks one way or another?* She grabs the bottle, opens it, and lifts it to her mouth. Just before it touches her lips, she asks herself, *So now I'm going to drink to prove to him I can if I want to? How screwed up am I?*

She lets out a sigh. *He's difficult, opinionated, odd, and . . .* She stops herself as she parks the car and stares at the yard and trailer.

Israel's horror story from yesterday of how he was repeatedly raped in prison was impossible to wash off in the hot shower last night. It ended up triggering nightmares during the night of her own abuse, nightmares that she thought she was finished with. Part of her felt like what happened to him was worse than what happened to her, although she knew that was just her way of downplaying the impact of her abuse. He would probably say hers was worse, *Not that it matters what he thinks.*

She heads inside the trailer, announcing herself as she steps through the door, and then proceeds to Israel's bedroom. She is struck by how dramatically worse he looks—cheeks more sunken, skin tone more yellow; even the whites of his eyes are tinged with yellow.

Taking a seat in the chair beside his bed, she returns his gaze and waits for him to speak. But he doesn't. Seconds tick by and become moments as they rest their eyes on each other. After a minute, they start to speak at the same time, then stop and say simultaneously, "You go first."

Maggie makes a motion like she's locking her lips, then points at him.

"I didn't sleep much last night," Israel says. "Lots of dreams. Some pleasant. Some sad. Some nightmares."

Yes, I know the feeling. "You look tired. Maybe I shouldn't have come by today. I'll come back tomorrow, if you want me to."

She starts to stand, and he shakes his head. "Don't leave."

Pleased by this, she settles back in the chair. Again, he just looks at her. "What is it, Israel? What do you want to say?"

"That's just it—I don't know. I've been thinking and trying to decide how much to tell you."

"About what?"

"About me, about my story."

Maggie nods. It was something she had to get used to when she started working hospice, that dying people would sometimes use her like a priest, someone to confess their sins to, sins that no one else knew anything about. To her, it felt like they were trying to use her as the fabled sin-eater of folklore, as if she had the power to devour people's sins and remove their guilt. *But the truth is, if anybody needs a real sin-eater, it's me.* "I'm here to listen, Israel. Are there things you need to tell?"

"Nobody knows me," he replies.

Maggie frowns. "But that's not true. I'm sure there are many people who know the Gravedigger."

"But that's just who I've been for the last several years. Nobody around here knows the story I told you yesterday of me being a convict. And even that's not all of who I am. I've been places and done things . . ." His voice trails off.

Out of habit, she nods as a way to let him know she's listening and following him, but it is also a nod of understanding and agreement that she, too, has been places and done things that no one knows about. "Israel, is there someone you are wanting to see and talk to? Someone I can contact to come, like a member of your family?"

He shakes his head. "Got no family."

"They've all passed away?"

He shakes his head again. "I was an orphan. Grew up in an orphanage. So I don't have nobody." His voice cracks, and she sees tears well up in his eyes.

For some reason, Maggie thinks of her sister, Rachel, the only family she ever had that mattered to her, and wonders whatever became of her. *Does she feel like I abandoned her? Did she grow up hating me? Does she even remember me?* The sour and bitter taste of regret fills her mouth and makes her feel nauseated.

When her aunt didn't answer the only phone number she had, she didn't know where else to turn to find out about Rachel. It was a riddle that would never be solved, one that left her with a heavy dose of guilt.

Out of the blue, Israel says, "I think I'm hungry."

It takes Maggie half a second to pull herself away from her memories. "Hungry? Tell me what you want, and I'll run to town and get it for you."

"No need for that. Got some cans of beanie weenies and plastic forks in the over-the-counter cabinet just to the left of the kitchen sink. Leastwise there's supposed to be some there, as long as none of them nurses that comes out here has stole them."

Maggie stands halfway up, but a sharp pain in her knee puts her back in the chair. She grabs her knee and rubs it.

"Got a bad knee?" Israel asks.

"Yeah, it's been on its way out for a few years. My doctor says it needs to be replaced, but I'm going to try to lose some weight first, then get it taken care of after I retire."

"Don't worry about the beanie weenies. I'll be all right."

"No, no," she says as she stands up, "I'm used to it. I'll be right back."

In the kitchen, Maggie glances at the white sink that shows the signs of abuse and neglect—multiple stains of unknown origin and a couple of chips in the porcelain. She hesitates before opening the cabinet, a little afraid of what else might be in there besides the beanie weenies, but she steels herself and pulls open the door. A little wave of relief goes through her as the only things visible are several stacks of the cans she is hoping for. She takes out a couple of them and the package of plastic forks lying beside them and heads back to Israel's room.

With her help, he sits up on the edge of the bed and uses the TV tray she's placed in front of him. After she lets him eat a few bites in silence, she asks, "When did you start hoarding things? Were you always interested in collecting stuff?"

Between bites, Israel says, "Didn't set out to be this way. Just sort of happened after I got out of prison. I've never had anything permanent, not my whole life. This here place that Darnell left me is the first place that I could call mine. I'd never thought about it before, but that really meant something to me. When you've never had nothing, you get used to it and expect that's the way it'll always be. Then when you suddenly have something that's all yours, it gives you a feeling of . . . a feeling of belonging, a feeling of permanence. That's when I started keeping other things, and they gave me the same feeling." He pushes aside the empty can, opens another, and continues eating. "I know all this looks like a bunch of junk and trash to other people. But it's all I've got."

Maggie's notices that his energy level is picking up, his voice sounds stronger, and his eyes are a little more lively. *Wonder when was the last time he ate anything. I bet his blood sugar had dropped pretty low.*

While chewing a mouthful of food, he points with his fork, swallows, and says, "You know you left your guitar."

"Yes."

"Sing me a song while I finish eating."

Although his words sound like he's ordering her, she knows that's not his intent. "I've never thought I had a voice for singing. I just enjoyed playing and hearing the songs in my head."

"Nonsense. Your voice is fine, sort of like the voice of Mama Cass. I enjoy how it sounds."

Normally she would feel too self-conscious to grant such a request to someone, but he has such a disarming, unassuming way about him, she reaches for her guitar. "Let me play you the first song I ever learned." She launches into "Beautiful, Beautiful Brown Eyes." From there, she goes to "Little Brown Jug," then finishes with "I'm So Lonesome I Could Cry."

On the third verse of that song, Israel stops forking beanie weenies into his mouth and joins in singing with her but singing a high harmony line. Two lost souls singing a duet of truth.

Maggie's heart fills to overflowing as she looks at him singing with his eyes closed. She closes her eyes, too, as she sings the last line. In those brief seconds, she takes a whirlwind tour of the heartbreakingly sad times of her life. She feels the guitar vibrating against her, and when she stops playing, she hugs it as if it were a long-lost child.

Light filters through the prism of tears on her eyelashes as she looks at Israel.

"I could die right now and be content," he says with a sweet smile on his face. He looks so relaxed and happy, nothing like he did when she arrived. "What about you? You ever think about dying? Bound to, seeing as you've been working with the dying for years."

"It's interesting, isn't it?" she replies. "I've been working with the dying while you've been working with the dead. And now here we are with each other."

"You go a long way to avoid answering a question, don't you?" He shakes his head. "Hey, if you don't want to talk to me or answer my questions, that's your business. I'd just like to meet one person before I die who I can be open and honest with and who will be the same with me. Guess you're not the one, huh."

For her entire career as a social worker, Maggie has steadfastly been careful not to share details of her life with clients. Occasionally she might share a snippet if it might prove to be clinically helpful to someone, but that's been rare. She stares at this strange man who has a way of cutting straight to the heart of things and, without thinking it through, decides she's going to take down some walls. *It's my last patient before retiring, so what difference does it make? Nobody's going to fire me for crossing some kind of artificial boundary. He deserves to get what he's always wished for.* She says, "Sometimes I think about dying."

This produces a smile from Israel, and he raises his eyebrows. "Now we're getting somewhere. I'm not afraid to die because I know I'm going to a better place, a place where there will be no heartache, no sadness, and no tears. Are you afraid to die?"

"Are you asking me if I know Jesus or if I'm afraid to die?"

"Your answer to the last question will tell me the answer to the first one."

She hesitates as she thinks through what he's saying. "I'm not sure how I feel about dying except that it's inevitable."

"That's what you *think* about dying. I want to know how you *feel* about it."

I know what he's going to do with my answer. It's going to be all about God. But I made the decision to be honest, so honest it will be. "I guess I'm a little afraid because I don't know what's on the other side—if there is anything."

"Thank you for being honest."

When he doesn't say anything else, Maggie says, "That's it? No preaching to me about Jesus?"

He shrugs. "The Lord says this isn't the right time. Maybe tomorrow. You asked me about my family. What about you? You got any family?"

She teeters on the fringe of the truth and says, "I used to. But not anymore."

Chapter Thirty-Two

Cocking his head to one side, Israel says, "What happened to them? Did they all die or something?"

"It's complicated," Maggie replies.

"Ha! That's life, isn't it?"

She nods. "I suppose you're right. Well, my mother did die, when I was ten, or maybe it was eleven; it's been so long ago I don't remember exactly. I had a younger sister, but she went to live with relatives, and I never heard from her again."

"What about your father? Did you have one?"

Maggie stops at the edges of the unvarnished truth. "He died in a house fire when I was a teenager." She's beginning to feel uncomfortable with her decision to be open and honest with Israel, fearing she might accidentally let her deepest secrets slip. *What I'd like to do is take a drink of vodka right now.* She tries to turn the conversation without it sounding like she's avoiding something. "You said you grew up in an orphanage. What was that like?"

For the next several minutes, he tells her of his life there, funny things that happened, difficult times of realizing he had no family, his relationship with Darnell, and the twisted house mother that kept him confused about sex. He concludes by saying, "But all that changed when I was adopted out at age eleven. That was the worst thing that ever happened to me, even worse than prison."

Maggie is stunned to hear this. "How is that possible? I thought the things that happened to you in prison were the most inhumane actions that could be perpetrated on a human being. How in the world could your adoptive home have been worse?"

He waves off her question. "Talked enough about sad things, don't you think? Let's talk about something else. I want to show you my treasure box."

"You have a treasure box?"

"Don't get excited. It's not a pirate's chest of gold doubloons. Actually, it's the opposite. It has worthless things in it, but they mean a lot to me." He starts to get up out of bed.

She stops him. "Where are you going?"

"I'm going to get it out from under my bed."

"You stay put. I'll get it for you."

He protests, "But you've got bad knees."

"And you are dying. I think that trumps my bad knees." She smiles at him.

"Okay, okay, you win. It's that cigar box you asked me about before."

Maggie easily finds the cigar box lying where she left it when she was getting his guitar out from under the bed. Handing it to him, she says, "I've got a cigar box of treasures, too."

"You're kidding."

"No. It has some keepsakes in it that I've had since I was little."

"Would you bring it here sometime and share?"

Why not? She shrugs and nods. "Sure, I will."

He gives her a pleased smile.

Uncertain what he might have in his box, Maggie peers in as he opens it. As he'd said, at first glance there appears to be nothing remarkable, no shiny coins or sparkling gems. There is what looks like an old envelope that time has turned yellow, some rocks of various sizes, a rusty key, a knife, and some old coins turned black by oxidation.

Israel lets his hands hover over the items, as if he were warming them on a fire. "They all tell a story, each and every one." He picks up one of the rocks and holds it in his palm for her to see. "It's a fossil, a trilobite. Leastwise that's what I guessed from looking it up in an encyclopedia. I found it when I was digging my very first grave here in Tennessee. That there fossil had been lying in the ground undisturbed for millions of years until I dug it up. When I learned what it was, I kind of felt bad for digging it up. But once something's dug up, you can't ever put it back exactly where it was to begin with, so I decided I'd hold on to it."

Maggie looks closer at the object. "It sort of looks like a beetle of some kind."

"Yep. Here, you hold it."

She takes it as he reaches into the box and pulls out another rock.

"Now, this here is a bullet from the Civil War. I found it in the old Coldwater Cemetery. I've often wished it could tell me what all it saw during the war, which side used it, and did somebody die from the wound it made, or did it just fly harmlessly through the air and drop onto the ground? I could probably get some money for it from a collector, but I've kept it because it reminds me that most anything can be used for good or bad. This bullet might have been used to kill a deer to feed a man's family, or it might have been used to kill a boy soldier who was fighting in a war he didn't know anything about."

He hands it to her, and she inspects the three circular grooves just below the tip.

"I've never cleaned these coins," he says as he picks them up. "Found all of them in the same grave, north of Palmersville. They might be really old, or they might not be. The thing is, though, they're worth something, even if they don't look like it. Maybe a little or maybe a lot; it don't matter. They're worth something. You see my point, don't you?"

She shifts her focus from the dirty coins in his hand to his questioning face, then back to the coins. "Every person has value, right? Is that it? No matter what they may look like, they still are important."

"You've cut through it like a laser," he replies. "No matter how people may judge them, they still have value because other people might not know the whole story behind why they are the way they are."

Pointing at another coin in the box, Maggie asks, "What about that coin?"

He places the coins he's holding on his bed and picks up the one in the box she's asking about. It's then that she sees it is not a coin but a button.

He lowers his voice and looks furtively around the room. "This is my most prized possession. I got it when I buried Governor McWherter. Once everybody left the cemetery so that I could fill in the grave, I opened the casket and cut a button off his sleeve. I know it was a terrible, wrong thing to do. I could get in real trouble for doing it, but I had to have something so that I'd never forget that day."

For the next few minutes, he details the story behind every item in the box until nothing is left but the weathered envelope. He looks up at the ceiling and speaks to it. "Yes, sir, I think you're right. It's time."

Maggie waits to see what this imaginary conversation between him and God means. *I wonder who convinced him he could talk to God like that.*

Israel gently picks up the envelope as if it is an ancient document written on papyrus. "When I got out of prison, I had two letters waiting on me, both from Darnell. The first one was telling me about leaving me this place. This here was the second one. He told me not to open it right then, that it would answer questions about me but that I should wait until I was sure I wanted to read it. I've thought about reading it lots of times but always decided that whatever it had to say really wouldn't matter, you know, wouldn't change anything, so what's the point? But for some reason, I feel this urge to read it, and the Lord says it's time, so I'm not going to argue with him."

She feels herself growing nervous for Israel, wondering what in the world will be in the letter.

His hands begin trembling, and he has trouble opening the envelope. He hands it to her. "Here, you open it and read it out loud."

"Really, Israel, I don't think I should. This is for your eyes."

"I'm feeling sort of scared right now. I'd rather you do it."

Accepting his explanation as sufficient reason, Maggie slowly tears open the envelope and pulls out a folded piece of notebook paper. When she unfolds it, a smaller folded piece of paper flutters onto her lap.

Both of them stare at it. "We'll look at it after we read the letter, okay?" she asks.

He nods.

She begins reading:

Dear Israel,

I see you decided to read this and find out more about yourself. I hope you are in a place where what I'm going to tell you will bring you some measure of peace and not frustrate or anger you.

You have to understand that people do all sorts of things for all sorts of reasons. Later in life they might come to regret those decisions, but it's too late to turn back time and change things. Please understand that and believe it.

Maggie pauses and looks at him. She feels like her heart is pushing up into her throat, knowing now that whatever is in this letter is going to be far-reaching and possibly hard-hitting for Israel. Part of her wishes she could unread the letter and reseal it in its envelope.

"I'm ready," he says. "Keep reading."

Lowering her eyes, she reads:

The man who owned the orphanage wanted all the kids to be adopted. He thought a home was a much better place for a kid to be raised than spending life in an orphanage. But he found that not every kid was being selected by the interested couples. So he made a decision to change the names of the kids, thinking that if they had a Bible name that that would make them more attractive to couples. I know, that sounds crazy, but that's what he thought.

You came to the orphanage when you were still a baby. I don't know anything about how you got there or who brought you. But I do know he changed your name.

Maggie stops and folds the letter. Her mind races in a hundred directions, trying to absorb the treachery of changing someone's name and wondering how all this sounds to Israel. But she also feels her hands tingling as a mixture of feelings she cannot identify races through her.

"Israel's not my name?" he whispers.

The letter shakes in her hands as she opens it back up and reads:

He changed your name to Israel McKenzie, thinking that either a good Jewish or Irish Catholic family would adopt you. Your real name, though, is Theodore Stinson.

Chapter Thirty-Three

Maggie's eyes blur so that she cannot see to read. It feels to her like someone has grasped the wheels of time and is spinning them backward to the morning she woke up and discovered that her baby brother was gone.

"That's a real coincidence, isn't it?" Israel says. "Me and you both have the same last name, Stin—" But he does not finish the sentence. He stares at her with his mouth agape as a look of shock spreads across his face. "You don't think—" Again, he stops short of completing the thought.

Maggie finally catches hold of her reeling thoughts and tries to see anything about his features that resemble the baby she used to care for. "Are you my lost baby brother?"

He shakes his head. "It can't be. Darnell said my name is Theodore."

She nods as her chest fills with emotions. "Yes, that was my brother's name, but we called him Teddy for short."

He closes his eyes and rubs his forehead. "This can't be. It's impossible. I just can't believe it."

Looking back down at the letter, she says, "There's more here." She reads:

You are probably going to have a hard time believing this, but I promise it is the truth. I'm enclosing a copy of your original birth certificate to prove it.

She picks up the small folded piece of paper that fell into her lap earlier, slowly opens it, and scans it carefully. Each word and number that she reads adds weight to the undeniable truth.

"Is it true?" Israel asks.

To answer, she offers the copy to him.

He reads it and looks up at her. "Columbus, Indiana? That's where we lived?"

"Actually, we lived in Waynesville. Columbus was where the closest hospital was and where you were born." She feels warm tears on her cheeks and realizes she's crying. "Only in my dreams did I ever expect to find you. It was just too unbelievable to think it was possible."

He stretches out his hand toward her, and she takes it in hers. In a trembling voice, he asks, "I had a sister? You're my sister?"

She puts the palm of his cool hand to her lips and kisses it. "Yes, Teddy. I'm your sister."

He pulls her hands to his cheek and bathes them in tears.

For a few moments they hold this pose, hearts communing through unspoken words.

Finally, he releases her and says, "Were there any other brothers and sisters? How big was our family?"

Before she thinks where her answer will lead her, Maggie says, "There was another sister, younger than me. Her name was Rachel."

Smiling, Israel says, "What a beautiful name. Where does she live?"

The truth sits on the tip of her tongue a million miles away. She turns away from him.

"What happened?" he asks. "Did she die? Is she dead?"

Sadness and regret that she has kept sealed in an iron chest find their way past the hinges and locks fatigued by time and make her heart as heavy as a ship's anchor. She looks at him. "I don't know."

He gives her a puzzled look. "You don't know where she lives, or you don't know if she's dead? What do you mean?"

"I mean, I don't know either thing." She starts to explain, but emotions clog her throat, and she has to cough to clear it. "Our family was no *Leave It to Beaver* TV show, Israel, as a matter of fact, it was the complete opposite. Our father was a sick and evil man. When you were still a baby, Mama died, and he gave you away to a social worker. I got up one morning, and you were gone—just like that. We never heard anything else about you. The other thing you need to know is that he sexually abused me for years."

Fresh tears spring up in Israel's eyes and spill over onto his cheeks.

"Don't feel sorry for me. I've been over that for a long time. But when I was growing up, in my own mixed-up way, I began to think that as long as he was abusing me, he would leave Rachel alone. In that way, I felt like was protecting her. The day she told me he was starting to bother her, I knew something else had to be done, so I convinced an aunt to take her to live with them. A couple of years later, I ran away. I had to." She suddenly winces as a sharp pain, like a knife in her back just below her shoulder blade, surprises her. Gasping for a breath, she reflexively reaches for her back.

In a voice etched with alarm, Israel asks, "Maggie? Are you all right?"

She holds up her hand in a disarming gesture, but it is a few seconds before the pain begins to subside and she can take a breath. "It must have been a muscle spasm of some kind." She reaches for a tissue and dabs the sweat off her face.

"I can tell you feel guilty about sending Rachel to your aunt, but you shouldn't. It was the right thing to do. You were just trying to protect her."

With all her defenses now taken down, Maggie replies, "But I abandoned her. I was so selfish! And I'm ashamed." Having uttered one of her most closely held feelings about herself, a floodgate opens somewhere inside her, and she begins to sob uncontrollably. In the midst of it, she cries out, "I've done so many shameful things!"

Several moments pass before she pulls herself together. A small pile of used tissues, a garbage heap of spent emotions, lies on her lap. She doesn't know when or how he did it, but Israel is squatting on his knees in front of her.

"My sweet sister, Maggie," he says. "I can tell that life's never been easy for you, but you hide it so well nobody would ever know it. You don't have to do that anymore because now you've got family you can share with. I'm here for you. Besides, when it comes to comparing our lists of shame, I think mine will far outweigh yours."

Although she doesn't believe him, she loves him for his tender and heartfelt words. When he struggles to stand up and get back in bed, she lends a hand, tucking the sheet around him. "My baby brother . . . what should I call you? Israel or Teddy?"

"I'd like it if you called me Teddy, just like you used to when you took care of me."

She peers through the haze of her emotions and sees that he looks spent from all of it. "You're tired and need to go to sleep and rest. I'll be back tomorrow, and we'll get to know each other even better."

"No hidden chapters?"

She shakes her head. "No hidden chapters."

His eyes close, and he appears to fall instantly asleep.

Maggie pushes herself up from the chair and begins making her way out. When she reaches the living room, she suddenly feels as though an elephant has its foot on her chest. Clutching her chest, she drops to her knees. Almost immediately, she breaks out in a cold sweat as a wave of nausea rushes through her. The pain in her chest gives no signs of letting up, and she finds it difficult to get a breath. *My God, I'm having a heart attack!*

She falls over on her side, and the contents of her bag spill out in front of her. She spots her phone and tries to reach for it, but the pain in her chest is now radiating down her arm, and she can't move it. Rolling onto her stomach, she manages to use her other arm to get hold of the phone. As she flips it open, everything around her grows dim. In the distance, she thinks she hears someone calling her name. It is her last conscious thought.

Chapter Thirty-Four

The sound of a siren blaring pierces Maggie's ears. Opening her eyes, she sees a stocky young woman with hazel eyes holding a stethoscope to Maggie's heart. There's something familiar about her, but she's unsure what.

"She's conscious," the EMT announces.

As the ambulance sways and bounces over a bump in the road, Maggie notices she has an oxygen mask covering her mouth and nose. She reaches to pull it off, but the EMT stops her.

"We need to leave that alone," she tells Maggie. "My name is Christine Mathis. It appears you've had a heart attack. We're rushing you to the hospital in Martin. Have you ever had a heart attack before?"

Maggie shakes her head no.

As Christine makes a note on a clipboard, Maggie looks around and sees a short IV pole with a bag of fluid hanging on it. Following the tube, she discovers it is attached to a needle in her arm. She's surprised at how calm she feels in the middle of this tempest and is especially thankful that the horrible pain in her chest has subsided. She starts to ask a question, but her voice is muffled by the mask, so she stops. *What about Teddy? He had to have been the one to call 9-1-1. How did he deal with them barging into his trailer? Is he okay?*

Christine returns her attention to Maggie and says, "We're almost to the hospital. I think you're going to be fine." She leans in close to Maggie's ear. "You don't remember me, but you helped me and my mother escape from my abusive father. You saved our lives. I'm glad I could return the favor."

Amid the swirl of emotions, physical sensations, and the swaying of the ambulance, Christine's words pierce Maggie's heart, not that she hasn't heard such sentiment before; it's just that she's never heard it when she was close to dying. She lays her palm on the side of Christine's face and nods her appreciation.

The last few minutes of the approach to the hospital are relatively calm. But as soon as the ambulance comes to a stop, the doors are flung open, and it seems as if scores of people are talking at the same time, with questions pouring in from the team that's been waiting and corresponding cryptic answers being supplied by Christine.

Even though Maggie's convinced she's going to be fine, the urgency with which everyone speaks and the swiftness of the transfer of her gurney to the ground and then through the hallways increase her anxiety. *Stay calm. Stay calm, or you're going to make yourself have another heart attack.* She concentrates on taking slow breaths.

Two hours later, the attending physician, whose name she can't remember, enters her room in the ICU, holding what appears to be an iPad. Using his finger, he taps, reads, and slides through pages. Finally, he looks at her and says, "Ms. Stinson, you definitely had a heart attack, but it appears to be a mild one. There are some constrictions in a couple of arteries but not serious enough for us to put any stents in. The best course of action is to start you on some medications and for you to change your diet and begin an exercise program. We'll supply you with some guidelines for each that, if you follow them, will make a huge difference in your overall health, not just that of your heart."

I wonder how many times he's given this little speech and if anyone really listens to him or follows his advice. "Diet and exercise," I've heard that for years from my doctor. I'm just ready to disconnect from all these monitors and get out of here. She says to the doctor, "Thank you for taking care of me. All the staff was so kind. Be sure you tell them all thank you for me." She starts pulling off the leads that are fastened to her chest.

"Whoa, whoa, there," the doctor says as he grasps her wrist. "What are you doing?"

"I'm going home."

"Not just yet. We're going to play it safe and keep you overnight. I just think it's smart to monitor you for several hours to make certain nothing else is going to happen."

Yeah, and so you can charge my insurance company another fifty thousand dollars.

Just then, Christine, the EMT, appears in the doorway dressed in civilian clothes. She smiles at Maggie and says, "How's it going?"

The doctor looks in her direction. "Oh, hey, Christine. Ms. Stinson is going to be fine, I think, but she's being a little stubborn about spending the night with us."

Christine walks to Maggie's bedside and takes her hand. To the doctor, she says, "Why don't you let me talk to her?"

The physician raises his eyebrows. "You know her?"

Smiling down at Maggie, she answers, "Yes, I do."

"Great. I'll leave her to you."

Once he exits, Christine says, "How do you feel?"

"I feel fine. I'm just ready to go home."

She squeezes Maggie's hand. "No, I mean, really, how do you feel?"

At that moment, Maggie lets in all the fatigue she's been ignoring, and her body sags into the mattress. "Tired."

"Exactly. You need to spend the night if for no other reason than to give your body time to rest and do a reset."

"I suppose you're right." Maggie thinks she sees a question flit across Christine's face. "Was there something you wanted to ask me?"

"That place."

"What place?"

"Where we picked you up—is that where you live?"

"Goodness, no."

A look of relief comes over Christine. "Oh, good. I couldn't imagine it was yours, but you never know."

Maggie's mind shifts from a relaxed state to spinning in concern over Teddy. She looks at the clock on the wall. "Is it really nearly eight o'clock?"

Christine gives her a knowing smile. "A hospital is a place where it's easy to lose track of time. But yeah, it's almost eight. You look worried. What's wrong?"

"I'm seeing a patient that lives in the trailer. I'm concerned about him. Did you talk to him when you were there?"

"Uh, no. There wasn't anybody there but you. I mean, as far as I know, there wasn't. Me and my partner called out when we went inside, but nobody answered. It's odd, though, because it looked like someone had been doing CPR on you before we got there. You were lying on your back with your head tilted back to open your airway, and the front of your shirt was rumpled like someone had done compressions. Was your patient there when you had your heart attack?"

Nodding, Maggie says, "I had left him in bed and was on my way out. A few minutes earlier I'd had a spell, but it passed, and I thought I was fine. He must have heard me fall." She chuckled. "I am a rather large woman, you know. It probably sounded like the floor was falling in."

"Well, I sure didn't see anybody else."

Maggie chews on her lip, wondering what she can do.

"Are you worried about your patient?"

"Actually, I am. He won't know what became of me and will worry."

"I can go back out there and check on him if you like."

Maggie thinks about all that Christine will face if she goes out there and also how Teddy will react to someone he doesn't know showing up this time of night. "I appreciate your offer, but I think it's best if you don't. I'm sure you could tell that it isn't the cleanest place you could be."

This time Christine chuckles. "You've forgotten about the kind of place my mother and I were living when you helped us. We didn't have running water, and most of the time, we didn't have electricity. There's nothing at your patient's trailer that will bother me."

"You're awfully sweet, but the other part of this is I don't think he would react very well to a stranger showing up at this time of night."

"You know him better than I do, so I'll let it go. Now when you go home tomorrow, you need to take it easy for a few days."

Maggie smiles to herself. *This is probably what it would be like if I had an adult daughter—making sure I take care of myself and trying to tell me what to do.* "Thank you for coming by to check on me. And thank you for saving—"

Christine cuts her off by holding up her hand. "We've already had this conversation. I'm just glad I got to return the favor." Bending down, she gives Maggie a hug and then leaves.

Thirty minutes later, Maggie is reliving the death of her baby, feeling sad that she will die one day without having someone at her bedside like Christine, when a nurse enters her room with a tiny cup.

"Here's something to help you sleep," the nurse says.

Thankful to be forced away from the tar pit of depression she was about to slip into, Maggie swallows the pill and, in moments, falls fast asleep.

Chapter Thirty-Five

Feeling fairly rested from the night's sleep, Maggie sits on the edge of her hospital bed, fully dressed and eyeing the clock. She swings her short legs impatiently. *It's almost ten o'clock. If someone doesn't come soon, I'm walking out of here.*

True to her word, ten minutes later, she walks out of her room.

"Ms. Stinson," someone calls from behind her.

Maggie turns around and sees a nurse, who looks as old and out of shape as she does, walking toward her at a fast clip, carrying a handful of papers.

"Where are you going?" the nurse asks, trying to catch her breath.

"I'm leaving. I can't sit around here all day. The doctor's already released me, and I'm tired of waiting."

In a low voice, the nurse says, "I don't blame you. These other nurses around here are more interested in looking at their phones than they are in doing their jobs."

Maggie's attitude softens. "I know how you feel. My administrator, who looks like she just graduated high school, can't keep her nose out of her phone."

They both laugh.

"I'm supposed to give you these papers before you leave. They are handouts on eating and exercising to improve your heart health. I will also reiterate what I'm sure the doctor told you, that you need to take it easy for a couple of days. But I suspect you'll do what you want to do."

Taking the handouts, Maggie replies, "You are correct." Before turning to leave, she adds, "Hang in there with these kids you work with. Don't let them get the best of you."

When she gets to the parking lot, it dawns on her that her car is still out at Teddy's trailer. *What the heck am I supposed to do now?*

"Looking for these?" a voice calls out.

Maggie turns and sees Christine walking toward her, dangling a set of keys.

"Me and my partner drove out to that trailer this morning and brought your car here. It's over by the second light pole. I hope that was okay."

Rather than pleased and relieved, the first thought Maggie has is to wonder whether or not Christine saw her bottle of vodka. Blushing, she takes the keys and says, "My car was probably a mess. It's sort of my office on wheels. I hope you weren't offended." She searches Christine's face for any hint that she felt odd about finding the liquor, but Christine gives no such indication.

Christine laughs. "You should see my car. It looks like a garbage can from McDonald's. How are you feeling this morning?

Relieved, Maggie says, "I actually feel pretty good, certainly not like I had a heart attack less than twenty-four hours ago. Thank you for bringing my car to me." With a laugh, she adds, "You can now put 'valet parking attendant' on your work résumé."

"I'll do it. It was good to see you again." She gives Maggie a hug and heads toward the waiting ambulance.

Maggie locates her car, unlocks it, and slides in. Immediately her eyes go to the passenger seat to see if the vodka bottle is still there. She can't remember if that's where she left it or if she put it back under the driver's seat. Not spotting the bottle, she reaches under her seat but feels nothing. Bending over, she reaches farther under the seat but still comes up empty. *What the . . . ?* She checks the glove compartment, looks behind her in the back seat and floorboard—still nothing. *Oh my gosh, did Christine find it and take it out?* A fresh wave of shame and embarrassment sweeps over her.

Glancing in her rearview mirror, she sees what a mess she looks like. *My hair looks like a rat's nest.* She pulls a wide-tooth comb out of her purse and restores a semblance of order to her hair. After putting on a touch of lipstick, she cranks her car and heads straight to Teddy's.

The closer she gets to her destination, the deeper she furrows her brow out of worry and concern about what state she will find him in.

As soon as she steps into his trailer, she knows something is wrong. All the neat stacks of magazines and newspapers look as if a cyclone has struck them. Garbage has been strewn on top of everything. Maggie feels a bit of panic. "Teddy?" she calls out. "It's Maggie. Are you here?"

"Maggie?" comes a tired voice. "Is that you?"

Paying no mind to all the sounds of scurrying vermin underneath her feet, Maggie treads on top of the trash in her path and hurries back to the bedroom. Standing in his doorway, she is struck by the change in his appearance since she last saw him. His face looks more drawn, and his bed seems to be made of quicksand that is slowly swallowing him.

He gives her a weak smile and stretches his skeleton of an arm toward her. "Maggie, you're alive."

She walks in, takes his hand in hers, and sits down in the chair beside his bed. "Yes, I'm alive, and I'm here."

A lone tear slips from the corner of his eye and trickles down his cheek. "I was afraid . . ." His unfinished thought hangs suspended in the air like a harrier hawk.

"What happened to your trailer?"

"I decided if you weren't coming back, what's the point to any of it?" In a half whisper, he adds, "What's the point of living?"

She squeezes his hand. "Hush talking like that. I'm far from dead, and you and I have a lifetime to catch up on. But tell me what happened yesterday after I passed out in your living room."

"I heard you fall and thought you'd tripped over something. When you didn't answer after I called your name, I went to see about you. One look and I knew it was bad. You were pale as a sheet, and your lips were blue. I checked your pulse and didn't feel anything." New tears brim in his eyes, and he looks away from her.

"I'm sorry you were so scared. It must have been horrible for you."

Turning back toward her, he says, "I saw your phone and called 9-1-1. They tried to keep me on the line to tell me what to do for you, but I didn't listen to them. I took a CPR class in prison and even did it on an inmate one time, so I hung up the phone and started compressions. The problem was that I've got no more strength than a baby has and couldn't keep it up. It was the most helpless feeling I've had in a long, long time. I knew what needed to be done but couldn't do it."

"You did plenty, Teddy," Maggie says, trying to reassure him. "I'm sure whatever small amount you did helped me survive. You did fine." Standing up, she says, "I'll bet you haven't had anything to eat or drink this morning. Let me get something for you."

In less than a minute, she's back with a can of beanie weenies and a can of cola. She helps him with the first few bites, and as before, he rallies and asks her to help him sit up.

For several minutes, she lets him eat in silence. Finally, he sets aside the food and appears more like he did when she last saw him.

"I need to tell you something else," he says. "Sometime during the night, I happened to think about your car still being parked outside. I knew you'd need it if you were still alive. I looked inside and saw that the keys were still in it."

Maggie purses her lips and squeezes her toes, anticipating where he is going with this.

"I was going to see if I would be able to drive the car to the hospital and leave it for you, but then I'd need a way to get back home. Just as I turned to come back inside the trailer, I saw the bottle on the passenger seat. If you weren't my sister, I don't think I would have done what I did, but you are, and I did. I took it, poured it out, and threw the bottle away. So there. You can be mad if you want to, but I hope you're not."

No words of condemnation. No preaching at her or trying to make her feel guilty. Just his truth. All of it is why Maggie cannot object to what he did because it was done out of love. "I'm not mad at you for doing it. It's really okay. I'd already been thinking about maybe I need to just give it up, so maybe I will."

A big smile opens up his face. "That's the way to think. And the good Lord will help you leave it alone. Just ask him to, and he'll jump onboard with you."

His reference to God rankles her, and anger bubbles up, but she decides now isn't the time to tell him her feelings. *He's happy. Why don't I just enjoy being happy with him.* Yet in the back of her mind, she knows she will tell him one day and that this topic might cause a rift in their newly formed relationship.

Chapter Thirty-Six

Maggie assists Teddy down his front steps and leads him into the front yard like he'd asked her to; he'd said he wanted to feel the sun on his face.

He tilts his face toward the sun and smiles. "Feels so good. It's one of the things you miss the most when you're in prison."

She imitates his pose and enjoys feeling the sun warm her face.

As he takes a seat on one of the metal lawn chairs, her phone rings for the fifth time since she got out of the hospital this morning.

"Are you going to keep ignoring that thing, or are you going to answer it?" Teddy asks.

Sighing out of frustration, knowing who it is, and of resignation, knowing she's going to have to answer eventually, Maggie flips open her phone. "Hello, this is Maggie." She listens for a moment, then says, "Yes, Sheila, I had a mild heart attack, so they say, but I'm fine." Again, she listens and this time rolls her eyes at Teddy. "No, Sheila, I don't need to take some time off work. I'm out here at Teddy's . . . I mean Israel McKenzie's, checking on him. I'll come to the office later today, and we can talk." Without saying goodbye, she closes her phone.

"Was that your boss?" Teddy asks.

Maggie nods. "She's a well-meaning person, but she wears me out sometimes with trying to micromanage things. I'm glad I'm about to retire."

"Close your eyes with me," he says, "and notice what you hear."

She obliges and hears nothing at first, but then come the sounds of grasshoppers sawing their legs together, the voices of a cardinal and a mourning dove, and high overhead, the warning cry of a hawk. As she listens she feels all the tension in her body going away, leaving her completely relaxed. With her eyes still closed, she says, "This is nice."

"Yes, it is. I've sat out here lots of times trying to imagine what kind of family I was born into and wishing I could find answers to my questions. And now I'm sitting here with my sister."

Maggie opens her eyes and sees him looking at her.

He tells her, "I guess wishes do come true sometimes."

"I'm happy for you."

"Are you not happy, too? Isn't this like a wish come true for you?"

"Oh yes, I'm very happy, Teddy, but not like a wish coming true. It's more like an unbelievable surprise. I quit wishing for things a long time ago when I figured out that they never come true anyway."

"But you've spent your whole career helping people and, I'm guessing, trying to get them to dream about a better life and convincing them they can achieve their dreams."

She considers his words for a moment, then says, "I'm a fraud, Teddy. You're the only person I've ever told that to, the only person I've ever admitted it to."

"What do you mean you're a fraud?"

"I don't believe half the things I tell people. In school, I learned what people want to be told and to believe in. They want to be given hope and a belief that things can work out for them. But here's the cold hard truth: life here is hell from the time you are born until the day you die." She takes a deep breath and lets it out. "I've been holding that in forever. It feels good to finally be letting it out."

He stares at her, slowly blinking his eyes, but shows no other reaction. She can't tell if he's mad, sad, or disgusted with her, so she says, "I'm sorry if that hurts your feelings, me not being the kind of wonderful sister you were hoping for."

Shrugging, he says, "Don't hurt my feelings. If that's your truth, I can deal with it. Might not agree with it, but it doesn't affect how I feel about you. I can't help wondering, though, what in the world has happened to you that twisted you up like you are."

Maggie feels the bile of anger and bitterness in the back of her throat. "How about this? How about me being used as a sex object by our father all of my childhood until I ran away with a used-car salesman who ended up beating me repeatedly and nearly killing me. Then I go to college and am seduced by a lecherous college professor who dumps me when I get pregnant, and then my baby is stillborn." Only by severe restraint does she hold off blurting out what she did to their father and to Professor Reed, although she would love to vomit it all out.

It's only after she stops speaking that she sees Teddy's pained expression, as if she has slapped him in the face or punched him in the gut.

He shakes his head and tries to speak, but nothing comes out.

Hoping to lessen the sting of what she's revealed, she says, "Don't feel sorry for me. It's all right; I'm past all of it and don't dwell on it. It just happened. Like I said before, life is hell. Look what happened to you. You've been through hell; you know how it is. You just move on. That's all there is to do."

"I don't feel sorry for you, that's a waste of energy," Teddy finally says. But I do feel sad for you, sad that evil has touched your life so many times. I used to be where you are, so I understand how you feel." He shakes his head. "This conversation's not going the way I wanted it to. I can't do anything about the things that were done to me, but I'd like to do something about the things I've done to others."

Maggie's surprised to hear him say he has felt the same kind of bitterness. Somehow, he's been able to wipe away any detectable semblance of it. She's also puzzled that he says he's done things to others, for she can't imagine this meek and humble creature hurting anyone.

He interrupts her thoughts by saying, "Maggie, I want you to help me do some things before I die. I want to try and make things right, as best I can. I never thought I'd be able to, that I'd never meet someone who'd be willing to help me, but now I have you. Will you help me?"

"What do you mean you want to make things right?"

"I've done bad things, and I want to try and make amends. I just can't do it by myself." He waves his hand at his body. "Not with this. I may not have time, but I'd like to die trying, if you'll help me."

"Maybe you need to tell me a little bit more about what happened, so I can understand better."

With a faraway look in his eyes, Teddy says, "Her name was Ada."

For the next little bit, he tells her the story of meeting Ada Lane in West Virginia, of falling in love with her and her family, of her getting pregnant and him deserting her. "I had everything I ever wanted right there in my hands: a wife who loved me, a child I could raise as my own, her parents who loved me. What a fool I was to leave! It makes me feel so ashamed. What kind of person does that?"

"Men do that for all sorts of reasons," Maggie answers. "Most of the reasons are just excuses for not being responsible and doing the right thing, but for you, I suspect the reason was because it was too good to be true, and it scared you."

He wipes his runny nose on his sleeve. "You're exactly right. I was scared I would be a horrible husband and a mean father. I didn't know anything about how to do either of those. How are you supposed to know how to do something you've never done or seen before? Even as I say it out loud, it sounds like a sorry excuse. I should have at least tried to make it work."

Maggie wants to say something that will assuage his shame and regret, but now that she's confessed to him the truth of who she is, she's afraid her words will ring hollow and insincere to him. So she tries for honesty. "Shame and regret make up a two-headed monster that will eat your heart up from the inside out and make sleeping an impossible exercise. It's how I feel about abandoning my sister, Rachel." At the mere mention of it, she feels a sharp pain in her chest and reflexively puts her hand on it.

Teddy's eyes grow wide in alarm. "Are you okay? Are you having another heart attack?"

Shaking her head, she says, "I don't think so. It's just the pain of a broken heart."

The concern on his face slides off. "I know how that feels. Turns out we have more in common than just being brother and sister."

"You said you wanted my help in making things right. What can I do for you?"

"Help me find Ada and take me to her so I can apologize."

Chapter Thirty-Seven

The next morning, Maggie places a few final things in her suitcase and zips it shut. Carrying it in one hand and her guitar in the other, she passes through the living room, pauses to pick up a sheaf of papers off the printer, and then heads out the door with the papers held between her teeth.

In town, she stops at the office and heads back to Sheila's door.

Looking up in surprise, Sheila says, "Maggie! How are you? You look remarkably well for someone who's had a heart attack. I still think you need to take off a few—"

Maggie holds up her hand. "Hold up right there, Sheila. I've just stopped to tell you that I'm quitting my job."

Sheila smiles. "I know. Your retirement's just around the corner. I'll bet you're getting excited."

"No, I mean I'm quitting my job today, as in right now. I just wanted to stop by and let you know." She reaches to shake Sheila's hand. "It's been real, Sheila. I wish you and the agency the very best."

Her mouth agape, Sheila reaches for her hand in slow motion. "But . . . but I thought . . ."

"Yeah—me too. But my plans have changed rather suddenly."

"Oh, Maggie, it's not your health, is it? There's not something more serious going on, is there?"

"No, not at all." Before Sheila can think of another rejoinder, Maggie hustles out to her car and heads toward Teddy's.

She walks in his front door without knocking. "Teddy, it's me, Maggie," she calls out as she makes her way through the strewn papers and trash from yesterday.

In the doorway of his bedroom, she holds aloft the papers she brought with her and says, "Baby brother, you and I are going on a road trip! I found Ada!"

Teddy pushes himself up on one elbow and stares in disbelief. "What are you saying? How did you do that so quickly?"

"It's the magic of Google and the internet. You told me you wanted to find Ada and make amends. Well, I know where she is, at least I'm pretty sure I do, and I'm going to take you there. I've got an address in Wheeling, West Virginia."

He shakes his head as if he's clearing cobwebs. "Me and you are going to West Virginia? But what about the shape I'm in?"

"What about it? You're dying, right? If you die on the way, at least you'll die trying. That's all that matters. I can help you with your colostomy bag when you need it. I'll be doing all the driving. All you have to do is sit back and rest. You do want to go, don't you?"

Smiling, he says, "How much coffee have you had? Your mind is running a hundred miles an hour."

She returns his smile. "I spent most of the night doing this research. I just got started and couldn't quit. It was like I was a private investigator. You're right—I've had a bit more coffee than I usually drink."

He laughs. "A bit? I'd say more like a pot or two more. Yes, I do want to go. But do you realize what you're doing?"

She puzzles over the question. "I don't know what you mean."

"You're helping me realize my dream. But you're the one who doesn't believe in dreams. Is that what they call irony?"

Shrugging, she says, "I guess you're just lucky this time."

"I don't believe in luck. I think it's God." He looks toward the ceiling. "You're welcome, Lord."

She opens her mouth to speak but thinks better of it. "We're wasting time, Teddy. We need to get you ready to travel to West Virginia."

He pushes his fist into the air and yells a weak, "Woo-whoo!"

*****

Maggie squints against the bright streetlights as they enter the outskirts of Wheeling. She looks at the clock: 12:14. For the past two hours, it's been all she can do to keep her eyes open. Her back and shoulders ache from the long drive, but when she looks over at her sleeping brother, she tells herself it's worth it.

He has slept most of the trip, but the times he roused himself, he couldn't contain his excitement. He filled her in on more details of his life with Ada and her family. It sounded like a bucolic life, the kind she used to dream of when she was a little girl. *Yes,* she admitted to herself, *I did have dreams at one time.* She tried to remember when she decided dreaming was for fools. *I guess it was after living with Jackson.*

Turning on her blinker, she takes an exit and pulls into a Holiday Inn Express. When she comes to a stop, Teddy awakens.

Rubbing his eyes, he says, "Are we here?"

"We're in Wheeling. It's midnight, and we need to get some rest. Let me ask you about something. I've been thinking about the motel situation and getting separate rooms but wonder how you'd feel about sharing a room. Obviously, it would save money, but that's not the reason I'm thinking of. I would just feel better if I could keep an eye on you. It's an unfamiliar place, and you might get disoriented or need some help. I'm okay with sharing a room, but if you're not, then I'll be happy to get two rooms."

His face crinkles with a smile. "You want to keep an eye on me, and you are the one who had a heart attack. That's sort of upside down, isn't it?"

"You think you're funny, don't you? Okay, we'll share a room where we can keep an eye on each other, how's that?" An extended chuckle is all she gets in reply.

*****

When Maggie awakens the next morning, she's completely disoriented for a moment until she remembers where she is. The green light of the digital clock on the bedside table tells her it's nearly nine-thirty. *Good lord, when's the last time I slept past eight o'clock?*

Looking over at Teddy, she notes he hasn't moved since she laid him in the bed. She gets up and tiptoes into the bathroom to take a long, hot shower in hopes it will ease the tight muscles in her back.

After she is finished, she checks on Teddy. Again, he appears not to have moved. A tingling alarm goes off in her head. *Please don't let him have died during the night!*

She moves closer and speaks his name. "Teddy? It's time to wake up."

Nothing happens.

Her heart gallops. *Stay calm. Stay calm.* She places two fingers on his neck in search of a pulse. It takes a moment, but there it is, a slow, steady heartbeat.

With his eyes still closed, Teddy says, "I was having this dream of being on a road trip with my sister. If you are not her, please be gone before I open my eyes."

Maggie lets out the breath that she's been holding. "My lord, Teddy, you scared me to death."

He looks at her. "Thought I'd kicked the can, didn't you? Well, I'm still here."

Though his words are a tease, neither his voice nor his face reflect any of that. "What's wrong, Teddy?"

His eyes close. "I am exhausted. I guess all that riding wore me out. Might need to stay in bed today."

Despite that not being part of her original plan, Maggie quickly agrees. "Sounds like a great idea. I'm tired, too. I can't remember the last time I made that long of a trip. Do you need some of your pain medication?"

He gives a slight nod, which sends her to the bathroom to get a cup of water.

Once he swallows the pill, she says, "I'm going to get us some breakfast." She transfers the "Do Not Disturb" sign to the outside door handle and heads to the lobby.

She spends the rest of the day alternately reading a book she brought, helping Teddy nibble at some food and sip some juice, and napping. But as evening approaches, he seems to revive a bit, asking her to help him sit up in the bed.

"Feeling better?" she asks.

"I think so."

"I want to show you something. You ready?"

"Sure."

Going to her suitcase, she takes out a worn cigar box. "It's my treasure box that I told you about."

A look of delight brightens his face. "You remembered!"

"Of course I did." She takes a seat on his bed and hands him a baby shoe. "This was yours."

If it had been a Faberge egg, he could not have held it more gently. "You've had this ever since I was a baby? I can't believe it." He lets his fingertips trail over the soles, sides, and laces. "They are so tiny."

"Hard to believe you were that small, isn't it?"

"Yes, it is. Do you remember me wearing these?"

"Absolutely. I thought of you as mine. That's why it hurt so bad when all of a sudden our father gave you away."

"I wish I could have grown up with you."

"Not me. I'm glad you didn't. Living there was like being in a prisoner-of-war camp. I know you didn't have it easy, but who knows, he might have killed you." She hands him the faded photograph from the box. "That's our mother, and here's the brooch she was wearing in that picture."

Tears drip from the tip of Teddy's nose as he looks at the items. In a broken voice, he says, "She was beautiful."

"Yes, she was."

"Will you go get our guitars and bring them here? Let's sing and play some."

Maggie smiles. "Sure, I will."

For the next couple of hours, back and forth they go, taking turns leading a song they know and then following along as they try to keep up with an unfamiliar one. All of his are Beatles songs, while hers are mostly songs by Patsy Cline and Hank Williams.

Finally, he sets his guitar aside and lies down. "We're going to see Ada tomorrow, aren't we?"

"Yes." She hears the apprehension coating each of his words.

"I'm scared."

"I know. It's okay; I'll be there with you."

Chapter Thirty-Eight

Except for a few catnaps, Maggie lies awake most of the night worrying and wondering if bringing Teddy on this quest for Ada was the right thing to do. She had been so excited about finding Ada online that she didn't pause and think through all the possibilities and consequences. But now her mind is plagued by them. *What if it's not the correct Ada? What if it is, and she has harbored hatred for Teddy ever since he left her? If she's married, what will her husband say about a man from her past showing up? What if that man has raised Teddy's child as if he were his own, and the child knows nothing about his true parentage? And most importantly, how will Teddy handle all this?*

Like a condemned prisoner who will be executed on the morrow, Maggie dreads the coming of dawn. But when she sees light pushing in at the edges of the heavy curtain covering the window of their motel room, she knows she cannot prevent whatever penalties will be exacted this day because of what she's done.

Quietly easing out of bed, she makes her way to the bathroom so that she can take a shower. While standing in the warm spray, her mind shifts to wondering what kind of night Teddy had. *Did he sleep any? Is he still scared? What did he do with all the questions that had to have been swirling in his head?* And then it comes to her: *He probably spent the night praying.*

What must it be like to have that kind of belief and peace? She searches her own heart to find what it is that she believes in that brings her peace. And while she finds many things she believes in, she admits to herself that none of them brings her peace. *Maybe that's why vodka became my best friend. It's always there when I need it and can be counted on to put my mind at ease.*

She laughs at the absurdity of her truth but at the same time begins crying, crying that turns into sobs. It is the emptying of a soul that has lived a life walled off from intimacy and a sense of security.

When her sobs finally subside, and she feels hollow inside, she surprises herself by saying, *God, if you are real, then you know Teddy and how much he loves you. I'm not asking anything for myself because I for sure don't deserve anything, but if you can see how much Teddy needs this miracle, then please make it happen for him.*

After dressing and stepping out of the bathroom, she discovers Teddy sitting up in bed. "Good morning," she says, trying to sound cheerful. "How did you sleep last night?"

A smile creases his face. "Like a baby. I guess I was so exhausted from everything that I just passed out. What about you?"

"How do you do that?"

"Do what?"

"Sleep so well when you know the next day is something you've looked forward to for decades?"

Patting the foot of his bed, he answers, "Have a seat, sister." When she obliges, he continues, "When I was in prison, I stayed eaten up with fear every second of every day because at any moment I could be assaulted. I'd lay awake all night dreading what the morrow might bring. Thankfully, though, I crossed paths with an old man who taught me a better way, a way that is simply stated but hard to practice. He told me to live in the moment because it's the only moment we have."

Maggie finds herself hanging on his every word, hoping that she might learn something from her lost brother that can deliver her from the plague of sleepless nights she's had since she was a child. "It sounds like the AA adage of 'one day at a time.'"

Teddy nods. "Very similar, but to live in the moment means you break your day down into moments, sometimes seconds. For instance, this moment right here, right now, with me and you talking in this room, is the only moment that matters because it's the only moment that exists. He holds her eyes with his as a second or two of time pass, then says, "And now that moment is gone, and here we are at another. There is no past, and there is no future. Only the present exists."

She tries to take his words into her heart, desperately wanting them to make a difference in her, but her cynical side pushes them aside as foolish and trite. Deep inside her chest, she feels a pain that she interprets as a tug-of-war between these two sides of herself—the side that wants to believe there's a better way of life and the other that says the way she has been is the way she will always be. As Teddy's eyes search her face, she wonders if he can see her inner turmoil or if her practiced mask is still intact.

"You know, sis, all those years that I thought about what kind of family I came from, I envisioned it as a perfect family with people whose lives were filled with happiness and contentment. Now, though, I've met my family, and I know that is not true. You've been sad your whole life, and that breaks my heart."

Warm tears trickle down Maggie's cheeks, and she swipes at them with the back of her hand. "When I first met you, Teddy, I thought I had met a tortured soul, a soul battling demons. I was the professional, and you were the one in need of help, but the opposite was true. Look at me now, figuratively sitting at the feet of a wise man who is trying to help me find a way out of my sadness. It's a stroke of irony that belongs in a book of fiction because things like this don't happen in real life."

"Or maybe they do," he answers. "But you're giving me way too much credit when you call me wise. Nobody's ever thought that about me. I'm only sharing with you what I've learned along the way. And I'll be honest, this whole 'living in the moment' takes lots of practice before it finally works and makes a difference, and I do mean lots of practice."

She leans in and kisses him on his cheek. "I love you, Teddy, and I love the person you've become. How lucky for me to have finally met you."

He puts his palm up and shakes his head.

"I know, I know," she says, "you don't believe in luck. Well, whatever brought us together, I'm glad of it."

His eyes sparkle as he says, "Me, too!"

Clearing her throat, Maggie says, "Now then, I'm going to go get us some breakfast things from the lobby and bring them to the room. And after we eat we'll set out on the last leg of this search for Ada."

Chapter Thirty-Nine

Even though she maintains what she hopes is a calm exterior, Maggie's heart races like a greyhound as she and Teddy get closer to the address she found for Ada. The address was unfamiliar to Teddy, but he admitted he never really knew what the family's actual farm address was.

"You know," he suddenly says, "this is looking familiar. Do you think she still lives on the farm?"

"It's possible." She hesitates before bringing up an idea she's been mulling over. "Teddy, I was thinking that perhaps it would be good if I went to the door by myself and just let her know what this is all about. You've got to realize that you've been thinking about this for a while, but it is going to catch her completely off guard. There's no telling what her reaction might be. I just want to feel her out and give her some background on your situation."

"You going to tell her about me being in prison?"

"No, no, nothing like that. That kind of stuff is up to you to tell. I'll explain to her how our paths crossed and our discovery that we are brother and sister. I think it's fair that I tell her how sick you are, so she won't be expecting you to look like you did all those years ago, if that's okay with you."

He's quiet for a moment, then says, "Yeah, I guess you're right. I sometimes forget that I look like death warmed over or like death on two legs." He laughs at his own description.

"Don't say that."

"Why not? It's the truth. Come on, Maggie, I could get a job at a Halloween carnival looking like I do." Suddenly, he stares ahead and points. "I know that place. It was where a neighbor lived. Ada is still living on the family farm; I just know it. I bet your directions say we turn to the right a mile and a half up the road."

Maggie looks at the piece of paper in her hand. "You're right."

The air inside the cramped space of her car crackles with the electricity of their mutual apprehension and excitement.

Slow breaths, Maggie, slow breaths, she tells herself, trying to calm her nerves.

"Turn in right here," Teddy says, pointing to a driveway that leads to a frame house bordered by what Maggie assumes are long barns on each side.

She parks her car and looks at Teddy, whose eyes are closed. *I can't imagine the thoughts and feelings swirling in him.* Gently squeezing his arm, she says, "It's going to be okay, Teddy. Cross your fingers."

"No need to do that," he says as he opens his eyes. "I've said my prayer. God's in charge now."

She exits the car, walks to the front door of the house, and knocks.

After a few moments, the door opens slowly and reveals a woman in a wheelchair. The small features of her face are framed by thick, chestnut hair with streaks of gray in it. Her eyes are the darkest brown Maggie has ever seen.

Looking up at Maggie with a pleasant smile, the woman says, "May I help you?"

"Good morning. My name is Maggie Stinson, and I was looking for Ada Lane, or at least that used to be her last name."

"That would be me. I'm Ada Lane." A wary look casts a shadow over her face.

"Don't worry; I'm not here to sell you anything or to proselytize you to a religion. I would like to ask you if you remember someone named Israel McKenzie."

The wary look falls away and is replaced by an expression of excitement mixed with wistfulness. "Israel McKenzie . . . most assuredly I do remember him. Don't we always remember our first love?"

Maggie feels a measure of relief that, first of all, she's found the correct Ada but also that Ada remembers Teddy and that she doesn't react angrily to the memory of him.

Ada asks, "Is Israel someone that you know, too?"

"Actually, I'm his sister."

"But that can't be. Israel went to an orphanage when he was a baby."

"I know. I remember when he was taken from us."

Shock registers on Ada's face.

Maggie asks, "Do you mind if we go inside? There are some things that I think you'll be interested in hearing."

Ada rolls her chair backward. "Yes, please come in."

Once inside, Maggie decides not to question Ada about her feelings and memories of Teddy, but instead, she tells her that she and Teddy found each other via her work. She does not mention the kind of work she does or how sick Teddy is, deciding to save that until later in the conversation. *I don't want her to change how she feels about Teddy just because she feels sorry for him because he's dying.*

"Wow, Israel is still alive," Ada says thoughtfully and in a half voice. "I've often wondered what became of him." She then launches into telling her version of her brief time with Israel, concluding with, "I knew he was fighting demons, not all of which did he share with me. When I told him I was pregnant, I think it excited him but also scared him to death." All of a sudden, she looks at Maggie as if she's startled. "But why on earth are you here? Why did you try to find me?"

Maggie treads carefully. "It's because he wants to see you."

All the blood drains from Ada's face. "Israel wants to see me, after all these years? Why? Where has he been?"

"I'll let him explain those things to you, but first of all, you must know that Teddy is dying."

"Teddy?"

"I forget that you know him as Israel. His real name is Teddy Stinson. I'm a social worker with a hospice agency, or at least I was until I quit my job and brought Teddy on this quest to find you. He has liver cancer and doesn't have very long to live."

Ada glances at the front door. "Israel, er, Teddy is here with you, outside in the car? I can't let him see me like this." She fusses with her hair while she looks down at her simple T-shirt and jeans. "He doesn't remember me like this." Tapping the arm of the wheelchair with the base of her palm, she says, "This became a necessity a few years ago. When we knew each other, I still got around pretty good."

"You look beautiful, Ada," Maggie says with sincerity. "Israel doesn't look like he used to either, especially now that he's so sick. He describes himself as a scarecrow, and that's a pretty apt description."

"Why didn't he come to the door with you?"

"I was afraid you wouldn't want to see him because you were angry and resentful for him abandoning you when you needed him the most. I wanted to sort of feel you out first."

"Angry and resentful? For having been with the most amazing man I've ever met? Never. Sadness, that's what I felt when I realized he'd gone. Sadness that he didn't trust our love to be strong enough to overcome whatever obstacles might lie before us."

"And there's no one else in your life, another husband, perhaps?"

Ada looks deep into Maggie's eyes. "How could I ever marry someone else when I was in love with Isra . . . Teddy? I've never stopped loving him."

The image of Ada blurs as tears spring up in Maggie's eyes. A warm feeling spreads through her, and she mutters, "Maybe miracles do come true."

"What's that?"

"Oh, nothing. Just sort of thinking out loud. I can't tell you how happy all this makes me. Is it okay if I go get Teddy and bring him in?"

"I'm scared."

"That's okay. So is he."

Chapter Forty

Teddy tries to read Maggie's face as she approaches the car, hoping she has good news but fearing it is bad. However, she has on her professional mask that gives no hint of what she thinks or feels. Not until she opens his door and breaks into a big smile does he feel a sense of relief. "Is it her? Does she remember me? Does she hate me? How did it go?"

"Slow down, little brother; it's all good. This is going to go well for you—I almost guarantee it. Come on, let me help you." She extends her hand toward him.

Reaching toward her, he puts his cold hand into the warmth of her grip and sees that she has been crying. He lets her pull him to a standing position, takes a moment to get his legs under him, and walks with her toward the front door of the house.

She stops and says, "You're on your own from here. Ada is inside, waiting."

"But why aren't you going inside with me?"

"This is something you need to do on your own. It's your chapter to write. I'm just going to walk around and look at the farm and see how much it resembles the one you've described to me." She gives him a hug and a kiss on the cheek and leaves him standing alone.

The relief that Teddy felt when Maggie smiled at him is now swamped by a tidal wave of nervousness. *Lord God in heaven, if I ever needed you to give me strength and to guide my tongue, it's now. Don't let me down.*

As soon as he steps inside the house, he's struck by how similar everything looks compared to how it looked the last time he was there. Even the smells are the same. He makes a turn and spies Ada sitting in a wheelchair, looking at him.

For several seconds, time stands still as they gaze at each other from a distance. The wheelchair means nothing to him, for it is her eyes, those dark, mysterious eyes, that he is fixated on—until she smiles at him. And then light and warmth fill the room, time resumes its march, and they move toward each other, she rolling herself along and he walking slowly and carefully. "Ada."

"Israel—or I understand it's Teddy now."

He stops when he's three feet from her. "You can call me anything you'd like." He watches her as she looks him up and down. "Quite a difference from when you last saw me, isn't it?" he says.

"The same could be said about me."

"I feel like I'm in a dream. I'm afraid to touch you for fear the dream will dissolve into nothingness, and I don't think I could deal with that much disappointment." As he speaks he feels emotion pushing up into his throat, threatening to cut off his voice. With difficulty, he gets on his knees in front of her, bends down, and kisses her feet.

He feels her hands on his head and hears her say, "My dear, sweet Teddy."

It is too much for him. His emotions erupt from behind a stone sepulcher where they've lain since the day he left from there. He hugs her legs and pushes his face into her feet as he sobs her name over and over. Eventually, he lifts his face toward hers and says, "Please forgive me, Ada. What I did was so wrong. I just ran because that's all I knew to do."

She finds his hands and pulls. "Come closer, Teddy."

He shifts to the side of her wheelchair, resting on one knee so that he is at eye level with her.

"You have nothing to apologize for, but I know that doesn't matter to you, so let me say to you that I forgive you. I forgave you the day I discovered you'd gone. I understood why you left, and I don't blame you."

Her words of mercy wrap around him like a cloak, and he takes in the blessing of them. "And that's just one of the reasons I loved you so much. You were the kindest, most loving person I had ever known, no, have *ever* known. There's hardly a day that has passed since then that I haven't thought of you. Every night as I lay in prison—"

A look of horror springs to her face as she covers her open mouth with her hand.

"Yes," he says, "I was in prison for a long, long time. I will tell you about it if you want me to. But the point is, it was the memory of you that helped me survive. I imagined us living together, working this farm and raising our child." A thought hits him. "Oh my gosh! Our child! Did you have the baby? Was it a boy or a girl? Where are they?"

As if on cue, he hears the back door close and someone walking through the kitchen.

"Mom?" a man's voice calls.

"I'm in the living room," Ada calls back.

A tall, lean, and tanned young man strolls into the room. "We're going to have a really good crop of—" He stops midsentence when he sees Teddy. "I'm sorry—I didn't know you had company."

Teddy grips the arm of Ada's wheelchair to help himself to a standing position.

Ada reaches toward her son and says, "Come here, Israel, there's someone I want you to meet."

Teddy looks at her, confused. *She's gotten our names all mixed up.*

She speaks to Teddy. "This is my son, Israel."

"How do you do, sir." Israel offers to shake Teddy's hand, but Teddy can only manage to stare at him in shock. Israel looks down at his mother. "Am I supposed to know him?"

"You've never met him, but you've heard about him your whole life."

Israel looks more purposefully at Teddy, and slowly a knowing comes over his face. "You're . . . ?"

"Yes," Ada says. "He's your father."

A deep furrow appears between his eyes. "So you're the asshole who left my mother after you got her pregnant! You deserted us and never looked back."

"Israel!" Ada says sharply.

Teddy feels as if someone has run a spear through him.

"It's true!" Israel says to her. "I've got nothing to say to him." Spinning around, he storms out of the house.

The slamming back door echoes through the house like a rifle shot.

"I've got to sit down," Teddy says, feeling his knees about to buckle.

"Quick, go lie on the couch."

Feeling too weak to argue, he follows her direction. Lying there with his eyes closed, he feels the bile of shame in the back of his throat. *He's right. I am an asshole. He gave me exactly what I deserve. It's probably what Ada wanted to say, but she's too nice.*

"Here, drink this," he hears Ada say.

He opens his eyes and takes a glass from her. He takes a sip and immediately coughs and feels his eyes burn.

She laughs. "Taste familiar?"

"It's your famous apple cider." He takes a few more sips and smiles. "Tastes as good as ever, maybe even better."

"I want to apologize for Israel. He's usually not like that."

"It's okay. He had a right to say everything he said. I deserved it."

*****

An hour and a half later, Teddy and Ada, with red-rimmed eyes, exit the house through the front door and are both surprised to see Israel and Maggie, standing beside her car, engaged in what looks to be a serious conversation. They turn to face the approaching handicapped couple.

The four of them meet halfway between the house and the car.

Israel looks with concern at his mother. "Are you okay, Mom?"

"I've never been better."

He shifts his attention to Teddy. "I want to apologize for how I acted earlier."

Teddy waves off his comment. "That's not necessary. I don't blame you for how you feel."

Israel gives Maggie a quick glance.

"Go ahead," she says to him.

"I said what I said because I didn't know the whole truth. I only had a tiny piece of it." Nodding at Maggie, he continues, "Miss Maggie here helped me learn more of the truth." He looks squarely at Teddy. "I'm sorry you had it so hard growing up. I had no idea . . ."

"That's no excuse for how I acted," Teddy inserts.

"Maybe not," Israel says, "but it sure does explain things. I admire you for coming here and trying to make things right. It was a very brave thing to do." He offers his hand.

Teddy takes it and shakes it. "Thank you. I'm glad I got to meet you. Whatever you do, don't let who I was define who you are. Be your own person. Be a man."

"I will, sir."

He turns to Ada. "Goodbye, Ada, my love. Don't be afraid to let yourself love again, to take a chance."

"I still wish you would stay with me," she replies.

A series of ragged coughs is the only answer Teddy can manage.

When he looks as if he's about to lose his balance, Maggie and Israel grab him and hold him up. After his coughing stops, he says, "My end is coming very soon, Ada."

She replies, "Then you could stay until . . ."

"Can't do that. I've got other things I want to make right before I die. I've got Maggie here to help me and to take care of me."

Ada embraces him, and they kiss, a kiss that will be their last.

Looking at Maggie, he says, "Let's go, sis."

He and Maggie drive in silence for a few miles before he says, "Thank you, Maggie. I would never have been able to do that without you."

"You're welcome, Teddy. I'm honored that I could be with you. You are a good man."

Instead of rebuffing her words, he lets them knit together the tattered pieces of his heart.

After she pauses, she takes a loud breath. "I've decided I'm going to tell you something about me. Something I did a long time ago."

Chapter Forty-One

On the drive back to the motel, Maggie searches for the best way to explain to Teddy the chapter of her life that led to the burying of her stillborn baby. Like a great tsunami, a rising tide of suppressed emotions—shame, embarrassment, guilt, self-loathing—starts in her belly and pushes up into her chest, triggering a rapid heartbeat and shallow breaths. *How can I tell him what happened without sounding like a monster of some kind? But I am a monster. No one does something like that unless they are unhinged. I'm just going to tell exactly what happened and let him decide for himself how to feel about me.*

About to hyperventilate, she sneaks a quick look at him before launching into the story. She discovers that he's fast asleep, head tilted back against the headrest, mouth open in a soft snore *How could I not realize how exhausted he must be?*

She tries to imagine what it would be like to have righted a wrong from the past, what deep peace and satisfaction that would bring.

Getting Teddy from the car to the motel room proves much more difficult than she expected, mostly because he barely rises to a conscious level and can't walk without lots of assistance from her. Thankfully, their room is on the first floor, and the lobby is empty as they pass through it.

When she releases her hold on him at the side of his bed, he silently collapses onto it like the bag of bones he is. She slips his shoes, pants, and shirt off him, knowing full well that he'll probably raise a ruckus with her about it when he realizes what happened. Despite her efforts to not pry with her eyes, she can't help but stare at how emaciated his body is. As she pulls the covers up and tucks them around his shoulders, she wonders with sadness if this is going to be the end. *Will he ever wake up again? Now that he's accomplished his dream of making things right with Ada, is there any reason for him to keep living?* Then it dawns on her—the comment he made just before leaving Ada's house that there is something else he wants to make right.

Her head is full of imaginings as to what that "something else" is as she lies down on her bed to rest. Like a merry-go-round, her thoughts circle around and around but never go anywhere until she finally falls asleep.

*****

For two days Maggie sits in the motel with Teddy, listening to his breathing grow shallower and shallower. A few times she gently shakes his shoulder in an effort to rouse him from his slumber, but all that produces is a semiconscious state so that she can at least try to slip some liquids into his mouth. Most of it, though, spills onto his chin and cheeks until she finally decides there is no point in it.

It's a familiar stage she's seen in her work with hospice patients. They are exhausted with the effort of continuing to fight whatever disease has ravaged their bodies, and they are ready to let go of life. She hears her voice telling the family members, who desperately want their loved one to hang on a little longer, "It's time, time for you all to say goodbye and let go. Let them know you're okay, that they don't have to be here for you any longer, that it's okay for them to move on to whatever awaits them on the other side."

However, this is the first time she's had to say goodbye to someone whom she doesn't want to leave. *Just another reason not to believe in God: at the time I finally have family, they die on me. There is just nothing fair about this life.*

She braces herself, takes a deep breath, and eases herself onto the edge of Teddy's bed. She lightly touches the back of her hand across his brow and on both sides of his face; then, taking his hand, she says, "Teddy, this is your sister, Maggie, your long-lost sister, Maggie." Her voice catches in her throat, and she coughs to clear it. "I know you're tired and ready to take leave of this earth. I don't blame you. It's a pretty shitty place to live a lot of the time. I can't tell you how much joy it has brought to me that we discovered each other. It's just rotten luck that it didn't happen until you were so sick." She brushes a tear off her cheek.

Suddenly, Teddy says, "But if I hadn't been so sick, you never would have come to see me."

She stares at him, dumbfounded. His eyes are still closed, so for a moment, she thinks she is hearing things.

But then he says, "Got no answer to that one, do you?" Slowly, his eyes open, and a thin smile creases his features.

Maggie blinks rapidly and swears in disbelief. "What's going on? Am I hallucinating, or are you really talking to me?"

"It's really me, sis. You don't happen to have any beanie weenies sitting around, do you?"

She grabs him and hugs him tightly. "Oh, Teddy, I thought you were about to die at any minute, that I would never see you again."

"Well, if you're not careful, you're going to squeeze what's left of my life out of me."

Releasing her hold on him, she wipes the tears of joy from her face and laughs. "You're just full of surprises, aren't you? You beat all, Teddy. Seconds ago, I was wiping tears of sadness, and now these same eyes are leaking tears of happiness."

"What made you think I was going to die? We just got back from Ada's, didn't we?"

She shakes her head and lays her hand on his arm. "You've been mostly unconscious ever since we left her house two days ago."

His eyes open wide. "Two days ago? How's that possible? It feels like I just woke from a nap."

Opening a small bottle of apple juice that was sitting on the nightstand, she puts one hand behind his head and lifts. "Here, you need to drink this. You've barely eaten or drank anything." She watches him as he manages several swallows. "Good job. Now, I'm going to run and try to find you some of those beanie weenies you love. Will you do me a favor?"

"Sure."

"Don't die while I'm gone." This produces the chuckle from him that she hoped it would.

As she starts to get up, he takes hold of her wrist and looks at her intently.

When he doesn't say anything, she asks, "What is it?"

"I know you don't believe in God like I do; I even understand why. But can't you see his hand in all this? Who in this whole wide world would have gone to the trouble to help me find Ada, except you? God wanted to answer my prayer to find her, but the only way he could work it out for us to find each other was for me to go to that orphanage and meet Darnell. That way I could move close to where you live. And the only way to get you to come see me in my trailer was for me to get cancer and begin to die. It's all part of his plan so that the worst things that have ever happened to me were the best things." He squeezes her wrist. "Can't you see that?"

Twice, she opens her mouth to speak and then closes it before she finally says, "I want to see it like you do. I really do. There's no alternative explanation I can give for all of this except to use the word *luck* or *coincidence*, which I know you don't believe in. And the truth is, our coming together goes beyond just luck and coincidence. But I've been mad at God for so long that I just can't make myself believe he's behind all this. I can't get past how there's so much evil and pain and suffering in this world." She sees tears pool in his eyes. "It breaks my heart to see how hurtful my words are, but I'm not going to lie to you just because I know it's what you want to hear. Can you forgive me for that?"

He lets go of her, and his hand drops to the bed. "'Be honest with me,' that's one of the first things I told you that first day we met. So I'll say thank you for telling me the truth even if it's not what I want to hear. Forgive you? There's nothing to forgive. I hope I didn't make you mad by trying to push and persuade you to see what I see. It's just that . . ."

She waits for him to finish his thought, but he falls silent. She spins through her mind to try to figure out what it is he wants to say, but there are too many possibilities to choose from. In an effort to encourage him, she nods and says, "Go ahead—tell me."

He swallows noticeably and says, "I want to see you again when I get to where I'm going. I want us to be together forever."

Nothing he could have said could have penetrated her heart through like these words. Leaning over and kissing his forehead, she says, "That is the sweetest thing I have ever heard in my entire life, and I love you even more because of it. But even if I believed in your God, even he couldn't save me from all the bad things I've done. You just don't know . . ." She trails off as she remembers what she had intended to tell him before he fell silent these past two days.

He closes his eyes and nods. "I understand that feeling all too well." Then he opens his eyes and looks at her. "But what I learned is that you can't out-sin God's forgiveness. That's how deep and wide his love is."

This stuns her, as it's a concept she's never heard before. But instead of pausing, taking it in, and thinking about it, she pushes it to the side and says, "I'll be back with your food as quickly as I can." Without waiting for a response, she heads out of the room.

Chapter Forty-Two

Maggie returns to the motel room, carrying a plastic grocery bag in each hand, and finds Teddy propped up in bed, watching TV.

"Do you have any idea how many TV channels there are out there? My lord, at the orphan's home, we only had three channels to choose from." Waving the remote control in the air, he adds, "And with this little thing right here, you can change channels without ever getting out of your chair." He flips through the channels, looking at each one for a few seconds before switching to another.

It dawns on Maggie that he didn't have a TV in his trailer. Emptying the contents of the grocery bags on a table in the room, she says, "Have you not had a TV since you got out of prison?"

"Nope. Never saw the need to. Matter of fact, I haven't watched TV since I was in the orphan's home."

"So what did you do to entertain yourself?"

With his eyes still glued to the TV, he replies, "I like to read."

She remembers the stacks and stacks of papers and magazines in his trailer. With a can of beanie weenies and a plastic spoon in one hand and a small bottle of juice in the other, she walks over to him and gives him a wry smile. "Do you think you can peel your eyes away from the TV long enough to eat?"

He points the remote at the TV, and the screen goes dark. Shaking his head slowly, he says, "Watching that thing, it's like it hypnotizes you. I've read articles about how watching it can be bad for you, and now I see why."

He reaches for the bottle of juice she offers him and begins drinking, so she sets the can and spoon on the bedside table. She then takes a seat in the only chair in the room and opens the Rand McNally road atlas she just bought.

"What are you reading?" he asks.

"I'm looking at some road maps."

"Don't you remember the way home?"

She nods absentmindedly but doesn't answer him.

"Hey!"

The insistent tone in his voice pulls her away from the atlas, and she looks over at him. "What's wrong?"

"Nothing's wrong with me. What's wrong with you? You act like you didn't even hear me. What's so interesting over there?"

Turning her chair to face him, she says, "How would you like to see where you were born?"

His mouth falls open, and he stares at her. "Really? You mean it?"

"The only time we have left, Teddy, is this time right here, right now. I don't know what's going to happen tomorrow, and neither do you. You might die tonight. Hell, I might die tonight of a heart attack. I just think we need to use whatever time we have left doing the things that are important, that would be meaningful. Why go back to your place and sit around waiting for you to die? It came to me while I was out shopping that you might like going to the place where we lived when you were a baby."

He gives her a big grin. "I love the way you think, sis. 'Live in the moment'—I told you that's what I learned in prison. You really think you can find the place? I mean, it's been a long time."

"That's why I was looking at the road atlas, to see if I could figure out if the town has grown much since we were there. Looks like Waynesville is still the small place it used to be. I'm sure I can find the street. Whether or not the house is still standing is another matter." It suddenly hits her that the house probably burned down when she set her father on fire the night she left. *How stupid to get so excited about an idea that I forgot something so important! Now what do I do? Should I just go ahead and tell him now?* She hasn't made her mind up about telling him that detail of her history. Telling him about burying her baby? Yes, she's decided she will do that, but what she did to their dad . . . she just isn't sure.

Teddy breaks into her thoughts when he asks, "What's going on in that head of yours?"

Taking a deep breath, she says, "This idea of going to Indiana was a spur-of-the-moment kind of thing, and that's not how I usually do things. I like to plan them out first."

"You're a planner, are you?"

She nods in agreement and averts her eyes from his face.

"What are you hiding, Maggie? You know it's okay to tell me, don't you? I mean, who am I going to tell, Saint Peter?"

She can't help but smile at his wry joke. "Okay, I'm going to tell you something that no one on the face of this earth knows. But beware that it might change how you think of me. The truth, though, is that I'm not ashamed of what I did. Maybe I should be, but I'm not. You'll decide for yourself about that part of it."

Patting the edge of his bed, he says, "Please, come sit beside me. I want you close to me when you tell me. It's easier to tell a thing when you have someone to listen to you who really cares about you. I'm going to tell you plainly that no matter what you tell me, I'm still going to love you. Nothing will ever change that."

Without warning, tears fill her eyes. Although she's said similar things to people many times through the years, it never came close to the sincerity with which Teddy expresses himself. "I don't think I've ever had anyone in my life who felt that way about me, maybe because I never let anyone get close to me. But still . . ." She can't find the words to finish her thought.

As she sits on the edge of his bed, she feels her heart racing, and she places her hand on her chest and pushes against it.

"Hey, hey, there," Teddy says. "You're not fixing to have a heart attack, are you?"

"No, I'm just nervous, I guess."

"Don't try to find the right words to tell me what happened. Don't edit it. Just spit it out as it comes to you. You're going to feel better when you do. I promise."

For the next thirty minutes, Maggie tells him the background that led to her killing their father—the reign of terror, the repeated sexual abuse, and her ultimate decision to take revenge on him. Teddy sits quietly through it all, alternately weeping openly and taking her hand and kissing it.

As she comes to the end of her story, she says, "The last time I saw him or the house is when I dropped the burning lighter into his lap. After that, I left town and never returned." She suddenly feels exhausted but also like a weight has lifted from her shoulders. Looking at Teddy, she says, "Thank you for hearing that, for just listening without jumping in and judging me. You were right; I do feel better."

He hands her some tissue, and she dabs her tear-stained face with them. She waits to hear his judgment of her.

"I'm so sorry that all of that happened to you, Maggie. It makes me sad, and it makes me angry, too."

"But was I wrong for what I did to him?" she asks.

"It doesn't matter what I think."

"It does to me. I don't know why, but it does."

"How can I sit in judgment on you when I've done nearly the very same thing you did?"

Maggie feels as if her head will burst at this confession. She tries to grasp hold of it and what it must mean, but it is like trying to hold dry sand in her fist; it keeps slipping between her fingers. The only thoughts that come to her are half questions with monosyllabic answers that make no sense.

"Hard to know what to say back to that, isn't it?" he asks. "Well, it's true. I killed my adoptive father, the one we called Sir. Or, really, me and my adopted sister did. She tried to kill him by spiking a drink with a bunch of nerve pills. But when we started moving him, we discovered he was still alive. That's when I garroted him."

"Oh my . . ." Maggie is finally able to speak. "I would never have dreamed you . . . I mean, you're such a gentle soul; I just can't imagine you being able to do something like that."

"Well, you know what? Sometimes things happen that harden you and put an edge on you. A person can just take so much."

Swallowing as she nods, she says, "I completely understand that. It's what happened to me. I just couldn't take it anymore, and I didn't want it to happen to anyone else, at least not by his hands."

"Exactly. That's the same reason we put an end to Sir. Sort of a death to the tyrant, if you know what I mean."

She takes a deep breath and exhales. "Whew! The more we get to know each other, the more we find how alike we are and how similar our lives have been."

"And the first time we met, we would never have dreamed all this about each other."

"It's like I've known you all these years, not just these past few days. So now, do you still care anything about going to Indiana?"

"Absolutely! This is what people call a road trip, isn't it?"

She laughs. "Yes, it is. On to our next adventure!"

Chapter Forty-Three

That same night, Maggie lies awake sorting through all that she and Teddy revealed to each other. *It's really true, all that social work stuff I used to say to people—unburdening yourself to someone you trust can make you feel better. "Unconditional positive regard," Professor West used to call it. I just never . . .* She searches for the truth. *I just never let myself get that close to anyone to find out if I could trust them.*

She turns her head and sees Teddy's sleeping form in the other bed. *Is it possible that there is a God who made all this happen so that we could find each other?*

She replays her conversation with Teddy, stopping at the juncture when he said you can't out-sin God's forgiveness. *Why have I never heard that idea before? Could it really be true? Is God someone who wants to help people and wants to forgive them, rather than the mean-looking, bearded being who sits in heaven throwing thunderbolts at people, the God that I've hated all my life?*

Not for the first time in the last twenty-four hours, she feels pain between her shoulder blades that pushes through to her chest, the same feeling she had when she had her heart attack. She tries to brush away all the questions and disturbing thoughts and focus entirely on relaxing her body, doing her controlled breathing and visualization exercise. When fear and anxiety try to push their way forward, she treats them as if they are fried eggs on a Teflon skillet and slides them off into the trash. Speaking directly to her heart muscle, she says, *Calm and easy, that's the path you need to take. Turn loose of your tension, open up your valves, welcome and push through the life-giving blood. It's not time for you to give up yet. There's more we need to accomplish.*

I'm sorry I haven't taken care of you like I should have. All I'm asking for is just a little more time.

"I'm praying for you, sis."

Teddy's voice comes to her as if it were a disembodied apparition, floating in her thoughts.

"I'm praying God will give us a few more days."

This time the voice seems more real, and she pulls herself out of her self-imposed semiconscious state. "Teddy," she says softly, "was that you?" She holds her breath, waiting for his reply. But all she hears is the sound of passing traffic outside. Pushing herself up on one elbow, she peers through the darkness at him. "Teddy?" she says, a tiny bit louder. Again, there is no reply.

Resting her head back on her pillow, she notices that the pain in her chest has dissipated. *What in the world just happened?*

*****

Maggie lies in the bottom of a small, aluminum fishing boat as it gently rocks back and forth. There is the hypnotic sound of small waves lapping at the sides of the boat, and a breeze brushes across her face, bringing with it the fragrance of coffee. *Coffee?*

She extricates herself from her dream world and opens her eyes to find Teddy pushing on her shoulder and holding a cup of coffee in front of her.

"You going to sleep all day?" he asks.

"Huh? Where am I? What time is it?"

"Boy, you were deep in a dream, weren't you? It's close to ten thirty, and we're still in Wheeling, West Virginia."

Sitting up in bed, Maggie rubs her eyes, then takes the proffered cup of coffee. "Ten thirty in the morning? Why didn't you wake me up?"

"You were sleeping so well I didn't have the heart to, but then I got worried that something might be wrong with you." Nodding at the cup of coffee as she sips it, he says, "Made it from the stuff they leave in the rooms. Don't know if it's any good or not."

She closes her eyes and enjoys the feeling of the warm liquid going down her throat. "Ah, it's wonderful. But I need to get up and get ready. We're supposed to be on our way to Indiana."

"How long a drive is it?"

"The best I can figure, about five hours to where we're going."

After cleaning Teddy's colostomy bag, they head out of town, grabbing some lunch along the way. As before, Teddy spends most of the drive sleeping, so Maggie keeps the radio turned down and focuses on enjoying the countryside.

But when she sees the city limits sign for Waynesville, she speaks to him. "Teddy, can you wake up? We're in Waynesville."

He raises the back of the seat from the reclining position it has been in and looks around. "This is the town we lived in when I was born?"

"Yes, but remember, you were only here for a little while."

"Does it look familiar to you?"

"Amazingly so. I guess it's like the rural towns back in Tennessee—nothing much changes from decade to decade." She points to an old two-story brick building. "That's my high school." She slows and reads a sign in front. "But it looks like they've turned it into government offices."

Like a homing pigeon running on some sort of biological GPS, she turns on her blinker as she approaches an intersection. An eerie feeling comes over her, and she shudders.

"Okay?" Teddy asks.

"Yeah. I just had a weird feeling. I guess I didn't think about what it would feel like to travel these streets again."

She makes a couple more turns, and it's apparent they've moved into the poorer section of town—houses with peeling paint, abandoned houses with broken windows, a burned-out car sitting on the side of the street.

Suddenly, she takes her foot off the gas and lets the car coast. Shock hits her hard as she stares in disbelief at their old house still standing exactly where it had been when she left. The screen door hangs on one hinge, and there are tiny seedlings growing in the stopped-up gutters running along the eaves.

"Is that it there?" Teddy asks, pointing in the direction she's looking.

She nods.

"Who do you suppose the old man is that's sitting under that big ol' elm tree?"

"I don't know," Maggie whispers.

The car rolls to a stop in the middle of the street, right in front of the house. Unable to think, Maggie sits, staring.

"What do you want to do, sis? Want to see if this guy remembers the family? Or we can just drive on if you want to."

Robotlike, she pulls into the broken and pitted concrete driveway. They exit the car and make their way across the yard.

Even though it is late afternoon and the yard is shaded, the white-haired man is wearing sunglasses. Cocking his head to one side as they approach, he says, "Whatever you're selling, I'm not buying. And if you're a Jehovah's Witness, you can get the hell out of my yard."

At the sound of his voice, Maggie instantly feels nauseated. She's flooded with memories of smells and sounds. It's when they get close to the man that she sees the scars on his hands, arms, and face—scars from being burned.

Teddy speaks up. "My family used to live in this neighborhood a long time ago. Haven't been back since I was a kid."

"What's your name?" the man asks.

"Uh . . . Israel McKenzie. Did you know the family who lived in this house?"

"I should. I've lived here for fifty years."

"Seems like I heard about a fire in the house," Teddy says.

"Oh yeah, there was a fire, all right. The whole house would have burned down if somebody hadn't heard me screaming and ran in and threw a quilt over me and smothered out the flames."

"So you were set on fire?"

"What do you think these scars are about?" He lifts his sunglasses and reveals that his eyelids are sealed shut by the skin that melted that night. "Damned cigarettes, that's what caused it. I fell asleep smoking."

An awkward silence fills the air.

He turns his head toward Maggie. "Who's the silent one there with you? I heard two people walking toward me."

Maggie feels like running away and like stabbing him through the heart and, in spite of herself, a sense of pity. Her childhood monster has been castrated and reduced to living in his own darkness, a darkness that she caused. She feels Teddy looking at her but doesn't know what to say to her father. What do you say when you face the dragon? She finally says, "I'm just a friend."

Her father cocks his head. "Do I know you? Your voice sounds familiar."

Above them, the air crackles as a bolt of lightning splits the sky, followed by an explosion of thunder.

The trio jumps, and Maggie screams.

"Didn't know it was going to rain," her father says, pushing himself to his feet. "You all come on in the house, and we can talk some more."

She looks at Teddy and shakes her head vehemently.

"Thanks," he says, "but we're going to be on our way."

Chapter Forty-Four

Maggie's hands tremble as she grasps the steering wheel and tries to start her car. Teddy reaches over and puts his hand over her hand that holds the keys. She looks at it, then at him.

"It's going to be okay, sis. He can't hurt you anymore."

"I just never expected . . ."

"Yeah, I know. You thought he died in the fire, but he survived it so that he could live in the hell he's been in for the past fifty years. I'd say he still got what he deserved. Right now, though, we need to find a motel to spend the night in. You don't need to drive anymore today. Would Columbus be the closest place to find one?"

Thankful to have something objective to focus on and for Teddy for giving it to her, she says, "Yes, it would be." She cranks the engine, backs out of the driveway, and heads out of town.

At the first exit on the outskirts of Columbus that advertises motels, she pulls off and chooses a Hampton Inn.

As soon as they get in their room, she says, "I've got to talk about what happened back there in Waynesville."

Lying down on one of the beds and putting his hands behind his head, Teddy says, "Thought you should, just wasn't sure if you would."

She paces back and forth. "I just can't believe it was him. I mean, it was him—there's no doubt about it. It was his voice; it just wasn't his body. I wanted to run away, and at the same time, I wanted to kill him. And then I felt sorry for him. How crazy is that? How could I feel sorry for someone who did what he did to me?"

"Maybe you saw him from a different perspective than you've had before."

"Tell me, when you looked at him, what did you see?"

"I thought it was a pretty pitiful scene. The house falling in due to neglect, that scarred body of his, and his eyes . . . what can you say about that? Pitiful is the only word I can think of."

Maggie sits down on the other bed. "He did look pitiful, sort of like a mangy dog that needed to be put down, except that people don't do that to their dogs anymore. But right now, I don't feel fear or anger toward him. It's like it all drained away. Do I think he deserved what happened to him? I'll have to say yes, whether that's right or not. One thing for certain, though, is that I'm done with him. All this time I thought he was dead, but he still haunted my dreams. Now, though, I don't think that's going to happen anymore."

"Why not?" Teddy asks.

She thinks about that before answering. "Maybe because I couldn't be certain he was dead, or perhaps because I thought he was going to rise from the grave and come get me." She gives an empty-sounding laugh. "That makes me sound like I'm six years old. Do you ever have nightmares about Sir coming after you?"

"How can a nightmare be any worse than the torture and pain you and I have been through? But no, I never worried about Sir coming after me because I know what happened to him after he died."

"Are you certain?"

"I'm positive. I buried him."

Maggie can't believe her ears. She never imagined she would meet someone who was guilty of the same offense that she was, and she especially never thought Teddy would be. Without intending to, she says, "The Gravediggers."

He rolls onto his side, facing her. "What do you mean?"

She tries to cover by saying, "I just meant that you're known back home as the Gravedigger, but you've dug graves far longer than anyone knows."

"That's true, but you didn't say the *Gravedigger*. You said *Gravediggers*."

She feels like she has crawled out on the proverbial limb, and Teddy has cut it off behind her. There's no way to avoid the truth without lying. *And I'm not going to lie to him.* She flexes her fingers, then clutches her hands together. "What I meant was that you and I are both gravediggers."

He raises his eyebrows. "You mean you've buried a dog or cat, but you can't mean you've buried—"

She cuts in. "I've buried humans, that's plural." She looks for shock or disappointment on his face, but the only thing that changes is a solitary tear that slips from the corner of his eye.

"Sis, you had to have been through some really bad stuff to have done that. I wish I could have been there for you. No, I wish I could have gone through it for you so that you'd have been spared all that pain."

"Don't you want to hear about who I've buried?"

"That's up to you. It doesn't matter to me, but if you need to let it out, I'm listening."

"How can it not matter to you?"

"Because no matter what you've done, no matter what path you've walked, it's not going to change my love for you."

This proves to be too much for Maggie. She feels crushed by the weight of such love, a kind of love she's never known. She wants to push it away from her because it scares her, because part of her tells her it can't be trusted and that it can't be real. Standing up, she moves away from him and begins pacing again. "We'll just see how you feel once you've heard the ugly truth."

And so, she begins and tells him about the affair with Professor Reed, how he jilted her and how she humiliated him, about losing her baby and burying it, and lastly about him finding her and their altercation that resulted in his death. Her clothes are soaked with sweat and her face awash in bitter tears by the time she delivers her final line. "I decided he didn't deserve a decent burial where people would come and praise him for being such a wonderful person, so I buried him in the backyard." She halts her pacing and stands, facing him. "Now what do you think of your wonderful sister?"

"You're really something else, you know it?" he says as he motions for her to sit down beside him. "You walk and talk like you've got your life together and that you've had a pretty straightforward life. People who know you would be shocked to learn what all you've been through and what all you've done."

Shaking her head even as she sits beside him, she says, "If they knew the truth, they would put me in the electric chair."

"Sure, some would, but it also might deepen the admiration and respect that people have for you. You've got a powerful testimony to share with others; it's a story of overcoming. Lots of folks need to hear it, people who feel there's no way to put the pieces of their lives together, that feel trapped by the mistakes of their past, that have given up and have given in to the darkness."

"Do you mean a testimony, like me standing up in a church and telling all this? Ha! Why, the roof would fall in, or God would strike me dead, if I walked into a church. You don't know how many mean and hateful things I've said to him and about him."

Teddy looks toward the ceiling. "Yes, sir, I know, sir. I'm trying."

"Will you just stop that?" Maggie snaps.

"Stop what?"

"This carnival act like God is talking to you." A long moment passes as he looks at her, and she regrets saying what she'd been thinking.

"It's no act," he says. "I'm not exactly sure when it started, maybe sometime while I was in prison, but I heard this voice in my head telling me what to do and say. It's not there all the time, just sometimes it shows up. At first, I thought I was losing my mind, like I had gone crazy, but the voice wasn't telling me to say and do bizarre, stupid stuff. Everything it said made perfect sense. The only explanation I could come up with was that it was God talking to me."

"So what was he telling you just then?"

"He told me that I need to convince you that he loves you, that he's always loved you and will always love you."

Maggie feels as if her heart is being torn in two because of what she longs to believe is true and what she cannot accept. With a feeling of earnestness she's seldom felt, she leans in toward Teddy and says, "Then if he has always loved me, how could he let all those awful things happen to me? What kind of love is that?"

Nodding his head, Teddy replies, "That's the question that trips us all, isn't it? All I can tell you is what I believe about all that, and I'll admit that I might be wrong. I think all the vile and despicable things that you and I have been through are because of Satan. He is the very embodiment of evil, and he wants to destroy us by turning us away from God. On the other hand, what God wants is for us to love him, but not just because he's some kind of 'sugar daddy' who never lets anything bad happen to us and who gives us everything we want. He wants us to love him no matter what happens to us."

"You mean this is some kind of test or a game with him?"

"I don't think it's a game at all. I think it breaks his heart to see what kinds of trials we go through. But a test? Maybe so. Otherwise our love for him is cheap and shallow."

Deep within her, she feels as though an ancient wooden door on rusted hinges creaks open, and beams from a light brighter than the sun shoot through her. She moves toward the light, passing between rows of people whose faces she cannot see. At the source of the light, she sees a smiling face, a face she doesn't recognize, although it seems familiar. As she gets closer, a feeling of utter peace and contentment comes over her, and she smiles. She grasps a hand that is offered her.

Suddenly, she hears a voice in the distance calling her name and feels someone pulling her away from the light.

"Maggie," the voice calls more insistently.

She feels herself being shaken, and she realizes she's moving away from the light. Conflicted over whether she should stay or go, she searches for the source of the voice.

"Maggie, it's me, Teddy. Wake up! Come back! Don't leave me."

Turning her back to the light, Maggie opens her eyes and sees the frantic expression of her brother.

"Oh, Maggie." He throws himself on her, and she realizes she is lying on the floor of the motel room.

Chapter Forty-Five

"What happened?" Maggie asks. "Why am I on the floor?" She starts to sit up, but Teddy pushes down on her shoulders.

"Don't get up, just lie still. At one moment we were talking, and the next you collapsed to the floor. I think you died."

She frowns at him.

Nodding at her, he says, "Yes. You weren't breathing, and I couldn't find a pulse anywhere. I thought"—his voice breaks—"I thought you were gone forever. Did you have a heart attack?"

"I don't know. I don't remember my chest hurting or anything."

"Should I call an ambulance? How do you feel right now?"

"No, don't call an ambulance. I actually feel better than I've felt in a long time. Help me sit up."

He does his best to help her to a sitting position, and she leans against the bed. "Let me get you a drink of water." Without waiting for a response, he shuffles to the bathroom, where she hears the water running, and in a second he returns to her side, cup of water in hand.

"Thank you," she says before emptying the cup in three big gulps.

"If you won't let me call an ambulance, at least let's go to the ER so you can be checked out."

Shaking her head, she takes hold of his arm and says, "No, I'm fine. But I have to tell you what happened while I was passed out or while I was dead or whatever I was."

He gives her a curious look, and she gives him a detailed description of her experience. "Don't know if that's what really happened or if it was just my imagination or something like a dream, or maybe it was what you might call a vision. But I do know this: I believe you now."

He frowns at her. "Believe what?"

"Believe that God is real and that he does love me. Love is what the whole thing—the people around me, the source of light—felt like. My heart feels warm and open and free."

"I've heard of near-death experiences, but I've never known anyone who had one. It gives me goosebumps to hear you describe it."

"Why don't you talk to God like you do and ask him what it was that happened?"

Looking toward the ceiling, Teddy says, "Lord, we're excited and confused. Can you tell me what just happened to Maggie?"

After a moment, he looks back at her, crestfallen.

"What the matter?" she asks. "What did he say?"

"Two things: what happened was what needed to happen to help take the scales off your eyes."

When he doesn't continue, she asks, "And the other thing?"

"He told me my job is finished."

She turns his statement over in her mind. "You mean . . . ?"

"I think so. Looks like it's time for me to go home."

"But I'm not ready for you to go. I don't want to let you go, not yet."

"And I don't want to leave you, but that's not my call to make. It's my turn to go toward the light, except I won't be coming back. First, though, I need you to get a paper and pen and write something down for me."

They rise together and sit down at the small table in their room, where Maggie picks up the complimentary pen and stationery and strikes a pose of readiness to write.

He begins: "I, Israel McKenzie, also known as the Gravedigger, and whose real name is Theodore Stinson, being of sound mind—"

"Stop right there," she says as she puts the pen down. "You're not about to do this right here right now."

"If not now, then when, sis? I don't know when the end is coming, but I want to get this taken care of and make things right before I go." Pointing to the paper, he says, "Do hereby leave to my sister, Maggie Stinson, all my possessions and property. Now start a new paragraph," he instructs her. "I want to confess to the murder and burial of . . ." In an even, measured voice, he recites the name of Sir, where he lived, and the cemetery he is buried in.

When he stops, Maggie looks up at him. "Why do you want to do this?"

"Because it's the right thing to do. My intention was for you to drive me to the police station there so that I could confess in person, but I'm not certain I'll be here long enough for that. Now, give me the paper so I can sign and date it."

She obliges and watches how uneven his handwriting is as he scratches his name across the bottom of the page.

Folding it in half, he hands it back to her. "Make sure this gets to where it needs to go."

With a nod, she accepts it, then reaches for a tissue and blows her nose.

As she does so, he picks up a can of beanie weenies and a plastic spoon and makes his way to his bed. Hoisting the can toward her in a toast, he smiles and says, "Got to have my last supper."

She smiles through her sadness. "You won't do, Teddy."

But when he gets to his bed, he sets the food on the bedside table, lies down, and closes his eyes. With a sigh, he says, "I'm tired, Maggie."

For the rest of the day, she sits and watches him hour by hour as the sound of his breathing grows fainter. The echoes of things she's told the families of dying patients ring in her ears, and she accepts that she must let him go. With a heavy and breaking heart, she takes hold of his hand and says, "Teddy, this is Maggie. Thank you for everything you have taught me. I love you and am going to miss you greatly, but I know you're ready to leave. Thank you for staying long enough to complete your purpose and for finding me and setting me on a path of healing." Leaning down, she kisses both his cheeks.

When she sits back up, his eyes open. "I look forward to seeing you on the other side." And with that, he breathes his last.

Maggie begins crying softly and cradles him to her chest like a baby, rocking back and forth.

With grief, there is no way to measure time because time stops, and so, how long Maggie cries and holds him means nothing to her. Eventually, though, her tears dry, and she eases him onto his pillow and pulls the sheet up over his face.

Grunting as she does so, she gets down on her knees beside his bed. She closes her eyes, rests her forehead against the edge of the mattress, and says, *Lord Jesus, I don't know how to pray, but I want to tell you how much it has meant to me to find my brother. Thank you for bringing us together. And I want to apologize for all the mean and hateful things I've said to you and about you. All I want to do from this day forward is the right thing because I want to be certain I'll be with Teddy after my time here. I'm for sure going to need your help to do that.*

She rises, takes a seat at the table where that morning she had taken dictation from Teddy, and starts to write.

Chapter Forty-Six

Blue and red lights from police cars, an ambulance, and the coroner's van flash through the night sky and against the rain-slickened trees, grass, and surrounding houses. A heavy rain pelts the shiny rain slickers everyone is wearing.

In the backyard of Maggie's home, Police Chief Toby Sanders's attention is focused on two men with shovels, digging through the mud. Turning to his chief investigator, Al Slater, he says, "Tell me the story again."

"It starts in Columbus, Indiana. One of the housekeepers at a Hampton Inn could not get into one of their rooms because it was bolted from the inside. When three days passed with the door still bolted and no one answering the phone in the room, the manager authorized the local authorities to force open the door. What they found was two dead bodies, a male and a female. The male was under a sheet in one of the beds, and the female was sitting at a table holding a pen in her hand. When their IDs were checked, they discovered that they both were from here."

Sanders says, "And you're certain they were Maggie Stinson and the Gravedigger?"

"All the information they sent to us checked out."

"What the heck was Maggie doing in a motel with him?"

Slater shakes his head. "Crazy, isn't it?"

"And they both died of natural causes?"

"Yep. The coroner there said he died of cancer, and she died of a heart attack." Reaching inside his jacket, he retrieves a clear ziplock bag with folded pieces of paper inside.

"Those are the letters?" Sanders asks.

"Yes, sir. One of them is his last will and testament, which included a confession to a murder that occurred over thirty years ago. And the other is a letter from Maggie confessing to murdering Professor Gary Reed and burying him here." He nods toward the diggers.

"Man, I've seen some mixed-up situations before, but this one is one for the books. Wonder why she decided to confess?"

"In the letter she gave two reasons. One was to make things right, and the other was that she was doing it for Teddy."

- THE END -

For a list of all books by David Johnson, visit his Author Page on Amazon: https://www.amazon.com/David-Johnson/e/B00915TYU2/ref=ntt_dp_epwbk_0

You are invited to follow his Facebook author page: https://www.facebook.com/DavidJohnsonbookpage/

He would also like to hear from you with any questions or comments. You may contact him at: davidjohnsonbooks@gmail.com

Made in United States
Troutdale, OR
09/25/2024